P9-DCP-870

## *About the Author*

JILL PITKEATHLEY was born in Guernsey in the Channel Islands of the United Kingdom. She has had a long career in social work as a successful campaigner, bringing the needs of caregivers to public attention, in the UK and worldwide. In 1997 Prime Minister Tony Blair made her a Life Peer in the House of Lords. She has twice recovered from cancer, and it was during her second convalescence that she vowed, if and when she survived, to write a book about Jane Austen, whom she had long admired. This was published as *Cassandra and Jane*, and its reception inspired her to write another novel about one of the most influential people in Jane's life, her cousin Eliza.

Jill now enjoys good health and divides her time between her duties as a Baroness in Parliament in London and cultivating, with her new husband, a wildflower meadow in rural Herefordshire.

# Dearest Cousin Jane

*Also by Jill Pitkeathley*

CASSANDRA AND JANE

# Dearest Cousin Jane

A JANE AUSTEN NOVEL

Jill Pitkeathley

HARPER

NEW YORK • LONDON • TORONTO • SYDNEY

*For my dear husband, David*

# HARPER

DEAREST COUSIN JANE. Copyright © 2010 by Jill Pitkeathley. All rights reserved. Printed in the United States of America. No part of this book may be used or reproduced in any manner whatsoever without written permission except in the case of brief quotations embodied in critical articles and reviews. For information address HarperCollins Publishers, 10 East 53rd Street, New York, NY 10022.

HarperCollins books may be purchased for educational, business, or sales promotional use. For information please write: Special Markets Department, HarperCollins Publishers, 10 East 53rd Street, New York, NY 10022.

FIRST EDITION

Library of Congress Cataloging-in-Publication Data is available upon request.

ISBN 978-0-06-187598-4

10  11  12  13  14    OV/RRD    10  9  8  7  6  5  4  3  2  1

# Cast of Characters

**Jane Austen (1775–1817)**
Reverend George Austen (1731–1805), *father of Jane*
Cassandra Leigh Austen (1739–1827), *mother of Jane*
James Austen (1765–1819), *brother of Jane*
Mary Lloyd Austen (Mrs JA), *his wife*
Edward Austen Knight (1767–1852), *brother of Jane*
Elizabeth Bridges Austen Knight, *his wife*
Henry Austen (1771–1850), *brother of Jane*
Eliza Hancock de Feuillide Austen (1761–1813), *his wife* q.v.,
    *known as Betsy as a child and later as Mrs HA*
Cassandra Austen (1773–1845), *sister of Jane*
Francis (Frank) Austen (1774–1865), *brother of Jane*
Mary Gibson Austen (Mrs FA), *his wife*
Charles Austen (1779–1852), *brother of Jane*
Frances (Fanny) Palmer Austen, *his wife*
George Austen (1766–1838), *mentally handicapped brother of Jane*
Philadelphia Austen Hancock (1730–1792), *sister of Reverend George*
    *Austen, mother of Eliza*
Tysoe Saul Hancock (died 1775), *husband of above and father of Eliza*
Jean Capot, Comte de Feuillide (executed 1794), *first husband of*
    *Eliza*

Hastings de Feuillide (1786–1801), *son of Eliza and the Comte de Feuillide*

Philadelphia (Philly) Walter Whitaker, *niece to Mrs George Austen and cousin to Jane and Eliza*

Warren Hastings, *first governor-general of India, godfather of Eliza*

# PROLOGUE

## *Jane Austen at Steventon Rectory*
### Christmas 1787

I have always found that the most effectual way of getting rid of temptation is to give way to it, so I shall accept both your offers,' said Eliza as she glanced from one of my brothers to the other. Smiling at them both, she took the hands that each of them had held out to her and stepped down from the stage. 'The wind is chill in here,' she went on. 'Now which of my two charming squires will fetch me my shawl?'

'I will,' they chorused eagerly, but while James waited for her to choose the messenger, Henry, younger and more agile, was already running down to the other end of the barn where the outdoor clothing was piled upon a chair. As he returned with the multicoloured shawl, a gift from Eliza's godfather, I saw him glance triumphantly at James. Because Henry was my favourite brother, I was always on his side in these silly competitions that had developed between him and James for Eliza's attention, but even I could see how she flirted outrageously with them both and played them off against each other. I had overheard my parents talking about it, too. They were not quarrelling, my parents never did that, but they were certainly disagreeing about Eliza and the way two of their sons were reacting to her.

''Tis nothing but harmless fun my dear,' said my father. 'After all, she is a married woman with a small child so can have no serious designs on them.'

'Mr Austen,' replied my mother, 'you may be a clergyman well versed in the sins of your parishioners, but you are innocent of the wily ways of a woman like her. Why, she has been headstrong and spoiled since the time we first knew her and that racketing life she has led in France has not made her conform to our simple country ways. I tell you both James and Henry are in a fair way to having their heads turned and it is not a good example either to our girls. Cassandra is almost fifteen now and we must think of these things.'

'But Cassandra is as innocent as her father,' he replied, 'and not one to think ill of anyone.'

'What about Jane then?' my mother persisted. 'I can see that she is fascinated by Betsy, and you know how easily impressed she is by anything out of the common way.'

My mother had never quite become used to the idea of the niece she had always known as Betsy being called Eliza, as she suddenly announced she wished to be known when she was fifteen years old, and found it even more difficult to refer to her as Madame la Comtesse, as she should rightfully be known since she became the wife of the Comte de Feuillide three years ago.

'Jane listens to everything Betsy says and takes it all in. Why only yesterday I overheard both girls being told how the Comte adores her and would never think of taking a mistress as most French counts do. I ask you, Mr Austen—is that suitable talk for a child of twelve?'

'If you are worried,' said my father, 'have a word with my sister. I am sure that Philla will reassure you that it is just Eliza's way and there is nothing to worry about. As far as I can see, both the boys are enjoying the acting scheme, and James's writing talents are being encouraged after all. Now that he is back from France and going up to Oxford, the parsonage might seem a little dull to him without our acting plans. After all, my dear, it is Christmas and we should all be enjoying ourselves. Look how we all enjoyed Eliza's playing last night.'

'Come Mr Austen, did I not arrange the hiring of the instrument especially for her? And you know I am the first to encourage the acting, but I do not want to risk encouraging anything else.' Glancing up and seeing that I was nearby and might be overhearing, she closed the conversation with a meaningful look at my father, telling him, 'I am sure you know just what I mean.'

Henry, fresh from his triumph with the shawl, was eager to begin rehearsals again, but Eliza told him that she must now spend some time with her son, little Hastings, and could rehearse no more until he was abed.

'Mama and your sister have watched him all day you know, and it must now be his mama's turn.' Her dark, wide-set eyes held his fascinated gaze.

'But dear cousin,' said James, 'you know that both my sisters are only too delighted to care for him, even if Aunt Philla needs to rest.'

I was out of humour that he should volunteer my services without asking me. I was, in fact, rather nervous about taking care of little Hastings because of his peculiar condition. No one mentioned it, but it was clear he did not thrive. He could scarcely walk and, though Eliza made light of it, I had heard my mother whisper that he reminded her of my brother George, who was similarly stricken and could not live a normal life at home with us but had to be boarded out at Monk Sherborne. As Cassandra and I had been away at school in Reading, I had not been to visit him at Monk Sherborne recently, but I knew my parents went regularly. We had first seen Hastings last Christmas when Eliza and Aunt Philla brought him to stay; his father, the Comte, was engaged with his estates in France. James was not at home on that occasion

as he was with the Comte in France. Eliza had invited him for a
visit there. Our family could not afford a grand tour such as many
young men undertook before Oxford, but my parents thought a
visit to France might be a substitute. The result was that Henry
had had all Eliza's attention that year and, although but fifteen
at the time, had been her escort and played quite the gentleman
to her in their first tries at acting. His nose was quite put out of
joint that James, older and taller and an Oxford man, was now
competing for her attentions. He was writing some of the scripts,
too, so Eliza gave him a good deal of attention in return, diligently
asking him how he wanted this line or that spoken. It was really
amusing and gave Cassy and me some fun to watch them making
fools of themselves.

'She is a married woman,' we repeated to each other in our bedroom, 'she can have no serious intent.'

I liked the idea of two men fighting over me, but Cassandra was
as ever sensible and serious.

'No, Jane, she is improper and our brothers are ridiculous. Have
you read the piece that James has written and Eliza is to act tomorrow?'

'Oh yes, and I think it very fine.'

'Fine? When it refers to women being superior and no longer in
second place?'

'But Cassy, why should we be in second place? Eliza does not
seem to take second place to anyone. She has plenty of money as
far as I can see, a husband who adores her, and yet she is free to go
about as she pleases. Do you not envy her?' But I knew what my dear
sister's response would be before she said it.

'No, I envy no one. I am content.'

The next day Eliza read James's piece and both he and Henry
watched her, fascinated.

Her dark curls hung about her face as she read and her voice, the tone always low for a woman's, became deeper and softer as she read.

> But thank our happier stars, those times are o'er
> And woman holds a second place no more
> Now forced to quit their long held usurpation
> These Men all wise, these 'Lords of Creation',
> To our superior sway themselves submit,
> Slaves to our charms and vassals to our wit;
> We can with ease their ev'ry sense beguile
> And melt their resolution with a smile ...

My aunt Philla sat nursing little Hastings and smiled encouragingly at James.

'Bravo James—we shall have a writer in the family yet.'

I could see that my mother, who also sat watching, was displeased by this remark. Though she liked to have James, always her favourite of her six sons, praised, she felt that her own skill with words should be acknowledged by her sister-in-law. I tried to make amends:

'He has doubtless inherited Mama's talents—you know how she is always dashing off rhymes and riddles for us and for the boarders.'

As ever, I could not manage to please her.

'What nonsense, Jane. James has a fine talent and shows it in this script.'

'But surely it is the way the lines are spoken that shows them off to advantage,' put in Henry, gazing at Eliza. 'Our neighbours will be in raptures when they hear us the day after tomorrow.'

'Who are we expecting?' asked my aunt, trying perhaps to avert any more strife between her nephews.

'Oh the Biggs and the Lloyds, of course, and perhaps even Tom Chute if he does not consider himself too grand now that his papa sits at Westminster. James was hunting with him yesterday and invited him I believe.' My mother got up. 'Come, sister, we must attend to our household affairs and leave these young people to their rehearsals—it grows cold in this barn and will do that little boy no good.'

I think it must have been Eliza who suggested the theatricals the previous year when she visited us at Christmas. We would not have taken much persuading—we were ever a family for readings and scenes. But through Eliza we grew more adventurous and soon the large barn was fitted up with a proper stage and we began to collect many a costume and piece of scenery, side wings and backdrops, too. It was most amusing and though the presence of Eliza added spice to it and she always had the best parts, we all participated and enjoyed it. As well as our neighbours, we had been expecting our cousin Philly Walter to join us that year, but in the end she did not. I overheard my mother and aunt discussing it.

'Eliza is most disappointed that Philly has after all decided to stay in Tunbridge Wells for the festive season,' said my aunt. 'Eliza is very fond of her, you know, and did so wish she might join us.'

'Well for my part,' said my mother, 'I prefer her to stay away rather than be with us only to disapprove.'

'Disapprove—would she?'

'My dear, Philly and her mother disapprove of everything— from the way I bring up my family to the number of times we have beef on our table.'

'Really? She and Eliza seem to get along tolerably well.'

'That may be because Eliza is too forgiving and does not realise that Philly will judge her most severely for what she sees as frivolous behaviour.'

'I hope, sister, that you are not suggesting my Eliza behaves frivolously?'

'Why no, but in her last letter to Mr Austen, Philly was wondering that Eliza does not join her husband in France. And even you, my dear, must own that the Comte ought to have had sight of his only child before this—he is near two years old and has never seen his papa.'

'We intend to return to France in the spring as you know, but things are so unsettled there at present.'

'Sister, it is not I who makes the criticism but that minx Philly. Betsy—pardon me, I mean Eliza, of course—would do well to be wary of her.'

Philly was not a person who found favour in my eyes either—especially as I know she had described me ill the last time we had met when we all travelled to Kent. She said I was whimsical and affected and, though I laughed with Cass about it, I found the judgement hurtful.

But I knew, too, that both Eliza and my aunt should be wary of Philly's opinions because she seemed to believe there was something very shocking in Aunt Philla's background. I had heard this referred to once or twice, but whenever I approached the subject was changed. Cass and I often speculated about what it was. We knew she had travelled to India as an unmarried girl and had met Uncle Hancock there very shortly before marrying him.

'Do you think it could be that Cass?' I asked her one night

'I think it makes her very brave to travel alone and so far, but I cannot see that it is shocking.'

I could not either and longed to know the truth, but of course it was not a subject we could raise before Eliza and my mother would have been very angry had she known we discussed such matters. She came upon us once, Cassandra and me, with Eliza, discussing her husband.

I was asking if she loved him very much, as I thought it very romantic to have a French Comte for a husband.

'Why no, I do not love him, but he provides me with a comfortable means of living and he adores me, which is, you know, the most important thing. It is a bargain one makes: I perform my conjugal duties and he provides me with an agreeable way of life.'

'Eliza,' said my mother, coming into the room in a great hurry, 'you forget yourself. These are innocent young girls and you are under my roof. You will kindly remember that in future.'

I do not know if it was this conversation that caused the prompt departure of my aunt and cousins. Of course, there was the excuse that my father's pupils would soon be returning to school and we would be short of space, but I could sense Mama's relief when they departed, in a hired carriage with their mountains of trunks and bags.

'Next time we come, dear aunt,' said Eliza, kissing my mother on both cheeks, à la française, 'I do hope it will be in our own carriage. It is so inconvenient to have to hire a chaise and four.'

As our family had never owned a carriage, I could see that this remark was not very tactful, but my mother merely smiled and said to her sister-in-law: 'Come again as soon as you might and take care of the dear child when you travel to France.'

I do not think she meant Eliza.

I am not sure who told us that Eliza was an heiress, but I think it might have been when our brother Edward visited Cassandra and me when we were away at the Abbey School. Our cousin Jane was there, too—how confusing it is to have so many in our extensive family sharing so few names. Edward and Jane's brother—also called Edward, but we always called him Ned—came to see us and to our great delight we were allowed to go into Reading with them. We took our dinner at an inn in town and while we were there I remember telling my brother about a novel I was reading in which an heiress was cheated out of all her possessions by an unscrupulous uncle.

'Why, it is good fortune then for our own family heiress that our father has the guidance of her fortune—he is, I think, unlikely to cheat her. In fact, I can see him being too indulgent with her and letting her have any monies she begs for,' said my brother.

'And anyway,' joined in Ned, 'if it were to be spent, there would surely be more coming from her benefactor eh? I hear Warren Hastings is worth a pretty penny.'

'But why,' asked Cassandra, 'does Warren Hasting endow Eliza? She is no relation is she?'

'Well that depends how—' began Ned , but my brother cut him off.

'Now now, *pas devant les enfants*, as they say in France.' He laughed and changed the subject.

I found it very romantic to have a cousin who was an heiress, and I expect I boasted of it to the girls at school. We were poor compared to many of them, judging by their tales of fine houses, carriages, and outings, so it was something to boast about, especially since Warren Hastings was famous enough for many of the girls, and certainly the teachers, to have heard of him.

I was not sure how much money you had to have to be an heiress, but I knew Eliza must have a considerable amount. My cousin Jane told me that my mother had told her mother that my aunt's 'abandoning herself' to Warren Hastings had done Eliza no harm financially, even though the scandal had harmed their reputations in India.

When I spoke of Eliza's being an heiress, though, my sister reminded me that upon her marriage all her fortune became the possession of her husband, so being an heiress no longer counted for anything.

'Is that not unfair?' I asked her.

But she replied patiently: 'Of course not, it is the way it is for married women.'

I could see that this was a disadvantage to being married, though upon the whole it seemed to be a very desirable state. But I wanted any man I married to be a dashing hero, much like I imagined the Comte to be. I envied cousin Eliza vastly and hoped that when I was older I might be allowed to spend more time with her. She was generous in her attitude and conduct toward me and made me feel important in a way that Mama never permitted.

'I am an only child,' said Eliza to me one day at Steventon, 'so I shall never have a niece to spend time with me as so many fortunate women have. So you, dear Jane, can be in lieu of a niece to me and we shall spend time together. I shall supervise your coming out and inspect all your beaux and teach you to flirt in the most acceptable way. How I long for that time!'

I longed for it, too.

# PART I

*Eliza Hancock*

# ONE

## *Philadelphia Austen Hancock Aboard the Madras Castle*

### April 1765

How lively little Betsy has become. She runs about the ship from morn till night and it takes all my energy and that of the two nursery maids to keep her amused. Sometimes Mr Hancock takes a turn to help out and once or twice even Mr Hastings himself has taken her upon his knee to tell her a story. It touches my heart to see him with her, to see how the curve of her cheek resembles— No, I will not think of that.

Her liveliness increases as the weather grows cooler. Four months since leaving Calcutta, and we begin to feel a chill breeze of an evening and shawls are needed as we walk the deck before dinner.

Perhaps it is as they say and the climate of India—and especially of Calcutta—is not conducive to the health of an English child. The Portuguese nursery maids are quite energetic themselves, especially Diana and Clarinda, and I am glad that we chose to bring them rather than Betsy's Indian ayah, though Betsy's heart quite broke when she bade farewell to her. One hears such tales about the Indian nursemaids—of their indolence and propensity to lie. I have even heard some ladies say that they believe their ayahs have drugged their charges with opium. I can only say that all my Indian servants have been most satisfactory. Mr Hancock believes that I have been insufficiently firm with them because I was not used to dealing with servants, but he, too, has been indulgent with our household staff. Why, he has offered to deliver their babies for them when he thought they might have trouble and would have done so had they not been shocked at the idea of a man—even though a doctor—being present when they gave birth. They were shocked, too, when he attended me but as he said: 'After eight long years of waiting for a child, I want to ensure that both you and the infant are in the best of hands, my dear, and that means a doctor's, even though he is your husband, not an Indian midwife's.' He delivered our dear little girl himself while attending me most discreetly, keeping my body covered with a sheet all the while, and the joy on his face when he held her for the first time was sufficient recompense for any embarrassment I might have felt—or any guilt, perhaps?

Betsy has been asking 'When shall we see the white cliffs, Mama?' almost since the moment we sailed in January, and it is impossible to explain to a child of four that the voyage will take at least half a year, perhaps longer if the winds do not favour us. But in truth it was the same with me when I made the voyage out from England twelve years ago. I could not really imagine the distance we would have to travel on the *Bombay Castle* or how long it would take. How frightened I was, how strange everything seemed.

My dear brother George came with me to the dockside and though we were not in the habit of demonstrations of affection, I shall never forget how he clung to me.

'Oh take care of yourself, my dear sister,' he said as he left me at the top of the gangway. I had been feeling quite excited on our tour of the ship, though a little taken aback at how cramped the ladies accommodation was. The *Bombay Castle* was known as a fast modern ship, one of the best owned by the East India Company and my uncle Francis, who had arranged my passage, had implied that it would be richly furnished and spacious. It was far from that, being very cramped and small and of course the ladies were to share cabins. I was fortunate to be placed in one with only two beds—or bunks as I learned to call them—while some had four in a very small space. There was a great deal of wood about the boat also so it was no wonder we had heard tales of fires aboard that caused the poor passengers to take to the lifeboats, awaiting rescue that sometimes never came. We had heard too that the mariners—many of them Portuguese—were not very skilled and quite often went off course, so it was no wonder George was anxious about leaving me.

'Oh my dear, if only I had the means to take care of you or that our dear mother had been able to pay more for your education—then at least you might be travelling with some gentleman's family as a governess.'

'Hush George, do not fret. Uncle Francis has paid my fare and given me letters of introduction. I may yet find a position as a governess—they do say that many an English family longs for a well-spoken English woman to take care of their children until they are old enough to be sent home to school. And brother, please remember that this ship, small as it may be, is infinitely better than being at Mrs Coles's.'

My brother had never visited me at Russell Street, where I had been an apprenticed milliner for five years. The long hours hunched over worktables in airless rooms meant an early death for many like me.

'You are right, Philla.' He sighed. 'And at least you will have six months or so on the high seas with fresh air to restore you to health.'

'Why yes, and I am not alone here you know—I believe from the passenger list that there are at least twenty young ladies who

are travelling alone as I am, and I shall surely find congenial
company among them. Some have husbands waiting for them,
I suppose, but there will also be some like me who have to shift
for themselves and undertake this voyage else die an early death.'
I did not add 'an early death as an unloved spinster,' but I knew
he caught my meaning. With no dowry, no one to give me an
allowance of any kind, and no means of meeting a respectable
man, what else was a young woman like me to do but try my luck
in India?

There was something else I did not mention either—I did not
feel I could to an unmarried brother. For me, at least as bad as the
conditions in which milliners worked was the attitude of some people
to workers in the millinery trade and indeed in other dressmaking
professions. Because we earned our living by selling our skills, there
were those who thought we sold ourselves. For this reason I had
asked my uncle to ensure that on the passenger list I appeared as
'governess' not 'milliner.' I was intent on bettering myself and would
use the journey to do so.

The first time I could send a letter to my brother and uncle was
from Gibraltar. By then we had been at sea six weeks and I had
made friends. My principal friend was Mary Buchanan, with whom
I shared a cabin. She was the wife of Lieutenant Buchanan, who
had been some years an officer in the Indian army. I thought it most
romantic that he had come back to England expressly to find a wife
and had become acquainted with Mary's brother, an officer in the
same regiment as they travelled home. They spoke a great deal about
their families as the voyage progressed, so that, as Mary put it: 'By
the journey's end he was quite ready to fall in love with me as soon
as we met, and my brother contrived to arrange that directly they
reached Portsmouth.'

So they married before the end of his leave, having known each other but three months and spent only one week as man and wife. So unlike me, she had a husband awaiting her in Madras and was able to help me a great deal by telling me all she knew of India and its customs and what might be expected of us there. I was able to be of assistance to her, too, when she began to suffer dreadfully from seasickness.

The first part of our journey was made surrounded by a thick mist and it felt very strange to be setting off for the unknown as we were, but with the visibility no more than the length of the boat and the fog horn sounding every few minutes. As the mist cleared away, the wind began to pick up, and the sailors told us that we should soon begin to feel the Atlantic rollers. When we did I was surprised to find that I was what the crew called 'a good sailor' and, though I was afraid of falling on the slippery decks and companion-ways, I was never affected in the stomach like poor Mary. For near weeks together she could keep no food down and grew so thin and pale that I feared she would die on the voyage, as many had before her. As we travelled south, the sea gradually became calmer and she began to be able to take the broths that I got the cooks to make from the salt meat they carried. Luckily they had gruel also, and Mary took a basin of thin gruel almost every day if I made it myself on the small stove in our cabin. If we left it to the cooks it was inedible, being either too thick or too full of lumps. We laughed a great deal over that gruel, dear Mary and I, and by the time we reached the Cape of Good Hope we had a very firm friendship, which lasted for the rest of her sadly short life.

I have thought of her on this present voyage also, especially when we were at the Cape and I took little Betsy shopping to buy bonnets and gowns so that we should look respectable when we reached England. I thought of how Mary and I had ventured out there, so pleased to have dry land under our feet again. How we wondered at the strength of the sun, at the numbers of native people in the markets, and how she pondered over what present to buy for her new husband. Little did we know on that carefree day that the poor lieutenant would soon be dead in the horrors of the Black Hole of Calcutta, when so many white people were crowded into an airless dungeon by the natives and dozens were dead by morning, leaving Mary with two small girls. But then, I reflected, had that tragedy not happened, Mr Hancock and I would never have become acquainted with her second husband, Warren Hastings.

'Mama, Mama,' Betsy's insistent voice called me from my reverie. 'Papa says we have just seen the first English gull—oh look there, look there!' she cried, running to the rail and pointing her chubby finger. 'If we are soon to be in England, shall I not ask Diana to dress me in my new frock and bonnet?'

'The little minx is ever concerned with her appearance—instruct her if you will, wife, that it is not becoming for an English lady as she is to be,' said my husband. But he looked at her with an affectionate and indulgent eye as he was ever wont to do. He is a good man and I am fortunate to have him for a husband and no one could have been a better father to Betsy. Even if he suspects, and I am almost sure he does not, there has never been an atom of blame in his behaviour either to her or to me.

'There is still a long way to go child,' he went on. 'You must learn patience as your Mama had to do. Come, I will take you below as it is time for Papa to change for dinner. Will you join us Philla, my dear?' And he held out his arm to me in his old-fashioned, very courteous way.

'No, you go with Betsy, I will come below presently.'

I needed a few more minutes to collect myself, as I had been deep in my thoughts about the first time I met my husband.

He was a business acquaintance of my uncle Francis who had arranged accommodation for me when I arrived in Madras and who would give me letters of introduction to English families with whom I might present myself as a potential governess.

On the voyage, though, I had confessed to Mary that I thought Mr Hancock was himself in need of a bride and that it was possible that he and my uncle had discussed, in the most delicate of terms of course, whether I might be suitable.

'Oh my dear.' said Mary excitedly. 'You talk of *my* marriage being a romantic affair, but this is surely more so. Only consider, to come all this way to marry a man you have never set eyes upon—why it is the stuff of which those novels are made.'

One of the other travellers was a great reader and had whiled away the long voyage reading to herself and aloud to us from one of a stack of novels she had brought aboard. So we were by this time quite familiar with tales of innocent young girls finding themselves adrift upon the high seas with handsome pirates or in the Indies meeting merchants who turned out to be princes.

'Well, it is not at all a settled thing you know,' I said nervously. 'My uncle was not explicit.'

Of course, he emphasised how everything depended on what Mr Hancock and I thought of each other.

'I say only, my dear'—he laughed his rich laugh—'the doctor is in want of a wife and would infinitely prefer an English one, even without a dowry, than to get himself involved in one of those native arrangements that—' He stopped abruptly, realizing, perhaps, that reference to such 'arrangements' was not suitable for an unmarried lady. Though after six months on board ship, overhearing conversations and whispered confidences from the other ladies, some of whom had spent time in India before, I was quite familiar with the widespread practice among men who lived in India of taking a native wife and knew that the problem of half-caste children was an acute one.

As I leaned upon the rail of the ship, I reflected how much more tolerant we had all become of such unions now—why even Mr Hastings, the governor-general himself, has half-caste nephews.

It was August 1752—the fourth to be precise—when our ship docked at Madras and I caught my first glimpse of Mr Hancock— he rarely used the title of doctor, though he was a fully trained and skilled surgeon. I could not pick him out among the crowd gathered on the jetty to see our arrival and, indeed, all I could think of was the oppressive heat—unlike anything I had ever known in my life. The heat and the noise—those were my vivid first impressions, to- gether with the confusion, the people shouting, the smells. Oh it was all too exciting, too overwhelming. But then I saw a tall and rather melancholy-looking man approaching me. He took off his hat and bowed courteously. 'Miss Austen?' he enquired, and when I nodded and dropped a curtsey, he said, 'Tysoe Saul Hancock at your service madam.'

To tell the truth, his appearance was a disappointment to me and when I presented him to Mary, who came over to make her farewells and to present me in turn to her handsome lieutenant, I was saddened to see the look of disappointment on her face, too. But as I took my leave of her, with many promises to 'write at once and often' I took comfort from how bereft I should have felt had Mr Hancock not been there to give orders to servants and to escort me to my lodgings. He had been in India for more than seven years and was fully conversant with all the many things a new arrival had to learn.

What I should have done without him I do not know, but as it was I was able to sit back in the carriage that had brought him to the harbour and take in the white buildings—how welcome to see buildings after so many months at sea. There were green trees almost down to the white sand and the walls of the fort were visible in the distance. I was amazed to see how civilised the town was, with long tree-lined avenues and fine-looking houses. When I remarked on this with surprise, Mr Hancock, who had been sitting back watching my reactions, said dryly, 'Why, did you expect us to be living as savages? My household contains thirty servants— perhaps more. I confess I have not totalled them recently.'

I must have shown my amazement for he laughed, revealing teeth that were sadly discoloured.

'I have taken the liberty of engaging two maidservants for you at your lodgings,' he said. 'I know you will need more but at least you will have someone to help you settle in and no doubt you will need more suitable clothes—the muslins and silks the ladies wear are easily obtained I believe.'

I could scarcely take it in that I, who had never had so much as one maid, was now to consider that two were not enough—perhaps I was going to like it here in India!

When did I decide that I should marry Mr Hancock? I cannot now quite remember except that he seemed to expect it and I quickly realised that Madras was a difficult place for an unmarried woman. There were too many men there without wives and while in some respects that should have been exciting, in truth their manners and conduct were not those one would expect of gentlemen in England. I often felt threatened and soon became aware how quickly a young woman could lose her reputation.

So Mr Hancock it was to be. He was a doctor and enjoyed a level of society I could not have aspired to even as a governess, let alone as a milliner. I was to be mistress of a large household, now increased to forty servants and with no fewer than four personal maidservants. When I wrote to my dear brother and my uncle to announce my engagement I knew they would think I had done well for myself in moving to a higher social level than they could have expected. Of course, the letter would not have reached them before our marriage in February 1753, and by the time I received their congratulations, we had been married almost a year.

I suppose we might have remained in Madras for many years more with our only sadness being that no children came along. I did not know why this was. Some of the ladies with whom I spent days and for whom we gave dinners referred delicately to our childlessness and I remember one who even implied that as my husband was a doctor, he knew how to avoid pregnancy! I had very little experience in these matters and felt sure my husband had very little more, and although I imagine that he, like most unmarried men who spent time in India, had had a native mistress at one time, in truth he did not seem to be excessively interested in our conjugal relations. Nonetheless, we were puzzled as to why no children came and in fact we were beginning to plan a return visit to England so that I could see a specialist doctor, when our plans were thrown into disarray by receipt of a letter from the governor of Bengal. When the servant brought the letter in, with its elaborate seal, I was very excited and could not wait for Mr Hancock to open it.

"'Tis from my friend Robert Clive,' he said, smiling. 'He offers me a post as surgeon general at Fort William. Shall you like Calcutta my dear?' he asked, looking over his spectacles.

I was overjoyed and kissed him warmly. 'Oh Mr Hancock, I shall be able to renew my acquaintance with my dear Mary.' We had not met since we parted on the quayside at Madras, but we had corresponded regularly and I knew that she had lately found happiness again after her bereavement with a man who worked for the East India Company called Warren Hastings. Had I known how that meeting would change all our lives, would I have been so eager to go?

The sound of the dining bell, loud in the still evening air, brought me back from my reminiscences. I turned from the ship's rail and went below to dine with my husband, my daughter and her . . . her . . . godfather.

# TWO

## *Tysoe Saul Hancock*
### 1775, Calcutta

I am once more feeling quite unwell and as I read the letter back that I am to send to my dear wife, I wonder if my state of health is reflected in its tone. Her last to me took less time than usual to reach me—just over five months—but it brought news of yet another addition to my brother-in-law's family. I have responded:

> That my brother and sister Austen are well, I heartily rejoice, but
> I cannot say that the news of the violently rapid increase in their
> family gives me much pleasure; especially when I consider the case
> of my godson, who must be provided for without the least hope of
> his being able to assist himself.

Poor little George, I reflected, had to be boarded out forever at Monk Sherborne and taken care of—he would never be able to shift for himself.

I wonder if the letter, which Philla will read many months hence, sounds bitter? I do not feel so, but I have more than a moment's envy for my brother-in-law, George. His family is increasing rapidly—three sons in the first three years of their marriage and three more children, with a little girl at last, in not much more. He is not well off—that much is clear from the number of times he has had to borrow from me or his sister, though to be fair he has always repaid us promptly—but his letters and those of my sister-in-law, Cassandra, are always cheerful and optimistic. He seems genuinely pleased about his large family and content to take in boarders at the school, as well as his parish work. How I should have hated to have so many growing boys about the place, intruding on my home. And yet again, here I am in this great house with an army of servants but with no one to talk to and neither wife nor daughter to minister to me in what might be my last illness.

I call for the servant to light the lamps as I return to my letter.

Mr Hastings was here today as we had, as ever, matters of business to discuss. He shares my concern about the uncertainty at present about the tea exports. Unlike me, however, he has not so much of his fortune there invested to be excessively worried.

How shall I put it to her that our dear old friend, who has already been so good to us, has made a generous gesture to my wife and our dear Betsy? We are already greatly indebted to him for the monies he has given us in the past, but this last is beyond everything. I do not wish to give my dear Philla an excuse to be more profligate with money than she already is, and yet I must reassure her that she and the child will be well cared for when I am gone.

'Old friend,' Mr Hastings had said to me, 'you must perhaps now face the fact that you are seriously ill and may never see your wife and daughter again.' He is right, of course, though I have been resisting the thought.

'You owe me nothing,' I returned, 'though you have a blamable generosity and would swallow your fortune as fast as you have made it. Why I have never known you to keep half a crown if a poor man wanted it.'

He smiled that warm smile of his. His hair, always sparse, is now almost gone, yet he still retains his youthful looks—his skin soft, his eyes clear, while I, at fifty-two, look and feel an old man.

'Dear Tysoe, you have not always had the best of luck and I feel that I am responsible for some of that ill fortune. In hindsight perhaps we were foolish to return to England when we did—it cost us dear'.

'Aye, it did, yet my dear Philla was so eager to see her family and I myself wanted to show my dear Betsy off.'

'But we reckoned without the expenses of keeping a household in England, did we not?'

'We had a good two years though, especially our times at Stevenage and of course with the Woodmans in London,' I said .

'How soon, old friend, did we realise that we should have to return here? Living in England, pleasant though it was, turned out to be simply too expensive—beyond our means—did it not?'

'I think we knew that within the year but I put off the voyage as long as I could. Perhaps I realised that I would never see my family again.'

I could scarce forbear from weeping at that and it was then that he told me of the new arrangements he had made.

'We must ensure that Betsy has the best education, that she is a lady in every sense. She can already sit a horse well, I understand, and her mother's engaging a French governess will do her well in terms of language and behaviour.' I had shown him Betsy's last letter to me— they are not frequent but they do show she has not forgotten me.

I could scarce believe what he told me he was planning to do for Betsy and now attempt to tell her mother:

He has given a lump sum of £10,000 to be invested in a Trust fund. I thought no persons could be more proper for Trustees than your brother and Mr Woodman. You must get your brother to come to town and with Mr Woodman to sign the Deed, taking care that the proper seals are affixed before signing.

The interest of this Money will produce to you while you shall live nearly four hundred pounds per annum and the whole, if she marries be a large fortune to Betsy after your death.

As you and the child are now well provided for I may venture to tell you that I am not well enough to write a long letter. Give my love and blessing to Betsy.

And now that he has gone and the letter is sealed, I suppose I must ask myself just why Mr Hastings is so generous. True, my Philla was kind to his wife in her last confinement and our Eliza is named for the wee daughter who died so tragically at three weeks, just after her mother. True, Mr Hastings is her godfather. True, we took care of their little boy and the two stepdaughters when he was in the first paroxysms of grief. But he has little cause to thank us for our recommendation that the little boy should be sent to the school of my brother-in-law in Hampshire. I am sure Mr Austen took the greatest care of him and that his wife looked after him as she would one of her own, but the fact remains that the child was dead of a putrid sore throat within months of being there and never saw his father again. Mr Hastings has never cast blame on them or us and I suppose he looks on Betsy as a substitute child. A substitute? Well, of course there has been talk. But it was mostly from that spiteful wife of the governor and I have never found Hastings's manners to my wife anything but proper, affectionate of course, but entirely proper. It was natural for him to give her financial assistance when I had to return to India. He followed the year later and could not leave his friends embarrassed for money. I frequently saw his letters to her and remember well how he used to conclude them:

> Adieu my dear and ever valued friend. Remember me and make my
> Bessy remember and love her Godfather and her Mother's sincere
> and faithful Friend

Surely no husband could object to that? The only time I had any
ground for suspicion was when I wrote to Philla the year after he
returned to Calcutta to tell her he had a new favourite among the
ladies. This was Mrs Imhoff—very vivacious but of course a married lady. I was astonished when on receipt of this news my wife
immediately proposed returning to India with Betsy, who was then
about ten years old. I was truly horrified at this idea—she had surely
seen the problems that could befall a young girl, especially if she
was without the protection of both parents, if one of them should
die, for example—we had seen young girls debauched or married
far too young and I would not put my Betsy at such risk. I wrote
immediately:

> You know well that no girl tho but fourteen years old can arrive in
> India without attracting the notice of every coxcomb in the place of
> whom there is a very great plenty at Calcutta.
>    I am glad to say that Mr Hastings shares my concerns and bids
> me tell you that he is to settle £5000 upon his goddaughter.

I am sure my wife did not want to lose her place in Mr Hastings's
estimations nor have the child lose hers, but I was relieved when her
scheme of returning was by this means averted.
    I feel that my end is near and I shall die content that my dear
ones are taken care of and that they remember me with affection. I
have left detailed instructions for Betsy's education and I feel she will
make a brilliant match with a man worthy of her. With her looks,
her fortune, and her connections, it is to be expected. How I wish

I had their portraits near so I could look upon them again. I loved especially the one of my dear wife in her dark blue silk, the pearls I gave her at her throat. But the damp air here threatened to spoil them, so I had to have them returned to England for safekeeping.

In my will, which leaves everything I have—I fear there is very little; I have been a poor businessman and an indifferent and reluctant practiser of physic—to Philla, I have left the miniature set in a ring of diamonds to Betsy and have requested in the will that she never part with it as I intend it to remind her of her mother's virtue as well as of her person.

Hancock died in November 1775. News reached his wife in England in the spring of the following year while she and Betsy were at Steventon helping Mrs Austen following the birth of her second daughter, Jane.

# THREE

## Eliza Hancock in Paris
### 1780

I hope dear uncle George likes the miniature portrait I dispatched to him yesterday. I thought that he, my aunt, and cousins would like to see me looking more a lady of fashion than they had seen me last time I was in Hampshire. It may encourage them, too, to stop referring to me as Betsy, since Eliza is a so much more refined name. My mother says the miniature is a remarkable likeness and, with my hair piled up and powdered, I am pleased that I resemble some of the elegant ladies of the court. The blue ribbons on the dress and threaded through my hair are remarkably becoming, and we took the idea from a portrait of the queen at Versailles, where Her Majesty had her hair arranged very like. I sent uncle George a note with the package, which I hope will amuse them all at Steventon. I imagine them all looking at the picture and laughing at my description of the liberal use of powder at court—indeed, no one would dare to appear in public without it, so the ladies look as though they had dipped their heads in a tub of flour.

Paris is a most remarkable place. I had heard tell before we arrived here of the dirt and dangers people encountered, but to my mind it is the most exciting place I have ever visited—even more than India, though of course I remember very little of Calcutta since it is nigh fourteen years since I left our home there. My only sadness is that my dear father is unable to be with my mother and me to experience the delights of this great city. I know it was his dearest wish that I should have the benefits of a French education, and my mother wished it very much, too.

It took so long to settle my father's affairs and the poor man was in such financial difficulties at the last that I know my mother worried at one time that we should not be able to afford the life she and my father wished for me. All our income, £600 a year, would not have permitted us to live in style in London, but it was sufficient for us to live tolerably well *sur le continent.* Our maid Clarinda and I both loved Germany, where we went first, and Mama was happy in Brussels, but it was in Paris that we all three felt immediately that we could settle— filling at once our desires and my dear father's wish that I should be given an opportunity to acquire French manners and develop fluency in a language he always called 'the most elegant in the world.'

By the time we arrived in Paris I noticed that my dear mother had once again that distracted air that meant she was worried about money and that my father's affairs—especially the amount still owing to creditors—were still uncertain even five years after his death.

'There was never a man of better principles than your father,' she said to me, 'but some people are born to be unlucky. He suffered such a concurrence of unfortunate events as to make him much distressed financially.'

'Are we distressed financially, Mama?' I asked her.

'Not immediately, my dear,' she reassured me, 'but this illness of Clarinda's will cause us difficulty. The operations are costly, but she has been so faithful a creature that we must support her no matter what the cost.'

'Could we not ask my godfather to help us again, Mama?' I put my hand on her shoulder and was sad to find it much thinner than I recalled.

Her face darkened.

'It has been nigh four years since I last heard from him and with his new responsibilities . . . He is a grand person nowadays and has a wife . . .'

I was concerned to see her sadness. I had once overheard some ladies talking of her connection with Warren Hastings and had, as a foolish girl , wondered if my mother had been in love with him.

'But he has no children has he?' I interrupted.

She looked at me closely. 'No, only stepchildren 'tis true. . . . Perhaps I may . . .'

'Come Mama, I will bring you writing materials and let us set to together.'

The letter began, of course, with apologies for being in touch after so prolonged a period but with the excuse of our concerns over Clarinda's long illness, beginning as it did with a mere whitlow on her finger but escalating into almost half a year of severe disability, resulting in very heavy expense and great anxiety for us all. My mother enquired if my father's affairs were yet settled and whether any monies remained for our benefit after all the creditors had been paid.

She would have ended the letter at that point but I encouraged her to add something more personal.

'He was ever a warm and affectionate friend to us, Mama—let him know that we still think of him with warmth and gratitude.'

She hesitated but then concluded the letter thus:

I once thought to confine this letter to business, but knowing your heart as I know it and being convinced that in spite of appearances it has not changed for your friends, I cannot refuse you the satisfaction of knowing my daughter, the only thing I take comfort from, is in perfect health and joins me in every good wish for your happiness—

you may be surrounded by those who are happy in frequent
opportunities of showing their attachment to you, but I will venture
to say not one among them can boast a more disinterested, steady,
unshaken friendship for you than that which for many years has
animated and will continue to animate the breast of, dear Sir,

Your obliged friend,
*Philla Hancock*

A tear fell on the paper as she wrote and I wondered again, could
it be possible that they were lovers? But surely not; my mother was
devoted to Papa. But yet it may be as well to be sensitive on such
a matter. If they *had* been, then surely this would be all the more
reason for him to be sympathetic to our plight.

'There, Mama,' I said. 'He will respond soon I am sure.'

'It cannot be soon, my love. Only consider how long letters take
to reach India, but I will send this one by my bank. Mr Philips at
Hoare's Bank may perhaps have a faster mode of correspondence.'

Mr Philips said he would help us and was as good as his word.
Though the response from my godfather was not swift, in seven
months or so we heard that Mr Hastings had settled a further
£1,500 upon us. That and the interest from the considerable fortune
he had already settled upon me would enable us to live tolerably well.
We began to enjoy ourselves and the only sadness was the loss of our
dear Clarinda, who died later in the year.

In truth I had not initially wanted to leave England when we
did a year or so ago. We had a nice house in Bolton Street and I enjoyed my lessons with the teachers Mama engaged for me. I learned
music, too, and best of all, I was taught to ride in Rotten Row in
Hyde Park. When my dear Papa had learned that I had become a
tolerably accomplished horsewoman he allowed Mama to purchase
a horse for me.

'The dear man is so anxious for you to have all the accomplishments of a lady,' said Mama, showing me his letter, which had this time taken more than a year to reach us, so that I had in fact changed the first horse for one more easy for me to manage.

I am glad Betsy is happy with her horse. My intention in giving it to her is more on account of her health than to please her. I am convinced that riding is the most wholesome exercise in the world, and tho I think fox hunting not only dangerous but in some degree an indecent amusement for a lady, I wish my daughter to sit gracefully on a horse and to ride without fear

'Oh Mama, we could not hunt foxes in Hyde Park could we?' I said, and she laughed.

Our manservant Peter would come with me on my rides and I was especially proud of the green velvet riding habit trimmed with black that Mama had had made for me in Bond Street.

We spent a good deal of time with our cousins in Hampshire and it was most agreeable to meet my boy cousins particularly. James and Henry were always friendly, and I liked Frank and Edward, too. Sadly though, Frank was to be sent away to sea within two years.

'Tell me cousin,' he said, 'about your voyage from India. I long to be on the high seas.'

I thought him very young to be going on his own but knew that the navy was a good career for a young man who had no money of his own. I thought his brother Edward infinitely more fortunate in what had happened to him. Some cousins who had no children of their own had taken a great fancy to him when he was but twelve years old and had adopted him. I thought it very romantic, but Mama was as ever very practical.

'Why child, it is not romance that drives my sister Austen to persuade my brother to let him go to their rich cousins the Knights, but money.'

'How so? Have they sold him?' I had recently read a story in which a child was sold to a prince.

She laughed. 'No, of course not, but the Knights are rich while my brother- and sister-in-law are always short of money. Your aunt Cassandra was candid in her explanation to me and said that it would do no harm to please those who are rich and have the means of helping others.'

'And then of course their family is large is it not?'

She looked sad, as she often did. 'Yes, my love. I shall never have any child but you, so you are most precious to me.'

I put my arms around her. 'Have no fear, my dear Mama. I shall not leave you for another family, no matter how rich.'

'No.' She laughed, cheered up as ever by my nonsense. 'And I doubt that you will go away to sea either, will you? Come, it is time for your harp lesson.'

We also visited our other cousins in Kent, where I made the acquaintance of my cousin Philadelphia—named for my mother but always called Philly in the family. We are exactly the same age and played many happy games together. She is rather timid and sometimes I feel she does not quite approve of me and Mama, but I can never quite understand why.

Anyway, with all these connections and occupation I was not very pleased at the idea of going to live in a strange country, even though I knew it had been an urgent wish of my father's that I should learn the French language and also the refinements of French society.

'I am tired of London, my dear, and do not feel quite at home here' was my mother's explanation.

'Then could we not take a cottage in the country as we did last year when we went to Byfleet?' I asked.

'No, I want a change from English society as much as a change of location, I think.'

I had guessed before that my mother somehow had not the right position in society to please her. We lived a proper life, but our level was not right. My uncle George had his place in Hampshire, my uncle John his in Kent, but ours was strange. My mother thought it was because our money had been made in India.

Mr Hastings was much respected now that he was governor of India and very rich, and he was after all my godfather. I would have thought that this would have counted for a great deal, but my mother was not easy for some reason.

And so we removed to the Continent and now that we have arrived in Paris I am sure I shall like it well enough. The country about is pretty and I am sure we shall pass our time agreeably. Unlike London, where the world seems to depart during the summer months, Paris seems to be a city for residence the whole year round. If the heat during July and August becomes insupportable Mama has had the promise of a house in the country from a lady of her acquaintance. Meantime, I shall walk and ride and attend salons with Mama and the friends we are beginning to make here.

May 1780

I have just returned from our first visit to the court at Versailles and am so overwhelmed by all we have seen and experienced. We were actually in the same salon as Their Majesties! We were able in fact to see the whole royal family dine and sup. It is a curious arrangement that one is allowed to peer at them as though they were so many animals in a pen, but it is what the world does here.

The queen is a very fine woman with a beautiful complexion and is indeed exceedingly handsome. Her gown was beyond everything—most elegant. She had on a corset and petticoat of pale green lutestring, covered with a transparent silver gauze, the petticoat and sleeves puckered and confined in different places with large bunches of roses. The same flower, together with gauze, feathers, ribbon, and diamonds, intermixed with her hair. Her neck was entirely uncovered and ornamented by a most beautiful chain of diamonds, of which she had likewise very fine bracelets. She was without gloves. I said to Mama that I supposed this was to show her hands and arms, which are without exception the whitest and most beautiful I have ever beheld. The king was much more plainly dressed but he too had likewise some fine diamonds. The rest of the family were very elegant and indeed I may say that the court of France is, I believe, one of the most magnificent in all Europe.

While we were in the Hall of Mirrors—the most magnificent apartment I ever did see—I thought Mama looked as though she might faint.

'May I find you a seat Mama? Do you need your salts?'

She looked into my eyes—I have lately grown to the same height as hers—and said softly, 'I am well, dear child, only scarce able to believe that I, Philla Austen, milliner, am here at the French court— on the same level as the many others in this great room and with a daughter as elegant as Her Majesty herself.'

'Shall you tell uncle Austen of our adventures here?' I asked

'Of course I shall, and when we take the house in Fontainebleau I shall ask him and my sister to visit us there, so that they may share some of them.'

I was overjoyed at the thought of seeing dear uncle George again.

'Oh how nice—will they indeed make the journey here?'

'I doubt it,' said my mother. 'Your aunt is in the increasing way yet again, you know, and would not be able to travel even if they could afford it.'

I understood.

'It is fortunate is it not, Mama, that our dear benefactor has provided for us so well?'

'We shall never cease to be grateful to him, of course.' Her face took on that faraway look to which I had become accustomed. 'And of course to Mr Hancock, that he took such pains to ensure that your education was so extensive that you can hold your own in an assembly such as this. It is so sad that he is not here to protect you and guide you now that you are nearly of an age to be married.'

# FOUR

## *Mrs George Austen at Steventon*

### 1781

'Mr Austen, it is not to be borne. You must forbid it. You cannot allow our niece to marry this, this adventurer.'

My husband looked at me over the spectacles he had recently begun to need. They had lost a rivet and sat oddly upon his face. A face I noticed was wreathed in smiles.

Without allowing him to answer, I went on: 'How can you smile so? You surely do not wish to contend that this news gives you pleasure? What are you about? You are her guardian and must surely protect her.'

'My dear, calm yourself. I beg you to consider the facts. I may be Eliza's trustee but I am not her legal guardian, and if my sister, who is, considers this Comte to be a suitable match, how can—'

I interrupted: 'Eliza is not of age and needs guidance in these matters as she herself says. Where is the line . . .'

I took the letter up and read it again. Eliza had always had a neat hand, no doubt as a result of her father's nagging her, since Philla's scrawl is almost impossible to decipher.

'Yes here it is:

I have acted much less from my own judgement than that of those whose councils and opinions I am bound to follow—

'She cannot mean her mother, as she refers to those who are of rank and title.'

'No' was my husband's response. 'I daresay she means Sir John Lambert—you remember that rich baronet she met in Paris last year, who now seems to have such influence with my sister.'

'What do we know of him? Ten to one he has something to gain from this betrothal.'

'Cassandra, what can you mean?'

'Why, 'tis obvious to anyone with half a worldly eye, which as we know my dear, you sadly lack, and your sister is too easily influenced by powerful men, as we have reason to know from her past mis—'

'My dear, you know we agreed never to refer to that sad business again.'

'Yes, well as I was saying . . .' I knew such a reference would displease him. He is a loyal brother. He is a loyal father and husband, too. A good man—too good perhaps to understand what was afoot in France.

I took a deep breath and decided to tell him my worst fears, even though I doubted he would take them seriously. At that moment we were interrupted by little Charles, who came toddling in, his rosy face cheerful as ever.

'Cassy,' I called, 'come mind the babe for a few moments longer, your father and I need to talk.'

'But Mama,' I heard Jane's voice, 'Cassy and I were just set to pick apples and Charles cannot climb the trees with us.'

'Hush, Jane.' Cassy's voice contrasted in its soothing tones with Jane's complaining ones. 'We can as well pick the apples tomorrow. Let us take Charlie to watch Frank riding his dear little pony Squirrel in the lane.'

Cassy is always the peacemaker and always does as she is bid—

unlike Jane. When Cassy goes away to school we shall have to take Jane in hand.

I returned to my task of trying to make my husband see what was very obvious to me.

'Mr Austen, you know that Eliza is an heiress—not a great one perhaps, but good enough for most men. When she marries, all her property, all her wealth, becomes her husband's. Perhaps Sir John, of whom after all we know nothing, has made a bargain with this Frenchman, that he—Sir John I mean—shall have part of her fortune in return for making the match.'

'Oh come, dear wife, I may have permitted you too much freedom in your reading—'tis the plot of a novel you are setting out here. Besides, my sister says that the Comte has great connections and expectations. She also says the match is entirely to her satisfaction, so how can we possibly—'

Again I interrupted, not something I was in the habit of doing to my husband.

'As I have said, your sister is too easily influenced by men and no doubt dazzled by this supposed Comte's title and such. You know she told you how amused she was to have Eliza introduced as the ward of *Lord* Hastings.'

'You do seem to be excessively concerned by this news, my dear. Could it be perhaps that you had hoped our niece would make a match with one of her cousins?'

'To which cousins are you referring?'

'Why, our own sons of course. Did you and Philla not once talk of the desirability of cousins marrying?'

'Mr Austen, you take delight in vexing me.' I was angry and showed it. 'Eliza is far too old for any of our sons, as you know well.'

'Oh come, my dear, there are barely four years between her and James.'

'Yes, and you know full well that James is to become a clergyman and take over this parish after you. You cannot seriously be suggesting to me that Eliza, with all that fancy education, would be content as the wife of a country clergyman—still less make him a suitable one?'

His eyes twinkled as he responded. 'No one knows better than I how important a suitable wife is to a clergyman and how fortunate I have been in my choice.'

He always knew how to placate me, and I could not help but smile back.

'I fear you must hold on to your doubts and bear it well, however hard you find it,' he said, apparently not at all perturbed, 'though I do confess that one thing does worry me.'

I heard this with some relief. 'Pray, what is that?'

'Why, the question of Eliza's religion, of course. I would be highly concerned if I thought she was to become a Roman Catholic.'

'So you do not mind if she is at risk of being drained of every shilling as long as she is not a papist?'

'If I thought there was a risk of her being pauperised by this alliance I would intervene, I assure you, but as we have heard, the young man has great estates in the south and loves her violently, so I do not think we need fear for her too much. And I do assure you that neither I nor Mr Woodman shall ever consent to having her fortune transferred to the hands of French bankers. Let us invite them to come to Steventon on a wedding visit, and then we can judge his character for ourselves.'

'I do not believe the French are to be trusted, 'I warned, 'but it shall be as you wish.'

I knew when to close such a conversation.

The visit, however, was not to be paid for some considerable time, but so began the situation in which we were constant witness to what Eliza herself called 'a racketing life' by means of her correspondence with us and other members of the family. In fact, her most frequent and fullest letters went to her cousin Philly, but that minx often forwarded them to us or allowed us to read them on our visits to Kent or hers to us. I knew my girls were very interested in Eliza's doings and adventures, especially Jane, and I did not consider that the letters from France were always entirely suitable for the ears of young girls. I did not so much mind the ones in which she wrote of fashions, powder, curls in the hair, and jewels, or even the long descriptions of life at the French court.

> Paris has been remarkably gay this year on account of the birth of the Dauphin. This event was celebrated by illuminations, fireworks, balls, etc. The entertainment of the latter kind given at court was amazingly fine. The court of France is at all times brilliant but on this occasion the magnificence was beyond conception. The ball was given in a most noble saloon, adorned with paintings, sculpture, gildings, etc. Eight thousand lights disposed in the most beautiful forms showed to advantage the richest and most elegant dresses, the most beautiful women, and the noblest Assembly perhaps anywhere to be beheld; nothing but gold, silver, and diamonds and jewels of all kinds were to be seen on every side. In short, altogether it was the finest sight I ever beheld and I cannot give you a better idea of it than the one that struck me at the time, which is this: it answered exactly to the description in the Arabian Nights entertainments of enchanted palaces.

No, I did not object to hearing these accounts, but when she came to accounts of her relationship with her husband, I would ensure that the girls were not present—or the boys, for that matter, for on one occasion Henry and Frank accompanied us on a visit to Kent, where we were shown a letter that in my view said far too much about her marriage. It is simply not fitting to talk so freely—I wonder if she realises that Philly does not approve?

> If I may be allowed to judge of the future from the past and the
> present I must esteem myself the most fortunate of my sex. The man
> to whom I have given my hand is everyways amiable both in mind
> and person. It is too little to say he loves since he literally adores
> me; entirely devoted to me and making my inclinations the guide of
> all his actions, the whole study of my life seems to contribute to the
> happiness of mine.

I was glad she felt thus but could not remove from my mind the uneasiness I had always had about the French and things I had read, though never even related to my husband, about most French nobles expecting to keep a mistress. Still, I must say that in her letters I always found two redeeming features. She continued to be devoted to her mother.

> My situation is everyways agreeable, certain of never being separated
> from my dear Mama, whose presence enhances every other blessing
> I enjoy.

I also was impressed that she seemed genuinely to be devoted to her wider family, especially dear uncle George.

> I have reason to be grateful to Providence for the lot fallen to my
> share; the only thing that can make me uneasy is the distance I am
> from my relations and country.

My husband was always pleased and flattered by her emotional responses but I must admit that I was touched and surprised when she wrote me a most warm and thoughtful letter upon receiving the news of the sad death of my cousin Jane Cooper from a putrid sore throat that she had caught from her daughter Jane and from my Jane and Cassandra when they were away at that dreadful school in Southampton.

> The only consolation you will be able to find, dear aunt, at this saddest of news is that your dear daughters were spared and that dear Aunt Cooper died, as such a devoted mother as she would have wished, in nursing her daughter and yours, back to the good health, which I trust they now enjoy.

She also expressed gratitude that she herself had not been sent away to school but had always been able to have governesses.

We should have wished it, too, I thought to myself, had our income allowed it. I had considered that Jane was far too young to be sent away to school when she was only seven but she would not be parted from Cassandra. I never felt easy about it and feared that the dreadful illness to which they almost succumbed was a punishment for being careless of their welfare. They did better when we sent them to the Abbey School at Reading, though I believe that Madame la Tournelle, the headmistress, rather gave herself airs. I do not believe she was French at all. When my husband said we could no longer afford the fees for the school, I was not disappointed and was glad to welcome my girls home again. In my view they have had quite education enough. It does not do to have girls too well educated. They write a neat hand, Cassandra's better than Jane's, and have the run of Mr Austen's library—that should be sufficient. I shall teach them housekeeping and how to manage servants. Already their sewing is neat and accomplished and they can play and sing tolerably well. Their main object must be to make a happy marriage. We can give them no dowries to speak of, so they will not make brilliant matches, but if they can be good wives to a clergyman or a small landowner, I shall be content. Such a husband would surely not relish too clever a wife—we must remember that. Jane has a tendency to be too questioning, too willing to put herself forward. Only yesterday I saw her reading something dear James had written for his tutor at Oxford—the dear boy has a real talent for composition—and she actually suggested ways to improve it! I must have a word with her father about this; I think he indulges her and this may be encouraging her in these rather unladylike tendencies. Cassandra cannot be faulted and Jane should be encouraged to follow her fine example. My daughters may not be sufficiently accomplished to catch a Comte as a husband, but they will do well enough in the sphere to which they are born.

# PART II

*Eliza de Feuillide*

# FIVE

## Eliza, Comtesse de la Feuillide
### Paris, May 1784

I have often joked about the many reasons I have for doubting my husband's constancy. After all he is young, reckoned handsome, in the military, and a Frenchman besides, altogether adding up to a perfect picture of an inconstant spouse. I have always assured my friends that I am not of a jealous disposition and that I would take the matter very patiently. Not that I have ever had any reason to suspect him, but I am beginning to think he does in fact have a mistress. 'But,' as I said to Mama earlier today, 'his mistress is not another woman but a parcel of land.'

'Come my dear,' said my ever sensible mother, 'he cannot be blamed for wanting to improve the land that is rightly his inheritance.'

She is right, yet I cannot help but miss my handsome husband, who left us here in Paris when we had scarce been married a twelve month and has now been resident in the Landes—his native land—for almost two years. Of course, I have Mama for company, else he would never have been able to go, and we do live here in more than tolerable comfort. Our acquaintance in Paris is now very large and there are not the same restrictions on ladies going about that there would be in England. We dine and sup with at least four and twenty families here, and there are endless entertainments to be had. Only last year we had the incredible excitement of the invention of aerial balloons and had the joy of seeing some of the ascents. I was so glad that my dear husband was paying us one of his infrequent visits at the time, so that he could be present at the wonderful event.

He had been rather melancholy as his project in the south was not going well, and he finally confessed to me that he was very worried because the whole project was proving a great deal more costly than he had anticipated and that he feared he would have to borrow more money in order to complete it.

'But your father left you an inheritance for the draining of the land, did he not?' I asked.

'Yes, but not enough, and though I have now received permission to drain the land, it took two years for the licence to be granted and there were many expenses associated with that.' I took this to mean he had had to lay out money to bring it about, which I had heard was often the case in France.

In his last letter he had told me that the work was proceeding but not swiftly. It seemed that some other landowners in the area of the Marais in the Landes were disputing his right to the land, even though it had been left to him and he had received his licence to drain the land from the king himself. And then, of course, there were the peasants. Everywhere in Paris nowadays one hears stories of peasants who are trying to assert themselves—who are actually saying they have a right to own the land where they have grazed their cattle and sheep. One of them asked the Comte how the draining of the land would benefit *him*, disregarding the fact that all the expense of the draining falls to my husband.

'I do not know what is to become of a country where the lowest of peasants now dares to address a member of the nobility thus,' wrote my husband.

It was my suggestion that he should approach my mother for money.

'After all my love, we shall all, my mother also, benefit hugely when the land is drained and can be used for agriculture.'

I was not present at the discussions they had, but I know that the outcome was that she wrote to my uncle and Mr Woodman asking for the release of some of my inheritance. My dear husband was very restrained and polite, though he knew as I did that in truth the money was his to do with as he pleased. It was not held in France, however, and therefore when my trustees refused to release any to the Comte there was nothing to be done given that I am not yet of age. But dear Mama had sufficient income to advance him the money, on the understanding of two things: first, that when I had control of my fortune as my uncle had promised I should once I was more advanced in years, the money would be returned to her; and second, that the two of us should be permitted to see the Marais at firsthand and should travel south that summer.

The Comte was delighted with this proposal and his only stricture was that we delay sufficiently to allow him time to find a suitable residence. He would install his mother there also, as she had been most anxious to receive her new daughter-in-law ever since our marriage. So now the day approaches when we are to leave to undertake the six-hundred-and-fifty-mile journey south. I am happy at the prospect not only of seeing my husband's family but also of seeing more of France. My only anxiety is that my mother does not appear to be at all in good health—she has grown thin and pale during the winter. I have a slight health worry also but think it likely can be attributed to a happy cause, and I wish that we may have hopes of issue for next year.

Château de Jordan, September 1784

They tell me that it is painful indeed to bear a child, but what is uppermost in my mind at present is how fearfully painful it is *not* to bear one. Perhaps it was the roughness of the roads, or the inadequacy of the accommodation Mama and I had on our long journey south that caused my sad loss.

'You can never know the reasons for these things, Madame,' said the old French doctor who attended me at the château following my accident. 'But you are young and healthy as is your husband the Comte. There will be other children, of that you may be sure.'

How sad my husband was and his mother, too. They had prepared such a welcome for us at the end of our terrible journey. The château is a most charming place, so beautiful that it might be in a fairy story. Of course, *château* does not translate as "castle" as many an English person would suppose, but is more a gentleman's residence with the sweetest chimneys, a fine roof, and dormer windows. Madame Belle Mere—how much nicer this sounds than mother in law!—was kindness itself, even though I was unable by virtue of the onset of my condition to truly appreciate the fine food and wine that had been set out in our apartments.

I seem to have been somewhat slow in recovering—perhaps it has taken longer than recovering from a lying in—but am at last beginning to feel a little stronger. Mama oversees the nursing and supervises my food in agreement with Madame Belle Mere and I have little to do but sit in the sun. I grow quite tanned because, though the summer is almost at an end, the sun is still strong so far south.

'Before you return to England, my dear,' said Mama, 'we shall have to bleach your complexion with buttermilk lest your

English relatives think you have been working in these swamps yourself.'

She was joking, but I long to be strong enough to accompany the Comte as he goes about his work. Never did I think that I should be so interested in farming matters, but the work he undertakes is so exciting and the buildings that are beginning to emerge are so fit for the landscape that I fail to see how anyone could object to them. My husband says this project will immortalise him and now that I have seen it, I believe him. To have been so singled out by the king and entrusted with this heavy task is indeed an honour of which we must all strive to be worthy. It had seemed to me to be impossible, but I now see how he will manage to change stagnant water to a fertile plain and will be a benefactor to the whole province.

## November 1784

The cold is now so acute that it is hard to grip my pen as I write the sad news to all my relatives. Dear Madame Belle Mere is dead. The event is all the more shocking because the dear lady appeared to have escaped the dreadful fever that is common in these marshes and that has affected Mama, my husband, and me. We are all weakened by it, but my mother-in-law seemed to be in the best of health in spite of the damp that penetrates to your very bones hereabouts, when a sudden seizure, of not more that three quarters of an hour duration, took her from us.

My poor husband is distraught and, weakened as he already was by the fever, is in very poor spirits. Indeed, I have never seen him so cast down. Shortly we are to go to Bagnères, a nearby spa, which I am told does wonders for depressed spirits, and I am hoping it will have the effect of uplifting us all.

New Year 1786

I could not have believed that we should find such pleasant society in this part of the world, but we have met with such elegant and fashionable people as I thought were to be found only in London and Paris. Dear Lord and Lady Chesterfield, whom we met at the spa last year, are now with us at the house party to celebrate the New Year. He has been ambassador to Madrid for some time and she could not be more affable and charming. They introduced us to several other English families—we were surprised to find so many in this far-flung place—and we have visited and corresponded these last few months.

We are to have theatricals at the house party and I hope that my condition will not prevent me from taking part. Lady Chesterfield was so delightfully solicitous of my health when I confessed to her the reason for my frequent digestive upsets.

'You are far and away the best actress among us Madame la Comtesse,' she declared, 'but we must take no risks with your heath. The Comte, after all, needs an heir to inherit his great new estate once his work is completed.'

These new acquaintances have greatly increased my enjoyment of this part of France and I feel now I could settle here for some years quite contentedly.

I have written to my eldest cousin, James Austen, to beg he would visit us here. My uncle, I know, feels he should travel before he goes up to Oxford and what better place to visit than our works, which will be well advanced by the time he gets here.

February 1786

My plans for my cousin's visit have been thrown into disarray by the urgent desire my husband has expressed for our child to be born in

England. I had not reckoned that he would feel this so strongly and had not considered that I might have to undertake the long journey again in my delicate state of health.

'Consider, dear wife, the advantages of an English birth for our son, and I am sure they will overcome all your doubts. To be born an Englishman will no doubt be of great advantage to him in future years.'

'But Comte, he—if it is indeed a son—will be born into the French nobility. Would that not be of equal—indeed greater—advantage?'

'In former times I would consider you to be correct in that assumption, but as things are here at present I am not sure that to be related to the royal family itself could be called advantageous. Only yesterday in Guines, I heard a group of ruffians talking about wanting to be able to vote and to have the right to food—imagine, my dear, what we are coming to. No, mark me, English gentleman is what we should aspire to for our son and heir.'

I was dismayed, for I knew that the Comte would never be able to accompany me to England because of the progress of his works here. At a time when I should most have wished for and needed his company we were to be so far apart, with no fixed time for our being reunited. Had I not had the comfort of my mother to be with me, I could never have contemplated undertaking the journey. But it was my husband's wish, so how could I gainsay him?

Rouen, May 1786

I have mixed feelings now about my arrival in England. I begin to yearn to see my dear relations and to be somewhere familiar, but I have grown so large that I am somewhat ashamed of my appearance and nervous about what my dear uncles and aunts and cousins will think of my nonexistent waist and my tanned and roughened skin. I am afraid, too, that I lack the maternal skills and commitments that will shortly be called for. I know nothing of nurseries, nor of how to care for brats. Mama is reassuring and tells me such skills are found when they are needed. I am taken up with fearing that I have miscalculated my dates and the baby will be born in some inn en route, which would be the greatest shame and not at all fitting for the son of a count.

I worry too that dear cousin James, who has been urged so persistently by me to travel to France, will now arrive to find me departed.

One thing only brings comfort to me and to Mama. Our great benefactor, my godfather, is returned to England at last and has undertaken the task of finding us suitable lodgings. I am immensely grateful for this, for Lord knows the dear man has troubles enough with those dreadful Whigs in Parliament seeking his conviction for heinous crimes of which I know he cannot be guilty. He has been known throughout the subcontinent for his kindness and consideration for the people of India. My father always said he was the most generous of men and that has been amply felt by me and Mama. That he has been working all these years to 'feather his own nest' as *The Times* has put it is an outrageous falsehood. Would that I were able to give evidence at his trial, for I am sure I could convince the gentlemen of England of the goodness of his heart. Though only his goddaughter, I feel for him the love of a daughter, but on that matter it is as well to be silent perhaps.

London, June 1786

I am brought to bed of a fine son. He is to be called Hastings François Louis Henry Eugene. How I long to know that his papa has received the news with as much joy as I feel.

## SIX

## *Jane Austen at Steventon Rectory*
### December 1786

O h it is so exciting! Cousin Eliza is to be with us for the Christmas holidays! She is to be accompanied by Aunt Philla, of course, but best of all by her little baby. How young he is to have so many grand names, some of them of kings, but what credit his mother pays to her famous godfather by making Hastings his first name. It is rather shocking that he is six months old and as yet unchristened, but Eliza's charming letter to Papa explained that she wanted so much to have 'dear uncle George' perform the ceremony and had been putting off the christening in the hope that the Comte would be able to join them. Alas, the Comte is still too occupied with his land in France to come, and we shall miss James, too, as he has gone to France himself—at least we hope he has reached the Comte by now, as the last letter from him told us he was marooned in Jersey by high winds and treacherous seas.

'How romantic that sounds.' I said to Cassandra. 'Imagine, to be marooned on a small island, what an adventure! I wonder if they speak English there?'

My sister, ever practical, replied: 'You would not find sailing over rough seas very agreeable I am sure. Did you not feel indisposed by the motion of the carriage when we last went to Monk Sherborne?

And that is not above six miles away. And anyway, even if they do not speak English I imagine James could make himself understood in French or even Latin—a man about to go to Oxford could be relied upon for that surely.'

'But Cassy, do you not wish that we, too, could go to visit the Comte? What he is doing with clearing the land sounds so courageous and perhaps we could help?'

My sister laughed: 'What, dig with picks and shovels like the French peasants?'

'No, no, but perhaps seeing plans for how it will be planted with grass and trees and what animals they may later keep?'

'Jane, we cannot even go into the lanes hereabouts in winter when they are muddy, as ladies' shoes are not robust enough. Do not let your imagination run on so—or if you do, put it into your stories.'

'Perhaps I may, but I do not know enough about France to set a story there—indeed I know nothing of anywhere except our village.'

'Well, talk to Eliza when she is here; she will tell you tales I am sure. My mother says she is a lady who has a vivid imagination, just like you.'

'I know Mama does not like me to scribble as I do, but she encourages the boys and she herself composes rhymes and odes, so why am I in the wrong?'

Cassandra soothed me as usual: 'You are not in the wrong dearest, but girls are expected to be modest and to be content with womanly activities, you know.'

I sighed. 'I know, I think I shall take to concealing my notebook under my sewing on the worktable. I think having our cousin here will give me lots to write about!'

December 17th, 1786

Yesterday Eliza and I celebrated our birthdays together! How lovely it is that this most enchanting of cousins shares my birthday. Well, not the exact day, of course, but only one week apart. It feels very old to be eleven but dear Eliza is twenty-five! She was here at Steventon when I was born—I am not sure I had known this before. Mama said she had told me the story, but I do not remember and of course I do not remember my birth! Aunt Philla was here to attend Mama and it was one of the coldest days in an exceptionally cold winter.

'My dear,' said Eliza, 'I remember so well that had they wished for a doctor none would have been available as the snow was so deep in the lane that no carriage had passed down it for days.'

'Well,' joined in my aunt, 'since my dear sister Austen had given birth six times before, it was hardly likely she would need a doctor.'

'And did you see me born, cousin?' I asked

'Jane, you forget yourself,' said my mother sharply. 'Unmarried girls do not attend lyings in, as you would do well to remember.'

Eliza looked at me and winked imperceptibly. She seemed to know already that Mama does not always approve of me and it was comforting to know she was on my side. Cassandra always is, of course, and often protects me when Mama is cross, but she would not openly take my side as Eliza now did.

'Oh, dear aunt, Jane is naturally curious about her birth, as we all are. Why, my own dear Mama has given me a detailed account of mine, and I assure you it was helpful when it was my turn to give birth.'

'It will be a long time before Jane is in that position,' returned my mother, 'or Cassandra either, so please let us be modest in our conversation.' My mother had reddened and soon made an excuse to leave the room on account of ensuring that the cook had set the fowl bones to boil before retiring.

Eliza and Aunt Philla Hancock have been here one week now. There was such excitement as we waited in the lane for the sound of their carriage. They were not to travel post as my aunt had said it was impossible to carry all that they needed for such an extended stay, but had hired a coach and four to bring them, baby Hastings, and their two maids to pay their first visit to Hampshire since Eliza was a small girl. We did not often see a smart carriage in our part of the world, so Henry, Frank, Cassandra, and I waited near the gate to see who would be first to hear the hooves.

How thrilling it was to hear the carriage and to see my aunt and cousin waving from the window! When they stepped down I was amazed by their apparel—so grand and rich it was. I had not seen such velvets and fine trimmings, even on her ladyship in the manor church. Eliza smelled divine, some sweet scent like lily of the valley, and greeted us all with kisses on both cheeks and little cries of *'enchanté'*, *'si jolie'*, *'quel plaisir'*. I saw Henry blush deep red when she drew back from kissing him and said: 'Why cousin, I should no longer embrace you as a boy, you have grown into a man and a handsome one at that.'

My aunt was more reserved, but you could see her real pleasure as she embraced Mama and my father, saying, 'Dearest brother, how I miss your wise counsel,' with tears of joy in her eyes. My mother, too, was pleased to see Aunt Philla, but I saw her frown a little as she took Hastings from the nursemaid.

'How does this little one?' said Mama. 'He is a little on the small side is he not? We must feed him up while he is here.'

'He is a little tired from our journey perhaps,' said my aunt, and I saw her and my mother exchange meaningful looks as they went indoors.

It seemed to take us hours to get our visitors settled in. There was so much to be unloaded and taken upstairs. It was lucky that our boy boarders from my father's school had gone home for the Christmas holidays, else I do not know how we should have fitted them in. As it was, one of their maids had to stay with a family in the village and the nursemaid had only a little mattress in the room she shared with Hastings.

'I am sorry, Philla, that you and Eliza must share a room.' said my mother, 'but this is a humble parsonage, as you know. And it cannot compare with the grand house I hear you have taken in London—Orchard Street is it not?'

Eliza laughed, such a pretty tinkling laugh she has. 'Why aunt, we hope that you and dear uncle and the children will visit us there soon, and as for sharing a room, my dear mother and I have done that many times before and in fact prefer it. But in one thing I can assure you, this parsonage is far superior to any London dwelling.'

I was curious, since I had never been to London, and plucked up the courage to ask this pretty creature who had descended on our plain house like some exotic bird: 'Pray why is that cousin?'

'Why, dear little Jane, because it contains all my beautiful family and for that, there can be no substitute.'

When Cassy and I went to bed that night, I could not wait to hear what my sister thought of our visitors.

'Is she not like a princess? Do you not think her enchanting?' I asked.

Cassy was reserved: 'I like her well enough, and she seems inordinately pleased to be here. Though I cannot help thinking it must seem very dull after the French court and the fashionable resorts that she seems to frequent.'

'But that is what is so lovely about her—she tells us these exciting tales yet seems more than content with our humble home.'

Cassy frowned. 'I cannot quite understand her, but one thing I do know is that the baby does not thrive.'

I was alarmed. 'How so? What do you know of babies?'

'Not a great deal I own, but I heard Aunt Philla telling Mama that she fears he is not developing as he should and Mama said that he reminded her of our brother George.'

'George? Oh no! Do not say that Hastings, too, will have to be sent away! There seemed no sign of those dreadful fits that poor George suffers and there is no sign either that he cannot speak.'

'He is too young for speech, of course'—My sister spoke with authority— 'but George did not start the fits until he was two years old, you know. We shall have to watch and wait.'

Cassandra's warning about little Hastings was alarming, but apart from that I have had nothing but pleasure in our visitors. I have never had such a birthday celebration as the one we had yesterday. We ate dinner later that usual—not until five thirty in the afternoon, whereas we are accustomed to dine not long after three in the winter.

Cook had dressed a turkey and we even had side dishes of stuffings and sauces. Wine was served throughout the meal, instead of just at the end, as Aunt Philla had brought some with her and Cassandra and I were permitted a glass each, watered of course.

Afterwards we had some sweetmeats that Eliza calls bon-bons and Henry told me my father drank two glasses of port when we left the 'gentlemen' at the table and returned to the parlour. Of course the gentlemen were only Papa, Henry, and Frank, Charles having already been put to bed, and I have never known us to follow this custom before, but Eliza said, 'Now, ladies, shall we leave the gentlemen to their port and nuts while we ladies gossip about them in the other room?'

I thought my mother would protest, but she smiled quite indulgently and agreed. 'Yes, I suppose we must teach our young men fashionable manners so that they know how to conduct themselves at Oxford, and no doubt James will return to us with his head quite full of such ideas,' and she rose quite grandly and led we ladies out. It was most exciting!

I could not wait to return to the parlour, as Eliza had been in the middle of telling me some wonderful stories of the French queen, Marie Antoinette, and the daring man who ascended over Paris in a hot-air balloon. As we sat by the fire I begged her to tell me more.

'Where, was I? Oh yes, the ball at Versailles. Well, there were thousands of lights and gold and silver as far as the eye could see. But that was as nothing compared to the opera at the Tuileries—do you remember Mama?—when they had five hundred horses upon the stage!'

'Yes, I remember,' said my aunt, 'and they made such a clatter you could not hear the music!'

'Talking of music,' said Papa as he returned to the parlour with the other 'gentlemen', 'we have hired a pianoforte especially for your visit. Will you not favour us, Eliza?'

'I will, dear uncle, but not until I have given my dear Jane her birthday gift.'

I was amazed. We were not accustomed to much in the way of birthday gifts in our household. Mama gave me a new thimble at breakfast and Cassandra had drawn me a sweet sketch of Frank's pony Squirrel. But Eliza now drew my attention to a parcel standing on top of the pianoforte.

'I notice, Jane, what a great reader you are and have decided always to bring you books that you would not receive elsewhere, though I know you have the free run of your father's library.'

I saw a slight look of alarm on my mother's face and knew she was wondering if the gift would be suitable. But I drew out of the package a set of Berquin's *L'ami des enfants,* which we had read at the Abbey School and which had always delighted me.

'Oh thank you, cousin,' I cried, truly delighted. 'Look Cassy, so you remember Madame La Tournelle making us read aloud and correcting our pronunciation?'

'Your French is very good,' said Eliza, 'and I am sure this will make it even better.'

I glowed at receiving such praise from her, even while being embarrassed that my birthday gift to her had been only a needle case that I had worked myself.

For the rest of the evening she played and sang to us. I noticed that Henry could not take his eyes off her. At fifteen, it was the first time I had seen him look admiringly at a woman. But then, I, too, wanted nothing more than to look at her and think of the stories I could weave around her.

## January 1787

*Quel horreur!* Our visitors are to leave us today. The boarders are to return and in truth there is no room for them after next Sunday. Eliza has said I may write to her in London and that she will look forward to receiving word from me.

'And, Jane, if you should feel inclined to send me something more than letters, I should be delighted.'

'More than letters?' I was puzzled.

She smiled. 'Do not think that you have concealed from everyone that you write as well as read—I have seen that small notebook of yours you know.'

'Seen it? You do not mean you have read it?'

'Of course not,' she reassured me. 'But I know your brothers compose a little. Have James and Henry not written sketches for your family theatricals?'

'Well yes, but that is for men to do, I would not presume—'

'Women must and should presume,' she interrupted. 'You need not tell your mama. I say only, if you should wish to send me something, I will read it with pleasure. And if not, why, it matters not, we shall be together again next Christmas.'

I can hardly wait.

## SEVEN

## *Philadelphia [Philly] Walter, Eliza and Jane's cousin, Orchard Street, London*

### 1788

I have never experienced before so thorough a racketing life and had no idea it could be equal to how I now find it.

When my cousin Eliza—or *cousine,* as she persists in calling me; 'My dear it is how my husband the Comte denotes you'—invited me to stay with her in London, I was, I confess, a little reluctant. I do not find myself equal to the social round in which she exists and prefer the quiet life that is our custom in the country. But to tell the truth, I did not want to offend her again as I felt I had done last Christmas when I had been invited to join her at my aunt and uncle's at Steventon. I know she thought I refused to go because I disapproved of the acting they were all so keen to undertake. True, I do disapprove of ladies appearing in public in such productions as were proposed and I was, as I told Eliza at the time, concerned about leaving my mother unattended during the Christmas season, but the real reason I refused was because I felt there would be no comfort and little privacy at the rectory. Indeed, Aunt Cassandra promised me 'only a place to hide your head' so that I was not even sure I would have a bed, let alone a bedroom, and also made it quite clear I would not be welcome if I did not act.

I knew that Uncle George and Aunt Cassandra were to visit Orchard Street later in the year, so I felt that if I showed I was willing to visit Eliza this might by a means of patching up any feelings that had been ruffled and enable me to do it in the comfort of what Eliza had assured me was a spacious and comfortable lodging.

In that she was right—the house in which she and Aunt Philla live in great style is large and even luxurious and they are kind and affectionate to me. But I cannot much longer tolerate the pace at which they live their lives. Our mornings are spent in ridiculous calls from one door to another without ever being let in, our afternoons in drinking tea with affable and lively company, our evenings at theatres, balls, and concerts. They are constantly trying to do things for my pleasure and the coach with the coronet emblem is ever at my disposal, but oh! how I long for a simple walk in Kensington Gardens, which I can only occasionally prevail on them to allow.

I confess though that it was splendid to be able to write to Mama and relate our visit to St James's and to tell her that we had been invited to a party given by the Duchess of Cumberland.

Of course, Eliza has some very fine apparel, which nothing of mine is equal to. She was able to lend me one of her dresses with an embroidered bodice and a skirt so large and heavy that I thought I should have toppled over. Rosalie, my cousin's maid, had to add some lace at the hem as Eliza is so much shorter than me, and I had to tuck more lace at the neck, else I should have been ashamed to be seen in anything cut so low.

I had great enjoyment in one of our outings, though its cause was a sad one. Eliza's godfather, the great Warren Hastings, is brought to trial in Westminster Hall and we attended one day from ten o'clock in the morning until four in the afternoon. It was very exhausting, but I had the satisfaction of hearing the great orators of whom I had only heard tell—Sheridan and Burke and Fox—the latter with a most dark and saturnine countenance. I was very struck by Sheridan's eloquence and by the long queues which formed to hear him, as though

this were an entertainment. Hastings himself looked pale, and I was
most amazed by how small in stature he is. He is impeached and
tales of his corruption abound. Of course, Eliza and my aunt refuse
to believe any of the accusations and defend him violently whenever
his name is mentioned. Clearly they believe his defence that his actions, however cruel or unjust they may have seemed, were entirely
necessary in the situation in which he operated.

'You simply must realise my dear,' said Aunt Hancock, 'that
India is not England, nor anything like.'

'Nor even France, nor anywhere in Europe,' Eliza joined in. 'In
India, arbitrary powers without any restraint are quite normal, and
it is the only thing that the natives understand.'

I did not say so to them, but it is my belief that even natives
understand oppression and injustice, and I can scarce believe that
charges as serious as 'high crimes and misdemeanours' would have
been brought if there were no evidence. I heard Mr Sheridan himself
assert that 'Hastings' transgressions are many,' and I believe it will
be so proved.

In spite of being on trial as a criminal, Hastings and his wife
continue to live in great style. They even have their own box at the
Opera to which we went one evening. I think there is a great ca-
chet—one of Eliza's words—to being his goddaughter but if I were
in her position now, I should be ashamed to be associated with the
scandal and humiliation of this trial. But the more intimately I know
Eliza, the more I realise that very little makes her ashamed. I know
not if she has heard the gossip about her parentage but do not think
she would even find illegitimacy shameful. For instance, she simply
refuses to believe that her son is not normal. He cannot yet stand
or talk, though he makes a great deal of noise. He has frequent fits
and to all who see him it is obvious that his faculties are impaired.
I know my aunt Cassandra compares him to her unfortunate son

George and fears he will never be right. But Eliza only talks lightly of him proceeding at his own pace or of his having inordinate trouble cutting his teeth.

They are to convey me home soon and go on to Ramsgate with the little one, as Eliza is convinced that the sea bathing will do him a world of good.

## Tunbridge Wells, Kent

Oh! How good it is to be home again. I understood that Eliza and my aunt were to return to France as soon as they came back from Ramsgate—what a scandal it is that the babe has not yet even met his papa—but I have heard today from Eliza that they have delayed their journey yet again because of some disturbance in a town called Rennes, which it seems would have made it dangerous to travel. This is the woman who has willingly travelled in pursuit of pleasure to areas where there are known highwaymen and footpads. She seemed to think nothing of danger when she travelled into Surrey last year, yet when it comes to rejoining her husband she fears for her safety!

But of course she is not to stay quietly at home as would be fitting, but is visiting Oxford. I know this is because her cousins James and Henry are there at present, and I suppose she continues to flirt with them both outrageously.

I could scarce believe the impudence in her letter that arrived this morning telling me of this visit. She actually aspires to be a Fellow—is there no limit to her outrageousness?

We visited several of the colleges, the museum, etc., and were very elegantly entertained by our gallant relations at St John's, where I was mightily taken with the garden and longed to be a Fellow that I might walk in it every day. Besides I was delighted with the black

gown and thought the square cap mighty becoming. I do not think
you would know Henry with his hair powdered and dressed in a very
tonish style, besides he is at present taller than his father. We spent
a day seeing Blenheim. I liked the outside of the mansion but when
we entered I was disappointed at finding the furniture very old-
fashioned and shabby.

How typical of Eliza to be taken in by 'ton' and so dismissive of one
of our great monuments. I hope she is not setting her cap at Henry.
He is ten years her junior and she is married. But now I have spent
time with her, I see these facts would be of no consequence to her if
she has her heart set upon him. I fear there will be trouble ahead.

# EIGHT

## *Eliza at Her House in Orchard Street, London*

### September 1788

D elighted as I am to have a visit from dear uncle George and his family I could wish they were coming at a more propitious time. I do pride myself on always keeping an elegant home, and it is hard to be elegant when surrounded by boxes and packing cases. But I have so much to accomplish before our return to France, so much to store away here, so much to purchase and pack for the establishment in Guines that the disarray cannot be helped.

In addition I am so concerned about dear little Hastings. In August he suffered a most alarming series of seizures—well, in truth I must call them fits. It is dreadful to see him at these moments and we can only try to hold him and prevent him from hurting himself until they subside. When they do, he generally sleeps a little and awakes his usual sunny-natured and smiling self. I have consulted several of the doctors who have been recommended but they all say he may well grow out of it. In my most depressed moments, I remember that little George Austen has not grown out of his condition and must needs be cared for away from his family. That I could not bear and have promised myself that come what may, he will remain with me always.

I am delighted that young Frank and Cassandra and Jane are to be of the party. They have all been visiting cousin Philly, so no doubt will have heard of her visit here. I am confident the food there will have been frugal, so I shall ensure they dine splendidly when they arrive, in spite of being surrounded by trunks.

A few days later

Oh, how foolish I was to worry about the state of my apartments! As if my dear relations would worry about such trivia. What merriment and enjoyment we have had! Dear Uncle George grows more amiable with each year; his hair grows whiter but his manner is even more pleasing. We all took special delight in the teasing about cousin Philly.

'Why, my dear,' said Uncle George, 'we were amazed to find you in the hall when we arrived. According to Philly, you were never at home, unless, that is, you were entertaining some grand personage!'

'Take care what you say to that minx,' said Aunt Cassandra. 'She is no friend to you, but criticises constantly.'

'Yes,' put in Jane, 'she thinks Cassy very pretty and modest but finds me whimsical and affected!'

'I am sure it is just her rather strange manner.' I always feel it necessary to defend Philly, for she has a rather lonely life, isolated with her parents and I feel sorry for her. 'And after all, Cassy *is* very pretty.'

'Of course she is, but I am not—'

'That will do Jane,' said my aunt, 'lest you become what she thinks you are.'

I was glad that Frank distracted us with a tale of how Philly disapproves of his ambitions to join the navy, for I could see that there was the usual tension between Jane and her mother. I noticed, too, that Jane had changed considerably since the winter.

She had grown, it was true, but there was something a little more confident, more mature in her manner. I was eager to talk to her alone.

What a delight I found her! Whimsical she may be, but what virtue there is in her dry wit, and as for her powers of observation! I was touched that she shyly offered me two of what she called her 'scribblings' to read.

The first was called 'The Beautiful Cassandra,' and it is about a wild girl who rampages through London streets, stealing ice cream, knocking people down, refusing to pay the coachman who has driven her all round the city, and deciding that this is a splendid way to pass the day! The other is a longer tale called 'Jack and Alice,' and I was rather shocked to find it contained a murder, a mutilation, and some rather violent passions. For a twelve year old . . . well, I was astonished!

She watched me anxiously as I read, following my every expression, and when I refolded the papers she said, 'Well, what think you of my first efforts?'

'Jane, they are a true delight. Have you shown them to your parents?'

Her face fell. 'I have not. You see they are so pleased with the writings that they are receiving from James and Henry from Oxford, that I do not want to seem as though I . . .' She hesitated.

'As though you are trying to compete with them?'

'Yes, I suppose so.'

'I, too, have received the advance copy of their magazine—*The Loiterer* it is called is it not?'

'Yes, it is to come out each month'.

'Well they have done very well to set up a regular publication and it is most amusing, in the style of—'

'That is the trouble with it, it is in the style of Mr Fielding or even Dr Johnson, but a very poor imitation and really just poking fun at literature for a particular group of people at Oxford.'

'You do not admire it then?'

'Oh it is tolerably amusing, I suppose'—she made an impatient gesture with her hand—'but I have spent the summer reading all the back copies of *The Tatler* and *The Spectator*, which my father keeps on his shelves, and believe me, *The Loiterer* is a poor, a very poor, imitation.'

I could see how she might have difficulty telling her parents how she felt about their sons' literary efforts, of which they were justly proud.

'Well, Jane, I said, 'it does not seem to me that your writing is a poor imitation of anyone else's. If you can write so engagingly at twelve years old, I cannot imagine what you will produce at one and twenty!'

'You will see, cousin,' she said, her eyes sparkling. 'I shall have pieces to dedicate to everyone in my family before very long!'

# NINE

## Cassandra Austen, Steventon
### June 1791

I really think you enjoy writing the dedication as much as writing the story,' I said to my sister as I watched her sign her name with a flourish and close the lid of her writing desk.

She ran her hand over the smooth top of the little desk my father had given her last year.

'Well, you know when you write the dedication you feel the work is finished and that gives me a sense of accomplishment.'

'Is Eliza pleased that 'Love and Freindship' is dedicated to her?'

'I think she is,' she replied. 'Well no, it is clear that she is but you know that dear Eliza is always so lavish in her praise of our accomplishments, whether my writing or your drawing—'

'Or more likely James's or Henry's efforts,' I interrupted with a smile.

'Yes, indeed.' Jane laughed, joining in the joke. 'She is never stilted in her praise so it is not easy to tell what she really thinks, but she certainly seemed excessively diverted when I read it to her and asked her permission to dedicate it to her.'

'As well she might.' I was always indignant at the thought that anyone did not admire what Jane called her scribblings as much as I did. 'It is *so* funny—especially the part where Laura and Sophia faint alternately upon the sofa.'

'Even Mama laughed at that, did she not? Though I fear she does not entirely approve that I have written about all those deceitful pleasures.'

'Perhaps not, but you know that both Mama and our father have been lenient about what we are permitted to read—in fact, I think the Lloyds are quite shocked about the contents of our library.'

'You mean Mr Fielding and Mr Richardson?'

'Yes, and the other novels that most clergymen would think unsuitable for young ladies to read.'

Our friends, Mary and Martha Lloyd, would certainly not have been allowed such access, and even though they too were the daughters of a clergyman we did not seem to have much in common on these matters.

'I have in mind several more ideas for stories and I have a notion to make something a little longer, too—what think you of a story that is told entirely in letters?' Jane asked.

'I would have to read it first—or have you read it to me—you know that my imagination is such a poor thing compared with yours,' I said. 'I have not the liveliness of you, my love, nor of Eliza either, I added.

She looked suddenly concerned and said: 'Oh, it strikes me of a sudden that you may have been hurt by my giving a dedication to Eliza when I have given none to you.'

I was reluctant to admit it but shrugged a little.

'What a selfish and inconsiderate creature I am,' said Jane, but fear not. It is my intention to set all my family's names upon my works before I am done. I have promised Frank to send him something now he is away at sea and we see him so little. But for you, my dearest, I have a better idea—to be sure I shall dedicate one to you but how much better if we produce it together?'

'Oh Jane you know I cannot—'

'No, a proper joint effort—with my scribbles illustrated by your wonderful drawings. What think you?'

I laughed. 'Well, I certainly could not draw the shocking goings on of Laura and Sophia.'

'No but you could of the kings and queens of England could you not? And what I have in mind is a history of England, which shall be dedicated to you and charmingly illustrated by you.'

She was as good as her word and ere long we were at work together on what she called *The History of England, by a Partial, Prejudiced, and Ignorant Historian.*

I was touched by the dedication:

*To Miss Austen, eldest daughter of the Revd George Austen, this work is inscribed with due respect by the Author.*

Compilation of the work gave us ample time for exchanging views about the latest news from our cousin. Jane loved the drama of what she perceived as her romance with Henry and the jealousy this inspired in James, but as I told her this all came to naught when James announced his engagement to Anne Matthews—the daughter of a general, a fine match for him that clearly pleased my parents.

'A fine match indeed for him,' said Eliza when she heard about it, 'but not a bad one for her, since she is two and thirty and he a fine handsome fellow of barely five and twenty.'

'But do not you always say,' teased Jane, 'that marriages are about money and he has a tolerably good position at Deane now he is ordained, with the prospect of inheriting my father's living at a later date?'

'No, it will not do, my dear,' returned Eliza. 'There would be too much disparity between the daughter of a general and a country clergyman, however tall and handsome, if her age had not made her willing to settle for him.'

Eliza's flippancy about marriage made me angry as it usually did. I hoped to marry for love and had the same hopes for Jane. I did not like the influence that Eliza seemed to exert on her when it came to discussing affairs of the heart. They seemed forever to be going into corners and whispering about such things, gossiping and giggling about love and marriage. The other day I heard her tell Jane that she would give her lessons in flirting. It is most unseemly, and I am sure Mama would not approve. She and Papa married for love as I hope to do and I do not think Eliza should try to turn Jane's head by talk of dowries and settlements and 'catching the right beau.' Jane has always taken my advice, and I worry about the manners she is picking up from Eliza.

We were very glad that Eliza, Aunt Philla, and the boy managed to return unharmed from France as things were very unsettled there and had given us cause of alarm about her safety.

''Tis right,' said my mother, 'that the poor Comte sees his son and heir at last, but I do not deny that I wish they would all return as soon as possible to these shores.'

Yet Eliza had been so happy when we visited her in London as she was packing to leave to join her husband. The house was in a very fashionable part of London and Jane was very excited to be there—I think what she liked most of all was riding around the streets in Eliza's coach, which actually had a coronet decorating the door.

'Can you not imagine, Cass,' Jane had said to me, 'that the populace will consider us to be princesses when they see this equipage?' She had begun to use French phrases since we had been again with Eliza—a habit that annoyed my mother, though I think Papa thought it rather smart.

'Of course they do not Jane. Do not let your imagination run riot so. There are many here who have coronets on their coaches,' I said.

'I do not imagine,' said my mother, ' that she will wish to ride around Paris in such a coach—things being as they are there. I would think it best to walk and dress in rags.' Our newspapers were full of stories of mob violence in Paris, and we truly felt at one point that Eliza, my aunt, and the boy would come to harm.

When Eliza returned, she came to spend the summer with us at Steventon. The pupils having departed, there was once again ample room for them. We were pleased to see that little Hastings was breeched at last as he seemed to have been kept in petticoats for far too long. I think Eliza was in hopes that putting him in breeches would enable him to make more progress with his walking, but he still finds it difficult and begs to be lifted up on every occasion. He grows so large and heavy that it is difficult for my cousin and even more so for my aunt, who seems to have grown thin and pale since the spring.

As Henry and James are at Oxford and Frank gone to Portsmouth, my mother has fitted up one of the first-floor rooms as a little sitting room for visitors, but the summer has been so fine that we spend most evenings sitting outside. Eliza regales us with tales of the new developments in France, though this is usually about the forms of dress rather than the politics.

'It is all so much simpler now. A simple chemise over a single petticoat is the style and the ladies wear fresh flowers in their hair rather than jewels.'

'Do they not wilt quickly?' asked Jane, more interested in fashion than either Mama or me.

'Why no, because the flowers are placed in tiny phials of water, which are hidden in the ladies' hair and can be refilled.'

'What will they think of next?' said Mama rather disapprovingly. 'I daresay we shall find such inventions spreading here.'

'Perhaps we could contrive such an ornament for our hair for the next Basingstoke Assembly?' said Jane, who had just acquired a new muslin for her first public ball.

My father, seeing my mother's look and trying as ever to avert the tensions that arise over the slightest thing between Mama and Jane, said: 'We may import French fashions but let us be sure not to import their ideas.'

'Oh dear uncle,' said Eliza, touching his arm in her familiar show of affection to him, 'my husband would so agree with you. He is most concerned about the hostility to the aristocracy that is so widespread now. In his last letter he tells me how it is evident even in the south and is no longer just confined to Paris.'

'We all thought the unrest would be put down by now but I was reading in the *Morning Post* today that violence to the nobility is becoming quite common. I do hope, my dear, that you will not think of returning to France until things are calmer.'

'I have agreed with the Comte that I should stay in England for a while. I have a mind to go to Margate with Mama and the little boy. I have heard that the sea bathing there is efficacious for conditions like his.'

She looked wistful and sad. This was the first time that I had heard any admission from her that Hastings was not normal and we were all taken aback. For a moment there was silence. Then Eliza recovered and clapped her hands excitedly.

'Now, my dears, let us talk of happier things. I hear that dear Edward is to be married—yet another of my cousins making a fine match.'

Edward had lately become engaged to Elizabeth Bridges, a baronet's daughter.

'Where is the marriage to take place? Is it to be in Kent? Are we all to attend? I confess I have attended only one wedding and thought it a very strange business.'

'Whose marriage was it?' asked Jane.

'Why my own, of course,' she replied.

My father burst out laughing, but he caught my mother's disapproving look and hastily collected himself.

'No my dear, we shall not travel to Kent, though they will call here on their wedding journey shortly after. But you know we expect another marriage here in which we shall all be involved? You remember that cousin Jane Cooper's father died last month? Your aunt and I have taken over arranging it all for the poor orphaned child.'

'Oh yes, of course,' Eliza said, her eyes brightening. She glanced at me.

'Does not our dear Cassy have an interest in that affair?'

I could not help blushing.

'Tom Fowle is a fine young man,' said my mother coldly 'and if he and Cassandra—'

'Mama', I interrupted, embarrassed. 'Mr Fowle is to officiate at the ceremony, that is all'.

Jane saw my discomfiture and suggested to Eliza that they walk together before bed. I was grateful to see them quit the group and walk off towards the shrubbery. Eliza's flirtatious ways are alien to me. I knew she would enquire about Tom's prospects, which in truth are not great. He is a curate but with no hope of advancement in his living he will have no prospect of marrying, though I have reason to think he admires me. I will keep my thoughts to myself though, and not even tell Jane lest Eliza plague me about falling in love.

After all, look how she teased Jane about what she wrote in the Parish Register. She was only trying out names for herself upon marriage, as many young girls do, and my father was mistaken to show it around. He meant it only as a joke but how Eliza played upon it.

'"Henry Frederick Howard Fitzwilliam of London"? Oh I like the sound him—Fitzwilliam is especially fine—could we not make him a baronet, too, for good measure? What about this next one? "Edmund Arthur William Mortimer of Liverpool." Edmund sounds like a clergyman to me and Liverpool is not a nice place so I am told.

'Now what is this last one? "Jack Smith to be married to Jane Smith, late Austen"? Oh Jane do aspire to something more than Smith I beg you!'

To my surprise Jane was not discomfited, but joined in the joke.

'I shall try hard to marry a man only if he has a fine name, I assure you,' and they all laughed.

I am often discomforted by Eliza's attitudes and frequently feel that she exerts too much influence upon my dear sister. Perhaps I am jealous? I own that may be the case but I do feel that desire to either shock or please Eliza leads Jane to be more outrageous in her writing than she might naturally be. I wish she would write of love and romance rather than murders, drunkenness, and madness. That story 'Jack and Alice,' which she has dedicated to Frank, has so many people in it who are described as 'dead drunk' and ruined by gambling that it may shock even a midshipman, and I doubt very much if he will tell his shipmates it is written by his younger sister. Still, the dear girl is so happy when she is writing that I do not criticise and am sure that when she falls in love herself she will write more romantically. I know that I, at present, want only to read of weddings and to dream of my own.

# TEN

## *Eliza, Comtesse de Feuillide, at Steventon*
### Summer 1792

How good it is to be here with my dear relations again after such a sad and turbulent period. Dear Uncle George is more precious to me than ever, now that his dear countenance helps me remember that of my beloved Mama. I can bear her loss easier when he is here. Even my aunt, who has often appeared to be disapproving of me, is kind. She even said to me: 'Eliza, my dear, I know I have not always been the most welcoming of aunts, but I have sometimes found your conduct unfamiliar to my notions of propriety.'

'Mrs Austen, there is no need for this,' interrupted my uncle, holding up his hand.

'No, let me speak,' she continued, 'for I wish only to commend her conduct towards our dear sister in that terrible illness. No one could have been more devoted. I have never known any daughter or son give so much affection and tender care and God will reward her for it. I am sure her dear mother rests in peace knowing how loved she was.'

My eyes filled with tears. I knew what it must have cost my aunt to speak to me so, as she had never hidden her disapproval of me in the past.

'I can only say that there never was such a mother or such a friend, and I was glad to do whatever I could for her. Her suffering was terrible but she bore it so bravely.'

'There are some in the family who were not sympathetic. Philly wrote after she had visited you and my sister-in-law to tell us that you were completely miserable and that she feared you would be unable to cope with what awaited. Moreover, she told us you would be left friendless and alone when the worst happened. I said to your uncle that you would never be friendless and alone as long as we were at hand.'

I could not help smiling to myself. Clearly this was one reason my aunt was being nicer to me—anything to contradict Philly, whom she has always disliked and tried to warn me against.

'It is truly good for my poor beleaguered spirits to be here with you all again,' I said, 'after such a year as I wish never to go through again.'

It was while we were at Margate that I first became aware of Mama's condition. Returning one day from taking Hastings for his morning bathe, I found Mama not dressed and in tears.

'Why Mama? What ails you?' I asked, indicating to Hastings's nurse to take him into the breakfast parlour of our lodgings.

'I can ignore it no longer,' she sobbed, 'the dreadful lump in my breast grows larger each day and now begins to leak fluid. Shall I show you?'

Mama and I had never observed much modesty in our personal connections—we had shared too many bedrooms in too many places to be concerned about such things.

She drew down the sleeve of her chemise and I could not but be shocked by what I saw. A lump as large as a plum and of the same shape was clearly visible, as was the fluid that soiled her linen.

I forced myself to be calm.

'We shall find you an apothecary instantly, Mama, and through him will find the finest specialist. I am sure it can be cured. Why, have we not heard about such skills that now exist for the treatment of growths and carbuncles and such things?'

She lifted her tear-stained face to me and tried to smile. She was ever a brave woman; her early struggles had given her a strength that I envied.

'You are right, my dear, I should have not ignored it so long, hoping for a miracle. We have always believed that God helps those who help themselves and we shall tackle it together.'

So it began: a year or more of terrible pain and suffering for her and anguish for me. The worst aspect was trying to be cheerful for her sake, professing hopes of a cure, sometimes indeed even believing in a cure. One particular surgeon, for we consulted many, assured us that in six months he would have cured the tumour and she would recover her strength. Sometimes she was even able to take a little sustenance and to leave her room for a short period. But for the most part there were violent bleedings, discharges, and above all intolerable pain. By last autumn I had to tell my relatives that there was no hope of recovery. They all wrote, most concerned, and even invited us to stay at various of their homes. But travelling was out of the question, since I could not subject my mother to anything that would cause her any agitation. Our house in London was a sombre place but I did not once miss the outings, calls, and salons that had hitherto been so important to me. We sat together most of the day, and I attempted to distract her with tales of our former travels and of the Comte's progress with his plans for our estate.

'How grateful he is, Mama, for the monies you have been kind enough to lend him, for this has helped him proceed tolerably well.' I did not add that I knew my husband had once more approached Uncle George about access to my own fortune, as he had almost exhausted Mama's loan.

'My child, you know I must soon make a will and we must ensure that its contents reflect the loan, as I fear there is little left for you and the boy.'

It was the first time she had alluded to the fact that she was dying, and it quite cut me up.

'We are well provided for, Mama, thanks to my godfather, so pray do not distress yourself on that account.'

'My concern for you is not a material one.' Her voice was low, but I could hear her clearly. 'I want only that you should be cared for the way I have cared for you these twenty-odd years.'

'I have my husband, my dear little one, and all our dear family—I shall be safe, do not fear.'

Her strength was gone and she could say no more. But I summoned the lawyer and the will was made. Warren Hastings and the solicitor Mr Baber were to be the executors.

At the New Year we did contrive to move Mama as far as Hampstead, as I had heard of a doctor there who had effected miracle cures in such cases. But alas, there was to be no miracle in our sad case and the dearest of mothers passed away. She was buried at the church of St John there and I had a simple headstone commissioned that bears the inscription:

*In memory of Philadelphia wife of Tysoe Saul Hancock Esq whose moral excellence united the practice of every Christian virtue. She bore with pious resignation the severest trials of a tedious and painful malady and expired on the 26th day of February 1792, Aged 61.*

I had been lost in my memories but now the sound of the teacups drew me back to the sitting room at Steventon. It was a sunny evening and as the windows faced full west, the room was now bathed in evening sunshine. My little pug dog, given me by the Comte to console me after the funeral, snuffled around my feet and I lifted her onto my lap

Cassandra poured the tea and Jane brought it over to me, bending down to stroke Pug.

'The book you brought me has such a fascinating title,' she whispered. 'I remember the first one you brought that Christmas—how do you always manage to bring something that widens my understanding?'

'Why, my dear, everyone in London is talking of Miss Wollstonecraft's book and I thought my niece who aspires to be a writer too should have the chance to read it.'

'Mama is a little shocked at the title—*A Vindication of the Rights of Women*—but Papa said I must be allowed to read it. He has many works in his library about the rights of man, so it seemed fair to him!'

'What a dear and farsighted man he is—how lucky you are to have him as a father.'

At moments like this, especially now that my dear mother is gone, I do long to be able to boast of my own father and his nobility and achievements, but it is as well not to dwell on this.

Cassandra has filled out since I last saw her and love has softened her face somewhat. Tom, her betrothed, is to call tomorrow, and I look forward to seeing him. Still my heart gives the preference to Jane, now the taller of the two and so lively in her disposition. How she will miss Cassandra when she is finally gone to Shropshire upon her marriage. I well remember my aunt saying earlier that if Cassandra had had her head cut off, Jane would have wanted the same.

'Now Eliza,' said my uncle, 'you must stay here as long as you wish. Your own health has not been good, we understand, and I must say I notice you are thin and pale.'

'Well the chicken pox was not pleasant and struck me down for some weeks. Though I felt embarrassed to be laid low by a child's illness, which even little Hastings escaped.'

They all smiled. Hastings is ever a favourite with my kind relatives, and they never draw attention to his undoubted back-wardness.

'Of course I was also weak from the accident I had recently suffered—the result, you know, of the kindness of the dear Comte coming over to England to comfort me after Mama's death.'

There was a sudden awkward silence, and I remembered too late that in the country one does not talk of conjugal duties or miscar-riages, especially in front of unmarried ladies. Cassandra reddened and looked at the floor, while Jane smiled slightly and glanced at her mother to judge her reaction.

My uncle recovered quickly. 'And did not you and your husband travel to Bath while he was here?'

'We did indeed, but I fear I could not fully appreciate the place as my spirits were so low at the time. We stayed but a fort-night.'

'Mr Austen and I love Bath,' said my aunt. 'We speak often of spending our retirement there.'

'The Comte found it excessively diverting, but of course he was often distracted by business in France.'

'And he was called away suddenly was he not?'

'Why yes, he was told by friends that if he did not return im-mediately he might be designated as an émigré, barred from ever returning, and all his property would be forfeit, so naturally he had to go back.'

'When shall you see him again?' asked Jane.

'I know not. Perhaps if things grow calmer there, when I am stronger I might perhaps—'

My uncle interrupted: 'My dear you must not think of it at present. You must keep yourself and the child as safe as possible.'

My uncle looked thoughtful, and I expected he was congratulating himself on refusing to transfer my capital to France. He would not want to see it confiscated and, to confess the truth, neither would I.

'We shall have a fine time while you are here. Our young men are mostly gone, but Jane has been scribbling mightily and you will be well entertained.'

I had been too bound up with all my distress lately to read much of Jane's latest work, but I know that she has indeed been 'scribbling mightily' and look forward to enjoying the new work.

'Now where do you advise me to begin Jane?' I said.

'Well, there is 'Lesley Castle'—that is the one I dedicated to Henry—and 'Frederick and Elfreda'—that one is for our friend Martha. Or you might start with 'Sir William Montague.' There is a good murder in that one and I am sending it to Charles.'

'Oh yes, poor little Charles is gone away to sea like his brother Frank is he not?'

'Yes,' said my uncle, 'and no longer poor little Charles, but midshipman C. Austen at Royal Naval Academy at Portsmouth. He will be at sea before his fourteenth birthday and plans to become an admiral!'

'Depending upon how long you are to stay with us,' said Jane, smiling, 'I may have something longer to show you. I am pondering on how a novel may be made from correspondence.'

I did not know how long I would stay; I knew only that Steventon was at this moment the most comfortable place I could imagine and settled down to read.

# ELEVEN

## *Jane Austen, Steventon*

### 1793

I f Henry came only to quarrel with Eliza, I wonder that he bothered to come home from Oxford at all. He is, after all, well established there now, a respected scholar and far from the callow schoolboy who was so besotted with her a few years ago. But none of us was surprised that when he heard she was to stay with us for a prolonged period after her sad bereavement, it did not take him long to decide that urgent business called him home. Just what this urgent business was we never discovered, since he seems to have time aplenty to walk and ride with Eliza. I often accompany them—it is a great pleasure to have her carriage at our disposal that we might call on our friends as we wish without waiting for the roads to be clear enough of mud to be able to walk.

We are especially grateful to be able to see Martha and Mary Lloyd more frequently. As James was to be married, the parsonage they had previously lived in was his now and they had to remove to Ibthorpe, a greater distance away.

I remarked to Eliza that I had noticed how married people were able to take precedence over single ones in so many ways and this was but one example.

'Yes indeed, dear Jane, never forget that marriage is all to a woman of small fortune, so try to ensure that you are not left an old maid.'

'But how shall I do that?'

'Why, with your pretty face and your wit, you should be able to make a good match and, you know, it is as easy to fall in love with a rich man as a poor one.'

'How shall I know when I am in love?' I asked. It was a matter I had often discussed with my sister.

'Now Jane, let me advise you. There are certainly not as many rich men in the world as there are pretty girls to deserve them, so do not make falling in love a prerequisite. In my judgement one can contrive to decide upon a suitable husband and then set about falling in love.'

I was hesitant to ask her about her own marriage, although in truth she had never been very reluctant to tell us about how she did not especially love the Comte but that he adored her. She continued: 'It is best to be a prodigious flirt and then one will always have gentlemen to hand to admire and flatter one.'

'Would your husband not mind if you flirted with others?'

'The French are more sophisticated about such matters, and after all I do not mind that he—' she stopped abruptly and changed the subject as Henry came into the room and they resumed their usual banter. 'Now Jane, here comes your accomplished brother— have we not heard that his writings at Oxford draw in many admirers? I believe he is quite the toast of the salons they hold there.'

'No cousin, not quite, but 'tis true that I edited the paper that James began with some modest success,' said Henry

'What think you Jane? Shall we see dear Henry a famous editor one day? Shall we see him in Parliament? At court perhaps?' Eliza smiled at him as she spoke.

'Well hardly, when he is to be a man of the cloth,' I replied, surprised that Eliza seemed to be ignorant of this.

A glance at her face told me immediately that it was indeed a new revelation to her that her favourite was to be a clergyman like his older brother.

'What, are you to go into the church?' Eliza asked, suddenly serious.

'Of course—is that not what most men do when they quit Oxford?' asked Henry.

'Indeed they do not,' she said sharply. 'They may go into the law, into Parliament as I said, or what is wrong with becoming a writer?'

'What is wrong with all those things is that they require more fortune than is at my disposal,' Henry explained with a tolerant smile and a shrug of his shoulders. 'Besides, a profession good enough for my father and my brother, not to mention so many uncles and cousins, is quite good enough for me.'

Eliza spoke sharply: 'My uncle and cousin excepted, I have not so much respect for the profession and to be sure I have rarely met a rich clergyman.'

'Perhaps my brother does not seek riches,' I said, feeling that Henry needed some support in what I thought was a most unexpected opposition.

'I never took your brother for a fool,' she said, 'and a man who does not at least aspire to riches is a fool. Ah but I know, he intends to make a rich match—is not that it, Henry? You have some young woman with thirty thousand pounds a year in your sights I suppose?'

'You of all people should know that is not true,' he burst out, looking very agitated.

She glanced at me and then back to him.

'Let us discontinue this for now,' she said. 'Our feelings run too high and I need time to accustom myself to having yet another clergyman for a cousin. Come, Jane, let us walk in the lanes here-abouts with Hastings, he is need of an airing.'

I was astonished that Eliza seemed so discomforted by the news of Henry's chosen profession. I thought it was understood by every-one that both James and Henry were to go into the church while Frank and Charles were to make the navy their profession. Edward, of course, was assured of an adequate—much more than adequate—income from the Knight inheritance. In any case, surely Henry's profession could be of little real concern to her? Unless, of course . . . but no, as we had often pointed out, she is a married woman and there can be no question of her marrying Henry, which might be the only circumstance in which . . .

I am struck though by the intensity of their disagreement about this and about other things. I wish that Henry would return to Oxford so that we might be tranquil again. It is true that Eliza is especially sensitive at the moment. I know that from some of her reactions to my scribblings. I showed her part of a work I called 'Catherine,' thinking it might divert her as she loves stories about romance and affairs of the heart that go awry. To my great distress, when I looked up from reading aloud I found her in tears.

'Oh Jane, how can you write so of my dear mama's experience? When I think of what she endured on those long journeys and how courageous she was . . .'

I was astonished and cried 'But of what are you speaking?'

'Why, the mock you make of young ladies who journey to India in search of a husband, of course'.

I looked down at the page, at a speech of Catherine's, and could have torn it in two.

*But do you call it lucky for a girl of genius and feeling to be sent in quest of a husband to Bengal, to be married there to a man*

*of whose disposition she has no opportunity of judging till her*
*judgement is of no use to her, who may be a tyrant or a fool or*
*both for what she knows to the contrary.*

'Oh, dearest Eliza, I do not write from life. I know full well that
my uncle Hancock was neither a tyrant nor a fool and that he and
my aunt were very happy together. I write only to amuse.'

She smiled through her tears and forgave me, but I was careful
to be more cautious in what I read to her, given her low spirits, and
in truth I never could quite resume 'Catherine' with the same enthu-
siasm as I had begun it. I have now left it on one side.

She and Henry seemed to get over the quarrel about his profession and for a while they seemed to be on easy terms again, but soon
another disagreement ensued. It was a fine morning in September
when Henry and my father came in from a visit to Basingstoke to tell
us some shocking news: 'They have abolished the monarchy—done
away with it,' my father almost shouted as he entered the vestibule.

'Great Heaven, Mr Austen, what do you mean?' asked my
mother, running in from the dairy, her cap awry.

'Just that, my dear, they have declared a republic in France and
imprisoned the king and queen.'

'Where is Eliza?' asked Henry. 'She must be told for this is serious news for her.'

'How so? How will it affect her?' my mother's face showed her
alarm.

'Now Henry, do not shock her I pray you,' my father said. 'Let
us discuss it calmly at the dinner hour and consider whether there is
anything useful to be done about the Comte.'

I could not truthfully see the import of this news but was aware
that so much in France seemed to be turned upon its head. I was
intrigued that their year now divided into ten instead of twelve

months. In truth I thought some of the new names for the months rather pretty and very descriptive—*Pluviose* for January and *Thermidor* for July, for example—but when I mentioned this once Mama immediately said how very unchristian it was. I did not point out that most of the names for our months came from pagan societies. I started to, but caught my father's eye and thought better of it.

At dinner I said not a word but only listened as the conversation swayed back and forth and tempers, especially Henry's, became more frayed.

His view was that as the monarchy had been abolished, it was only a matter of time before the king and queen were executed and that anyone with aristocratic connections would soon be in similar danger. He and my parents both urged Eliza to beg the Comte to return to these shores as soon as was possible. Eliza refused to believe that any such outrage could happen and declared that in no circumstances would the Comte abandon his birthright for the whims of a mob.

'You simply do not understand the seriousness of the situation, do you?' said Henry in exasperation. 'Make no mistake, if you do not act now to urge your husband to flee, your son may well never see his father again.'

Eliza burst into tears. 'How can you be so cruel? Have I not endured enough this past year without having to face such news as this?'

'Now my dear, Henry may be exaggerating somewhat but I am sure he speaks only from concern for you and the boy,' said my father.

'If he were really concerned he would not frighten me so,' said Eliza petulantly.

'You never can face the facts can you, cousin?' Henry's voice was fierce. 'Very well, I shall return to Oxford tomorrow if my presence upsets you so.' So saying he fled from the room and slammed the door.

How sorry I was that Cassy was visiting the Lloyds at Ibthorpe, as I should have liked to ask her what she made of this violence of feeling on both their parts. I had to content myself with planning another story, and I thought I could make something amusing of a character who was a little like Eliza, although I would make her considerably more wicked. I am struck by how Eliza seems not to be a very good judge of character. I know she writes to our nasty cousin Philly in the most affectionate terms, for example. I have seen an ending to one of her letters:

> Do me the justice to believe than no one can be more affectionately or more sincerely attached to you by all the pure and sacred laws of love and real friendship than your Eliza.

Whereas I know that Philly constantly condemns Eliza's lifestyle and even gloats over her misfortunes when she herself writes to others. I shall try using letters between a series of people perhaps, none of them knowing what the other thinks of them.

I am seated at my writing desk making a note of the names I shall use when Henry comes into the room to tell us that as England has now declared war on France, he intends to go straight to Oxford and enlist in the militia.

'What, will you give up your studies?' asks my mother.

'For as long as this war lasts, I will,' he replies.

'How smart you will look in a red coat Henry,' says Eliza, their quarrel evidently made up.

Better than in a surplice, I expect she is thinking. At least she has her wish.

# TWELVE

## *Comte de Feuillide in La Bastille Prison*

### February 20th, 1794, 2 Ventose II

To:
Madame la Comtesse de Feuillide
Orchard Street
London

Ma chère Femme,

It is scarce possible to believe that this is most likely my last
night on this earth. That things have come to this, who would have
believed? I still hope for a miracle. You will understand from your
knowledge of me as your husband these twelve or more years, I am
ever a man to live on hopes and dreams and that is the way I can pass
this terrible night—in hope rather than in despair. Perhaps those
who have betrayed me may yet recant and may be believed. Their
consciences may be troubling them after all—they took my money
and yet did not keep their promises.

But dear wife, if indeed I am to die tomorrow as I am
condemned, then I must spend the time in writing to you that you
may know the facts and that I may convey to you and our son my
love and gratitude. Also my sorrow for bringing yet more sorrow
to you both so soon upon the death of your dear Mama. I have not
been the best of correspondents I know since I returned to France

so suddenly after our all too short stay in Bath. How many times
I have thought of our days together there. The walks with our dear
boy and most of all our early morning together in our lodgings,
your dark hair spread upon the pillow, your eyes filling with tears
as we realised I must return here. How a large part of me wishes I
had heeded your pleas to stay in England. Though I would have been
branded an émigré and my lands would have been forfeit, it seems
they are lost to us anyway through the madness of the times.

I know you heard little from me but I hope you have had
occasional news of your husband through the communities that are
now established in England. These folks have left our dear France
and set themselves up to wait for the restoration of the Monarchy,
when they will be able to return and, they believe, claim their lands
again. I hope with all my heart that they may be able to do so and that
you and dear Hastings may one day be able to benefit from all my
investment of time, money, and, I may say, my soul, in those parts
of the south with which you are familiar. I pray you keep in contact
with these good people who will, I feel sure, take you and our little
one to their hearts. You will have the names of those in Bath, but I
believe they are now established also in London and in Reading—
close, I understand, to the place where cousins Jane and Cassandra
were at school.

To continue the sad account of my fortunes here—I returned
to Le Marais and was delighted with the progress made while I had
been absent. At last the place was looking as I had always imagined
it would. So much of the land was now dry that a vast deal of crops
were sown in the expectation of a great harvest the next summer.
There were cattle grazing where only marsh had been and now that
the buildings were repaired and our dwelling fully restored I was
able to send for the furniture that you, dear wife, had had sent over
from England. As the housekeeper supervised the arrangement of it

and we began to list the linens we would require I imagined how it would all look when you and our son were restored to your rightful place there.

Even as I planned though, there was unrest in the village. One day my carriage was stoned and I found the field hands had fled when I went to oversee the next stage of the drainage. The very next day I received a visit from the blacksmith—you will not believe that he has become the prefet for the area and no one may move about without his written permission! He told me that the local 'citizens' had made complaints that my improvements had deprived them of the fish and wildfowl that they were formerly used to take freely from my lands and so were in danger of starving! In vain did I point out how many of the so-called citizens had been given employment by my developments—employments that were not seasonal but had brought them wages all year. He told me that unless I restored free access to my lands for all the peasants, he would have to report me to the 'authorities' as a betrayer of the republic.

I was tempted to rage and threaten him in return and I hope you will not think me a coward that I did not. As you know, my dear, I have been a good card player in my time but on this occasion I felt that the trumps were all his. I told him I would consider his proposal and left with as much dignity as I could gather.

I realised, perhaps for the first time, that which I daresay you have known for some time—that for the present the cause of the nobility is lost. I decided that I must make my way to England if I were to preserve my life and hope for a return of my property when this madness that engulfs my country is over.

I managed to make my way to Paris—some good friends remain even to a nobleman—and there took lodgings while I sought a means of travelling to England. I think with pleasure of the days when we had free access. You would not recognise the process of

travelling about now—papers are required and there are checks at
every town and sometimes it seems at every village. People who
we would not have thought fit to groom our horses, still less wait
upon us, are now in official positions and act as the whim takes
them in forbidding your passage. You will perhaps remember my
good friend the Marquise de Marboeuf, with whom we dined
several times during one of our visits to Paris. She took me in and
was about to put me in touch with those who could help my escape
when she was herself arrested. You will scarce believe that a troop
of men came to her house in the middle of the night and searched
her kitchens. There they found, not unnaturally, large supplies of
food. They accuse her of keeping provisions for the Austrians and
Prussians she was expecting to come and attack Paris in order to
restore the monarchy. I know this charge seems almost ludicrous
when considered from a country that is sane. But my country is not
at present. The Marquise cried so bitterly when she was taken that
I determined to help her. I had large amounts of money concealed
about my person and thought that money must surely count for
something even in these times. I sought out those who had accused
her—two neighbours—and offered them money to retract their
accusations. To my infinite relief they agreed to do so and I waited at
the house for what I truly believed would be her safe return. Imagine
my horror when instead of her horses I heard the footsteps of the
prefets once again. Yes, my dear, they had taken my money and yet
shamelessly betrayed me also.

There is little delay here between arrest, trial, and execution
and they immediately threw me into this dreadful prison. I was
taken thence to a court that I can only call a sham and given but
five minutes to explain my actions. No one listened to me and to
my further horror I found they had a witness in the form of my
housekeeper at the Marais who attested to my traitorous impulses

and my lack of respect for the Republic. There was another witness also and I pray you not to believe the designation given to her. She was not my Mistress dear wife, believe me, then or ever. I have not, as I think you are aware, been an entirely faithful husband and have been grateful for your forbearance but I never, never, betrayed you with this woman.

I have written so long that the sky grows light outside. I fear there is no hope of reprieve now and I must pray to die with dignity as befits my class and breeding. I send my fondest love to you and my dear boy and to your family. Pray tell them I commend you both to their safekeeping.

Adieu, your husband
*Jean Capot, Comte de Feuillide*

# THIRTEEN

## *Letter from Henry Austen to His Sister Jane*

### June 1795, Portsmouth

My dearest sister,

I know that you will have heard tell of the disturbances here and will I hope have heard by my letters to Papa that I am unhurt. In fact, when the so-called mutiny occurred I was not here. I had been allowed to return briefly to Oxford to continue my studies. Some of the foolish men from my regiment joined with the poor of Newhaven in rioting for food. To tell the truth, if one sees the condition in which they live it is hardly surprising. It is of no use Mr Pitt, our Prime Minister, telling them to eat meat instead of bread as it becomes too expensive. They are used to and want bread and who can blame them? Nonetheless it was foolish in the extreme of my fellows to join the rioting, and they have paid the price. They were executed yesterday by firing squad. Do not be shocked, dear Jane , when I tell you that I saw this dreadful deed, for the whole of the regiment was drawn up in lines to witness it. I suppose this is thought to be a deterrent to anyone else to mutiny. I myself knew the rising had been brutally put down but did not imagine that they would all, every last man, be shot so summarily and with scarce a trial. But that is war and we grow used to news of violence do we not?

Have you news of how dear Eliza is faring after her dreadful news of the Comte's execution? I know that she is fled to her friends in the north—Durham County, I believe—and have been hoping to hear from her. She must at least be glad that her dear godfather is at last acquitted, as she was always faithful that he would be. In view of his many instances of his kindness to our family—you will perhaps know that he has spoken to the Admiralty about preferment for brother Frank and he is, as a result, made lieutenant?—I wrote to the great man in the following terms:

Dear Sir,
A humble and hitherto silent spectator of national concerns, permit me at the present interesting moment to transgress the strictness of propriety and though without permission, I hope without offence to offer you the warm and respectable congratulations of a heart deeply impressed with a sense of all you have done and suffered. Permit me to congratulate my country and myself as an Englishman.

I hope you, and more particularly he, do not think my tone too ingratiating, but you will perhaps understand that I have particular reasons for wanting this great man to approve of me. I will not say too much at this stage but I know that our cousin, dear sister is a great favourite of yours. I know, too, that you have ever thought highly of me. It is therefore my earnest hope that when and if a certain event comes to pass you may be willing to intercede with our mother and father to help them see that the match is a good one and all that I could desire. You and I know her faults all too well, but I am perfectly convinced that I can love no other woman but her. She has now been a widow above a year and I do not think it improper to be considering these matters. When she comes south again I shall put the question and believe from all the favour she has shown me in the past that I shall not ask in vain.

I am happy to hear that our dear sister Cassandra and Tom Fowle have pledged their troth and intend to marry. As you know, he was more James's friend than mine at Oxford but I always thought him a fine, upright, and principled young man, sincere in his beliefs and entirely to be trusted. I know that Cassandra and he have long admired each other and only their natural reticence has kept them from such an announcement for some while. It is indeed sad that they have not enough on which to marry and, although I would be reluctant to say this to either directly, I fear it may be some years before they may. What a curse poverty is to the wishes of our hearts!

But now, dear sister, because of the love we bear each other I must take up a matter with you that pains me to write and I daresay will pain you to read. I was very pleased to receive from Cassandra a copy, done by her own hand, of what I believe is your longest work yet. Lady Susan is its name and I was expecting to read another of your comic works that have afforded us all such pleasure in recent times—lighthearted, funny, and entirely suitable from the pen of a well-bred young lady such as yourself. But what can I say of this work? Lady Susan is as a character without redemption. That my own young sister could be writing of adultery, deceit, and intrigue in such a way! The entire lack of respect for the institution of marriage, for parental love, for the nobility, were greatly alarming and I must beg you not to circulate this work any farther else ruin your reputation entirely. And Jane, there is a further matter of concern that I cannot ignore. I believe that in creating the character of Lady Susan you have drawn most injudiciously on our dear Eliza. She is not, of course, as wicked as your character is but we cannot deny that she can seem a flirt at times and occasionally speaks her mind rather too freely for a respectable woman. This is not her fault—rather it is the result of the bad influences she has had to bear at the French Court and in her life in London. She has perhaps lacked guidance and been too indulged, but do not, I beg you, paint such an unflattering portrait. I know she would be shocked and hurt to read this work and I ask you please to put it to one side and begin on something more suitable for a young writer of your age and background.

Now to less weighty matters. Has the news reached Hampshire that there is to be a tax on hair powder? It seems the government needs to raise more money for the war and thinks this is a way to raise it without taxing the poor! My brother officers and I are determined to thwart the plan by simply giving up the use of it. I consider my own hair, cut short and combed back, to be quite gentlemanlike enough. Are the gentlemen of our neighbourhood doing the same?

Ever your devoted brother

*Henry Austen*

Letter from Jane Austen to Her Brother Henry
Steventon, June 1795

My dear Henry,

I received your letter some days ago but confess I put it to one side so that I might compose myself before answering it, as it distressed me greatly. However, before I was able to take up my pen certain events have occurred with which it is my sad duty to acquaint you before I come to the substance of your letter.

You will, I know, be shocked to hear that our dear brother James's wife is dead. We are all still quite overtaken by the suddenness of such news. She had seemed perfectly well but was taken abruptly unwell after dinner five days ago and was dead within hours. James is devastated, of course, but the chief of our concern is with little Anna, just two years old as you know. She is brought to us here, as James has his own grief to bear, and if I could just but explain to you the heartbreak we feel as she goes around the house looking for her Mama. What is to be done for her in future we cannot speculate, but we have told James we shall care for her here as long as he wishes it. Anne was not yet forty, and we had hopes of a brother or sister for the dear little one, so it is a great tragedy. James, I daresay, will in time see the advantage of marrying again as most widowers do and we must hope he might find someone who is kind to Anna.

You may perhaps be thinking that James, too, admired Eliza once but on this it may be as well to be silent for the present.

The other piece of family news that I must impart is that Cassandra's fiancé, Tom, is today departed for the West Indies as a chaplain to a regiment. His cousin Lord Craven has offered the position and it seems has promised him a good living in Shropshire when the regiment returns. Both he and Cassandra appear to think there was no option but to accept this proffered favour, although I think both are aware of the dangers and discomfort that surround such a posting, not to mention the perils of such a long voyage. It is their way of overcoming the disadvantage of their poverty, which you mention in your letter. My view is that it is too dangerous an undertaking for a man who is engaged, but I could do nothing as Tom was so determined. Cassy herself is distraught, as you can imagine, and begs me excuse her for her lack of correspondence with you at present. She is much taken up with the care of dear little Anna and I trust and pray that the little one may be of some comfort to her.

We, too, were glad to hear of the acquittal of Mr Hastings at long last, and Papa was most gratified to receive a letter from him praising British justice and expressing his thankfulness that, as he put it,

'my name shall not be blasted from infamy to posterity but be recorded with the many other victims of false opinions, some of higher worth, none of better intentions.'

Frank is indeed proud to be made lieutenant and would like to show off his new uniform when he visits us next week did not navy regulations forbidden him from wearing it except when engaged on His Majesty's business. It seems he, too, intends to eschew the use of hair powder. If all young men do the same I doubt that much will be raised in the way of tax.

Now, dear brother, I can no longer avoid responding to the severe scolding contained in your letter. I think of all my family you are the one who understands how much my writing means to me. This is perhaps because you yourself have created works of fiction and know the effort involved. You will also be aware of how much the approval of those close to us means. Therefore I will not disguise from you that your censure was hurtful and wounded me greatly. I do not write from life, as I think I have said to you on more than one occasion, and I will therefore pass over your accusation of Lady Susan being drawn from our cousin. Indeed, if you are intent on marrying Eliza, I am astonished that such a thought could have entered your head. It would seem to imply that you believe Eliza to be a character beyond redemption, which is exactly what I created Lady Susan to be. I intended her to be a character so outrageous, so wicked, that no one could take her seriously. She is clever, true, but without warmth or decency. Above all, she is devoid of any maternal feelings, which makes it all the more incredible to me that you could ever have thought her based on our cousin, who is surely a model of

maternal and filial love and duty. I intended people to laugh at Lady
Susan, to be shocked and wondering also, but above all to laugh
at her outrages and those parts of the society in which she moves.
Clearly I have failed in my intentions if you, my most devoted
brother, can have so mistaken me. I will therefore be putting her
aside for the present as you suggest. Do not imagine this is because
I have accepted your censure of her morals. It is rather because I
have perhaps not yet learned how to create such a character in a way
that creates mirth as well as outrage. But be warned brother, Lady
Susan, in some guise or other, will live again!

Meantime I have embarked on another work that I have so
far only read to Cassandra. Be assured it is quite respectable and
concerns two sisters, handsome but poor. Both behave, let me
assure you dear brother, in a most ladylike way throughout. One
has a tendency to be a little wild but she is always contained by her
sister, much as I am by Cassy and, on occasion, by yourself!

Be not afraid, dear Henry, I know your criticism was kindly
meant and as you see my good humour is now quite restored. I long
to laugh and joke with you again when next you return home. This
household is sad at present and we all long for the sight of you to
cheer our melancholy evenings.

Your devoted and chastened sister
*Jane Austen*

# FOURTEEN

## *James Austen at Deane parsonage*
### June 1796

I did not want to attend the ball—of that much I was certain. It was not so much that I thought it improper. Sufficient time had passed from the death of my dear Anne for that not to be a consideration. No, it was more that I have never been of much merit as a dancer and could not see myself in a ballroom in the role of a single man, or, rather, a recent widower. How did one go about choosing which young lady to engage for which dance? Were the dances I knew still in fashion or would I be expected to know a whole series more? Was it now the custom, as I had heard, to escort the lady back to her seat instead of leaving her immediately the dance was ended? There was so much I did not know.

'Nonsense James,' said my sister Jane briskly when I confided my fears. 'None of this is of any consequence whatsoever. A widower such as yourself, especially one with a young child to consider, has a duty to seek another wife, and what better place to do it than at a ball?'

Cassandra, too, was encouraging and so I decided to attend the next Assembly ball with them. Basingstoke was not too far away and would have the added advantage of being populated with many of our neighbours, so that I would not lack partners.

'Lack partners?' said Jane when I confided this to her. 'Indeed, there will be no question of that. Sadly, ladies always outnumber gentlemen at these affairs and many a fair young woman is forced to sit down for half an hour together for want of a willing partner. You will be in great demand, never fear.'

Cassandra smiled and added, 'And your sisters will give you instruction before the evening in order that you will be the most proficient gentleman there.'

So it turned out that by the time of the next Assembly I felt much more confident in my ability to tread the measure and really enjoyed my evening. I danced the two first with Mary Lloyd, the two next with Althea Bigg Wither, and by the end of the evening had not got around to favouring either of my sisters because of the number of other young ladies who were eager to favour me.

'You see James,' said Jane in the carriage of the Bigg Withers on our way home, 'how much more valued a man is than a lady in such circumstances. Why, both Cassy and I were forced to sit down during the course of the evening whereas you were never off the floor.'

I did, in fact, find this most gratifying and bethought me of the times before I was married when Henry and I used to vie for Eliza's attention like young bucks. Of course she, too, is widowed now. I must take up my pen to write to her. I believe Jane has her location. In truth, I found myself looking forward to the next ball.

'What do you think, girls?' I said 'Shall we make up a similar party next month?'

They both smiled as they glanced at each other.

As things turned out though, my next experience in a ballroom was not in Basingstoke but at Manydown, home of the Bigg Withers, and this time only Jane accompanied me, as Cassandra was gone to stay with her betrothed's family in Berkshire. Once again I enjoyed the evening greatly and found myself flattered by the numbers of young ladies who greeted me warmly and expressed a desire to be my partner. Even I felt that my dancing was improving, and I began to feel quite the eligible young man once again.

The evening was marred for me in one way though. I overheard two of the older ladies who habitually sit by the fire on such occasions and act as chaperones. Rather, perhaps, they act as commentators on what passes and exchange gossip. I was most discomfited to hear one of them describe my sister Jane as 'madly husband hunting' and another agrees that she was indeed becoming 'quite the flirt'.

I was sorely tempted to remonstrate with them but knew that the ballroom of my friend's house was not the place to do so, and was perhaps also made rather uncomfortable myself by observing some of Jane's behaviour during the evening. Her great friend Mrs Lefroy had her nephew visiting from Ireland, and it was apparent almost immediately that he and Jane were attracted to each other. He asked her to dance and I saw how animated their conversation was as they went down the line. After she had favoured Harris Bigg Wither, Lefroy asked her again and this time took her in to supper. I was seated on the other side of the room during supper, but could not help but notice that they talked to no one but each other and, to my astonishment, when her agreed partner for the first dance after the supper interlude came to claim her, she refused him and continued her nonstop conversation with Lefroy. I did not know what to do. I felt that had Cassandra been there she would have upbraided her or at least reminded her of the rules of good manners at a ball, but as her brother should I feel that it was my duty to do the same? I am not a person who feels able to make quick decisions about such matters, but, in any case, before I had time to decide what should be done, I actually observed her walk back into the ballroom with Lefroy and take her place in the set! To refuse the gentleman to whom you had promised the dance and then accept another was simply the worst insult one could pay in a ballroom, and I resolved that at the end of the dance I must take her discreetly to one side and remind her of her manners. I could not ignore the disapproving looks the couple were receiving from all sides, even though they themselves appeared to be in ignorance or oblivious. Accordingly, at the end of the dance, I left my partner at her seat and turned to look for Jane. She was nowhere to be seen! I did not want to make it obvious to all that I was seeking her but tried to stroll up and down casually while running my eyes over the ballroom crowd. Still no sign of them, nor in the supper room or in the vestibule. Eventually I passed Mrs Lefroy at the entrance to the hall and she whispered from behind her fan, 'Try the conservatory.'

I walked in and there they were, sitting among the palms, talking as earnestly as before. I could not believe my sister would be so indiscreet. Anyone would think she had not been set a good example at home, and I felt that my position both as her brother and a clergyman made it vital that I tell her immediately that her behaviour was bringing shame upon her family.

'Jane . . . ,' I began as I approached them.

Her smile was wide and warm and showed not the slightest degree of discomfort.

'Why James,' she said, 'allow me to present my newest acquaintance, Mr Tom Lefroy.'

He rose and turned to face me, bowing slightly. 'Delighted to meet you, sir. Miss Austen here has been telling me all about her fine family and I had already marked out her eldest brother by the proficiency of his dancing.'

Well, I thought, 'tis true what they say about the Irish having the gift of the gab. I returned his bow. 'But I fear I must ask you to return with my sister to the main party in the ballroom. Her parents would not approve of her sitting out here with a young man not known to them.'

I saw Jane colour and look most annoyed.

'Really James . . . ,' she began.

But Lefroy took the point immediately. 'My dear fellow, of course. I must apologise for monopolising her. I had quite forgotten the rules about such things are stricter here in the country than in town, and I do hope I have not caused any distress to you or our hosts.'

I could do nothing other than reassure him while feeling all the time that if he did not know the rules, my sister certainly did and was choosing deliberately to flout them.

'Perhaps,' the smooth-tongued charmer went on, 'when I call upon Miss Austen at home tomorrow, she may do me the honour of presenting me to your parents and allow me to apologise in person if I have done anything to offend them.'

Jane has certainly never met a more articulate and polished young man—it is impossible not to be impressed by him. Whether he is to be trusted is another matter though.

The following morning I had my own calls to pay, as was the custom, on the young ladies with whom I had danced at the ball. I had promised Mama to take my cold meat at Steventon and when I got there she greeted me with raised eyebrows and lowered voice.

'Who is this young fellow? He has been here above an hour sitting with Mr Austen and Jane in the library. They seem to be vastly entertained by him, judging by the laughter we are hearing.'

Indeed, I could myself hear peals of laughter and animated chatter from my father's room.

'Am I to invite him to take some refreshment with us?' went on my mother. 'His family are respectable enough but he seems a little forward for my taste.'

Before I could answer, the door opened and the three of them emerged.

'Mr Lefroy must leave us now,' said my father, 'but I hope we shall see him again during the course of his stay with his aunt. We rarely have the opportunity for such stimulating company.'

I tried to ignore the look of triumph that Jane shot at me behind my father's back as he shook hands very warmly with our visitor.

When I rode over from Deane the next day—I was to take little Anna home with me as her grandfather the general was to visit—I found that the 'stimulating company' had been there again. Jane was seated at her desk, writing to Cassandra, and was, I must say, looking remarkably pretty, her hair tied up in a green ribbon and her cheeks glowing.

'Only consider, James, what dear Cassy will make of my profligate behaviour with my Irish friend,' she said, seemingly rather proud of such behaviour. I am telling her that the only fault I can find with Mr Lefroy is that his morning coat is a good deal too light.'

I did not trust myself to respond. If my parents will not take a hand in correcting or restraining her, what am I to do?

Besides, I have other things on my mind. Mama has just told me that Eliza is finally returning from her long stay in the north and that she will be at Steventon within a sennight. My mind is made up. I shall court her while she is here. She has shown herself to be a devoted mother to that poor little boy of hers and I know she would be kind to my Anna. I must put my domestic affairs in order. It is no longer right for Anna to be constantly with her aunts, though they love her dearly, and I need someone to order my household and tend to parish matters. I have long admired Eliza and I believe she cares for me. It must surely be likely that she, too, wishes to remarry, and her long sojourn in the north country must have shown her that she is ready to relinquish that rather fast life she was leading in former times. She would, I am sure, find contentment at Deane, which is after all a fine house if not a grand one. Yes, I shall woo her and will even go back to writing verses. She is a romantic and poetry will appeal to her. I will start writing tonight.

# FIFTEEN

## *Philly Walter at Tunbridge Wells*
### March 1797

My cousin Eliza certainly is unfortunate in some ways, though she always has a pretence of cheerfulness even in her misfortunes.

When we were in Brighton together recently she told me she had an abscess on her breast and even went so far as to show it to me—though truth be told I thought I should faint when I looked upon it. She consulted a physician when we were there but I advised her most earnestly to seek the advice of a specialist when she returned to London. Always in my mind was the fate of her poor mother, and I daresay she, too, had such thoughts before her.

I have heard that she has consulted some famous knight surgeon—Eliza may be trusted always to have such people dance attendance on her, and she can in any case afford it. She assures me the condition is improving, though she has had to bear the horror of having leeches applied—I shudder at the thought of it. In spite of this rather serious indisposition she still seems to drive out all the time—she told me in her last letter that she was in Hyde Park that morning alongside the Princess of Wales, and she continues to attend the salons that she adores. I hope with all my heart she may not be sorry for her propensity for indulging in such pleasures.

She seems quite content about her eventual rejection of cousin James's proposal. I could have told the fool that she would never have him. Eliza as the wife of a country parson—it is too absurd! He clearly thought that because they were both widowed with a child to raise they could suit each other. Is he surprised that she preferred, as she put it, 'dear liberty'? Well yes, he did seem surprised, as I have heard not only from Eliza but from cousin Cassandra also. I suppose he thought his literary aspirations with poems and the like would conceal from her that life at Deane parsonage would have been very dull indeed compared with a life where you dine with exiled French aristos and curtsey to Her Majesty. How could she have ministered to his parishioners? She cares for little Hastings, 'tis true, but cares for little else except her beloved Pug. Neither I nor anyone else could see her taking soup to the poor of the parish. I suppose it was when she returned to London to think over his proposal that she saw the disparity in their persons and realised that she could not give up the style she so much enjoys, however much poetry he wrote for her and however pretty the countryside was looking in the spring.

So now she has rejected both the Austen brothers, and Henry I hear has found consolation with a Miss Mary Pearson. She has fine black eyes, I understand, and her father is in charge of the naval hospital at Greenwich, so she will have a fine dowry. Eliza writes of this a little wistfully, but you cannot blame Henry after all—he made her the offer and she refused him as she has now refused James. I do not believe that Aunt Cassandra will find this very flattering to her sons, though I imagine she would not have much welcomed Eliza as a daughter-in-law—there is no love lost there.

Mind you, I wonder if Eliza herself is not at present counting herself fortunate that she has escaped a closer connection with that part of the family, for I hear that Jane has been behaving in a way like to bring shame upon it. Eliza herself always professes such admiration for Jane and admires her compositions excessively. While she was at Steventon this time she heard reading from what she called 'Jane's best effort yet'—this is a full length novel if you please—about two young ladies called Elinor and Marianne. I do not know if there is any limit to cousin Jane's impudence— does she think herself a Miss Burney? I am astonished that Uncle George permits it and he a clergyman, too. Does he not know that lady novelists are considered profligate and shocking by decent people?

Anyway, it seems that the writing is not the limit of Jane's impropriety, as she has developed a reputation for madly husband hunting and recently behaved in the most indecent manner with a visiting young Irishman named Tom Lefroy. It is my belief that Cassandra's being absent visiting her future in-laws may have been a factor here, as I have always observed that Cassy is by far the steadier of the two. In my view she is the handsomer, too, though I know that others do not agree with me. This Mr Lefroy is the nephew of Jane's old friend Mrs Lefroy, and he and Jane met at a ball. My correspondents in the neighbourhood were profoundly shocked by how she set her cap at him and threw all good manners to the wind. I believe she even refused one of her promised partners in order to sit out with him and was seen entering the conservatory quite alone with him. Well, of course, it came to nothing—how could she have expected anything else? He is one of a large family with no money, and he is entirely dependent on some great-uncle who pays for his law studies in London. The boy's family depends on him to make a great match with a wealthy young woman, and Jane has not a penny. He probably just intended to have a few days amusement and she took it all too seriously and had her head turned. She is a shameless creature and, as she writes of romance, no doubt thought that love could overcome all obstacles. Well, she soon learned the truth. His aunt sent him packing pretty smart and Jane is left looking foolish and duped. They have now packed her off to her brother Edward's in Kent till the neighbourhood have forgotten that she behaved so ill—and perhaps until Cassandra is safe at home so she can keep her in control.

I received a nice letter from cousin Frank, who is also in Kent, on leave before his next venture on the high seas. He and Edward have been out shooting together and he told me—I suppose he thought to amuse me—that Jane had expressed a desire to go out shooting with the gentlemen instead of sewing shirts for her brother! There is no end to the impudence of that young lady.

A few weeks later

There is more bad news from Steventon. Tom Fowle is dead. Even as poor Cassandra sewed her wedding clothes he had been dead some weeks—of yellow fever in the West Indies. How sad for her—but really he should never have gone, engaged as he was. Where was his duty to his family and fiancée? But I suppose the sad truth was that without such a venture they could have no hope of marrying. Cassandra will bear it well—there will be no hysterics for her, no wailing, just bravery and dignity, I am sure. Indeed, Jane herself clearly admires her self-control—no doubt thinking that in similar circumstances she herself would not be a model of restraint. Jane told Eliza that her sister behaves with a degree of resolution and propriety that no common mind could evince in such a situation. There is some consolation for her, too; it seems that Tom has left her £1,000. Those girls could never have imagined the receipt of such riches. I wonder how she will spend it? It will give her at least some small degree of independence, which Jane can never hope for unless she makes a living with that much admired pen of hers. I shall believe that when it comes to pass!

James, too, is mightily afflicted by Tom's death, as they were friends from boyhood. I believe he gave a most moving oration at the funeral service. Well, not a funeral, of course, because Tom was buried at sea long ago. I believe that both Jane and Cassandra wished to attend the service and would have done so had not their parents forbade them. How unseemly that would have been.

James, I hear, is finding consolation for his disappointment with Eliza. He seems to be courting at Ibthorpe. Mary Lloyd will be far more suitable a wife for him than Eliza, and I am sure my aunt Cassandra has had a hand in this. I have heard her express great affection for both the Lloyd girls, but for my part I never cared much for Mary. Martha is altogether a kinder soul and gentler. It is a thousand pities that James has been so open about his pursuit of Eliza, for everyone must know that Mary is his second choice. What woman would be content with that? I am sure that Eliza will never be a welcome visitor in that house!

Eliza has recently been taking the waters in Cheltenham, a little town that begins to fancy itself another Bath, they say. She reports that the waters have done wonders for her abscess, which is now completely cleared. She tells me often in her letters now that she is desirous of taking control of her financial affairs herself instead of being reliant on Uncle George and Mr Woodman.

'After all, dear cousin,' she writes, 'I am a mature woman, well versed in the ways of the world and quite capable of managing my own money.'

She asks me to intercede on her behalf with my uncle, that he may be persuaded to grant her wish. In vain do I tell her that I can have no possible influence with my uncle, and in any case am not likely to see him in the near future. She has invited me to accompany her next time she goes to Steventon—what cheek she has to issue an invitation to a house that is not her own!—but I do not wish to see those girls again. Jane has returned home from Kent and I think Mama would not wish me to associate with someone who has behaved so ill. Cassandra, meanwhile, is surely too distraught from her own sorrow to welcome visitors.

I advised Eliza to seek the approval of her godfather for her plans as I am sure that neither my uncle nor Mr Woodman would hold out if the great Warren Hastings consented—Mr Woodman is his brother-in-law after all. She told me joyously some weeks later that my advice proved entirely right and Mr Hastings had replied:

> As Madame de Feuillide is desirous of taking the money which is now in trust with you and Mr Austen, into her own hands, you certainly ought to comply with her desire if you have the power to part with the trust. If you have doubts respecting this, it is your business, not hers, to satisfy them by applying to some able counsel for advice upon it and this I think you ought to do.

Upon receipt of this advice, all the trustees needed was proof of the death of the Comte, so that he might not have a claim on her fortune and this is easily furnished.

So she will soon be in complete control of her assets. I have a curiosity to know why she is so set on this. Has she another husband in her sights for whom this would be an inducement? She is now begging me to accompany her to Lowestoft—this lady never stays still for more than a month together. I have heard her speak of a certain Captain Smyth and it is possible she pursues him there, but I remember that I have heard Henry's regiment is now quartered in East Anglia. I shall not go. She wants me only to confer respectability on what is a far from respectable journey. She is set once more upon Henry, I think.

## SIXTEEN

### *Eliza de la Feuillide, London*
#### December 30th, 1797, or 10 Nivose VI

As I write the French version of the date I think of my dear husband, the Comte, writing to me from his prison cell the night before his death almost four years ago and fall to thinking of my decision and if it is the right one.

But the die is cast. Tomorrow is my wedding day when I shall change my name to Austen. So is this my last day as a countess? I suppose so, yet Henry, my dear husband-to-be says I shall always be noble to him. In truth, I daresay he likes the use of the title and the effect it has on those about us. His commanding officer was clearly impressed by it, and it never comes amiss to impress those who can advance or, for that matter, hinder one. Henry has been courting me for so long that I think even he was a little taken aback when I finally said yes, and as I write letters to my dear godfather, my dear uncle, so soon to be my father-in-law, and dear cousin Jane, now to be my sister-in-law, I have been gathering my thoughts as to why I acquiesced after having resisted him for so long.

Attending James's wedding at the beginning of the year made me envious, I suppose. Not of Mary—I long ago decided I did not wish to marry James and did not regret my decision. In truth, I was rather amused by the unfriendly looks that passed from Mary to me and by how she contrived to take his arm whenever he chanced to look my way. No, it was not them I envied, nor even the state of being married, but rather the state of being in love. That careless rapture, the pounding of the heart when the beloved comes near, was what I found myself missing. And then, too, it can be comforting as well as occasionally exciting to have some physical affection and to enjoy the moments of intimacy when one is preparing for bed in one's chamber.

It is not as though I was ever madly in love with the Comte, but we had our moments of passion and intimacy and I would not wish to think I shall never know those again.

Then there was the reading I heard from *First Impressions* while I was at Steventon. Dear Jane's talent is developing magnificently and there was one scene she read to us that was particularly fine. It concerned her heroine—I suppose that is what we must call her and she is in many ways rather like Jane herself, although she has been kind enough to give her my name—and a suitor, a man of large fortune whose name I have now forgotten. They were dancing partners and the conversation between them was so alive, so flirtatious yet so guarded, that it quite made me long to be involved in such matters again. They were on the edge of intimacy, so suspicious of each other yet so attracted somehow. I told Jane that she had quite inspired me to read more and begged to know the fate of the two characters.

'Pray tell, dear cousin—do these two marry or have you other plans for them?'

Jane smiled a touch mysteriously. 'I have not yet decided. I think they may but many difficulties are to be overcome, you know.'

'You mean that he is wealthy and she is poor?' I asked. 'Why, to be sure, a writer as clever as yourself must surely find a way around that.'

Henry had been listening to the reading also.

'At least there are no other obstacles to their marrying—they are each unattached and are near enough in age I fancy.' He looked at me meaningfully as he said this and I thought how handsome he looked now that his hair was its natural colour and curled a little around his ears.

I wondered if he was indicating to me that for him the disparity in our ages was still of no concern to him, and perhaps it was then that I began to consider whether I was growing tired of being single after all.

It is a considerable burden to be a woman alone when all one's affairs have to be dealt with, and I do miss my dear mama, who was always so good to talk to about such things. I was indeed most anxious to have charge of my own fortune and grateful to dear Uncle Austen and Mr Woodman for agreeing to give me control of it—spurred on, of course, by the recommendation of my godfather and yet . . . when one has the charge of it, it proves indeed to be a great responsibility and one might imagine the relief of giving it over to a husband, even though the law does mean that the husband is himself totally in control. Yet I reflected that Henry—a mild-mannered man and not worldly—might still let me be in charge of the money and the decision making.

When I saw Henry again in the spring of this year I could see he was recovering well from the jilting he had experienced by Mary Pearson and reflected that his attachment to me might be as strong as ever.

I resolved to test it out by going to East Anglia, where he was stationed with the militia. I did *not* pursue him, whatever opinion Philly or Cassandra have on that subject. I went to Lowestoft solely for the health of dear Hastings—the sea bathing there did him a power of good—but the sojourn there was of material importance in persuading me that a match with Henry *might* just suit us both.

The officers in his regiment were of the greatest gentility and held me in such respect that I felt entirely at ease. Their conversations worried me somewhat though, as the talk was constantly of invasion and of the French arriving at any minute. What was a poor widow and her sick son to do for protection in such circumstances? In addition, I was made anxious by their musings on the financial situation. I had already reflected that with rents rising—especially in London—and with the increased costs of keeping servants and carriages, it might be that my fortune was not as secure as it had seemed hitherto.

I may be a mercenary creature and own it with some shame, but I state with great conviction that the principal factor in my considering Henry once more was his great kindness, nay, I must say love, to dear Hastings. Henry seemed not the least embarrassed by his backwardness, but played with him robustly as a father should. Hastings, who had hitherto been mostly in the company of women, responded with such happiness that any mother would have begun to wonder whether it was her duty to ensure such a stepfather. When my dear little one had convulsions and fever earlier this winter, no blood relative could have been more devoted than Henry at that time. Hastings has need of a father; that does not admit of a doubt.

So all in all, it seemed the right decision to report to my godfather when I wrote to him thus:

> For some time in Possession of a comfortable income, and the excellence of his heart, Temper and Understanding, together with steady attachment to me, his Affection for my little boy, and distinguished concurrence in the disposal of my property in favour of this latter, have at length induced me to an acquiescence which I have withheld for more than two years.

I believe Henry will allow me sufficient separation that we shall be tolerably happy, and he is a dear soul and having courted me so long should have his wish granted at last.

I have written to Jane telling her of our marriage—she loves Henry dearly, but I will hazard she will be content with the news. How I wish I could contrive happiness in marriage for her. She would perhaps be content to earn her own living with her pen if such a course were not nigh on impossible for a respectable woman. She bears it well but how downcast she must have been with the rejection from Thomas Cadell this November. *First Impressions* is such a fine work that I can quite understand my uncle sending it to Cadell's in the hope of publication. To have it returned so swiftly with a dismissive 'Declined by return of post' scrawled across the first page—oh the disappointment, the humiliation! But Jane seems to feel it not and merely writes in her latest letter of how she is revising a former work. This is the one that was written as letters between the two delightful sisters, Elinor and Marianne. I heard her read parts of it some years ago and thought it most engaging. I remember that one of the sisters disapproved strongly of second attachments, but I am sure Jane will not share that view.

Well, as I have no such ability and can never earn my living by my pen or any other way, marriage is the way for me and I go, content and happy, to St Marylebone tomorrow.

# PART III

## *Eliza Austen*

## SEVENTEEN

## *The Reverend George Austen*
### Steventon, January 1798

I know that my dear wife does not approve but it is a fine match for Henry. I know she is ten years his senior and has been married before, but she is a countess when all is said and done and his first cousin, too, so has good Austen blood. He was determined to have her from being a young lad and has had eyes for no other woman, despite that little interlude with Miss Pearson. In addition, she is well provided for, as I have reason to know. I have told Mrs Austen so but she retorted, 'We shall see how long this so-called fortune lasts when the two of them set about spending on their carriages and fine wines. Henry, as you know Mr Austen, has no sense when it comes to money and she has always been so spoiled and indulged I doubt she knows the value of anything.'

'But my dear,' I protested, 'she is a wealthy woman and will be more so if this trouble in France comes to an end and she can come into her French property again.'

'How can you hope for such a thing—why, did you not tell us only yesterday that this General Bonaparte or whatever he is called is raising a huge army and intends to conquer the whole Continent? He is as opposed to the old order as the others were and will surely never allow the wife of someone who was guillotined to inherit.'

'Well, even without that,' I replied, anxious to calm her, 'she does not want for resources and Henry is now in charge of her affairs and will manage them sensibly.'

'Nonsense, Henry is not sensible at the best of times and certainly not when it comes to money. No sensible man would ally himself with our niece—she is too much trouble'.

'I know she has a tendency to be a little overdramatic—'

'A little?' interrupted my wife.

'But you remember how thoughtful and caring she was to my sister as she was dying and she quite dotes on the little boy. I am sure she will make Henry a good wife.'

'We shall see,' she responded and left the room.

In retrospect, it was a good thing that the marriage took place quietly in London with no family member present, as I am sure Mrs Austen would have refused any invitation to attend, while Cassandra and Jane have been in Bath these last few weeks, so would not have been available to make the journey either.

I confess that I am rather worried about Cassandra. She is still in deep mourning for Tom and has grown thin and pale; all her previous bloom seems to be disappearing. Mrs Austen and I thought a few weeks in Bath with their uncle and aunt Leigh-Perrot might do her good but in truth it does not appear to have been a successful visit. From what I can gather the girls found their aunt very tiresome. She seemed to spend too much time either telling Cassy that she must pull herself together and stop grieving or teasing Jane about Tom Lefroy. Neither subject was likely to endear her to the girls, who have always preferred their uncle anyway. Also it rained a great deal and they could not be out of doors but were compelled to spend most of their time indoors at Number 1, The Paragon. I have always found that house so gloomy—too much dark furniture in too little space, and it gets no sun at all. I believe they did go out each morning with their uncle to the Pump Room, but according to Jane:

The evening assemblies were not a patch on those of Basingstoke. My aunt and uncle could not contrive to have us introduced to any partner, so we sat out dance after dance and the main entertainment was in listening to my aunt complain that the crowd was so thick she could see no one she knew or hearing a detailed description of my uncle's five rubbers of whist.

I had hoped that they might have found more diversion in Bath—to help Cassandra over her loss and to veer Jane's interest away from Tom Lefroy. They are both in need of husbands, that is the simple truth, though Mrs Austen and I rarely discuss this. I worry about who will take care of them when I am gone, though I know their brothers would always be good to them. But they should marry and have families of their own—what fine mothers they would each make! I fear that Cassandra, having given her heart so completely once, may never love again, but for Jane to live as a spinster would be a sad waste. She finds comfort and fascination in her writing, I know, and was more disappointed than she allowed at that rejection from Cadell's. She tells me that Bath, although not very enjoyable, has provided her with material for another story. It seems that she and her sister read some fanciful novels—Gothic romances she calls them—to enliven their dull mornings during their stay there and she intends to write a story about a young girl who is too much under the influence of such books and the trouble it gets her into. It is to be set in Bath it seems, so as I said to Jane: 'At least your visit, however disagreeable, may have some positive outcome.'

I have been wondering whether Mrs Austen and I have quite done right by our two daughters. Our quiet country life may not be putting them in the way of suitable acquaintance who might in turn contrive to introduce them to suitors. I was rather struck by the lines attributed to Mrs Bennet in the rejected novel, *First Impressions*, when she upbraids her husband about shirking his responsibilities so far as the matrimonial prospects of his daughters were concerned. Have I, I wonder, been similarly irresponsible? When James inherits this parish as, of course, he is set to do, should we perhaps consider a move to Bath, where the girls could have more of a social life?

Or perhaps Edward will be the one who could help? He is well set up in his estate now and he and Elizabeth are constantly entertaining—perhaps I should suggest a long visit there? We are all in need of some relief after what was a difficult year.

The more I think about it, the more I find pleasure in contemplating Henry's marriage, even if my wife cannot. I think I shall send them a gift of money so that they may treat the regiment to a celebration. What would be an appropriate sum? £25? No, I shall make it £40—it is not every day one has a son who marries a countess after all. They will visit us soon on their wedding journey, and I believe they will lift the spirits of us all—even Mrs Austen.

## EIGHTEEN

## Philadelphia [Philly] Walter, Tunbridge Wells

### April 1798

I knew it! I knew she had set her cap at Henry again, so I was not surprised to hear of the marriage. The countess herself has only just seen fit to write to me, but of course the marriage was the talk of Hampshire and in a letter sent not two weeks after the event Uncle George told me they were married. He, poor foolish man, seemed to think it gave him nobility to have a son married to a countess. I have often thought him naïve—Aunt Cassandra is the realistic one in that household—but I had never thought him stupid. But without a doubt it is stupid to send a large sum of money to Henry's regiment so that they might toast the bride and groom. No doubt the militia drank a toast to the 'Good Parson Austen' too—everyone knows that the military indulges in alcoholic beverages far too much anyway, without encouragement from a misguided clergyman.

Uncle George did not tell me himself but I heard from another source that he has bought a carriage and actually had a coronet emblem engraved upon the side. I was always under the impression that money was too tight for them to afford a carriage—indeed Jane and Cassandra have often in their letters to me expressed regret that lack of a carriage is very disadvantageous for young ladies who like to attend balls as they are always dependent on being conveyed hither and thither by others. Now their father seems to think that a man in his position must have a carriage. What position is that, pray? He is a country parson and no amount of fine carriages will change that and neither will having a countess in the family. Of course, she is not really a countess at all now as she has re-married, but I cannot see Eliza easily giving up the title. Indeed, in the letter I have finally received from her this week she signs herself 'Eliza, Comtesse de Feuillide, Mrs Henry Austen.' The letter contains the shocking phrase that she does not like the word *husband* and will continue to refer to Henry as her cousin!

She is full of apologies that she has neglected me for so long, though she knows I will have heard of her marriage long ago. She is also extremely sorry to hear about the death of my father, though she knows that in truth this was a happy release as he had been senile for years. It seems that a new bride has little time for writing, as she is receiving so much attention from all Henry's regiment and other acquaintance. Her time has been taken up with all the officers and their families who wish to pay their respects. There have been parties and balls and what with driving out with Henry in their new curricle every day—has everyone in the world a new carriage apart from me?—she has scarcely an hour free, and this explains her silence. The curricle cost fifty pounds at least, so Uncle George says, and also tells me they make a fine sight—Henry in his scarlet cloak with Eliza beside him in a fur pelisse and carrying a large sable muff. The inhabitants of Ipswich are 'more fashionable' than she had expected and it seems that they vie with each other to be hospitable to the military. In her letter she tells me that she has given up flirting now that she is married, but I notice she remarks how Henry's friend Captain Tilson is 'remarkably handsome' and that she was already 'quite in love' with Colonel Lord Charles Spencer! How does Henry put up with this? But he has always thought her endearingly outrageous and I suppose it reflects well on him to have secured a well-looking and aristocratic wife. I will allow that Eliza seems to appreciate his tolerance and devotion. She writes:

> But all the comfort that can result from the tender affection and society of a being who is possessed of an excellent heart, understanding and temper I have at least ensured—to say nothing of the pleasure of having my own way in everything, for Henry well knows that I have not been much accustomed to control and should probably behave rather awkwardly under it, and therefore like a wise man he has no will but mine, which is to be sure what some people would call spoiling me, but I know is the best way of managing me.

I hope Henry continues to be devoted to Hastings as well as to his wife. The boy does seem to have benefited by a change of surroundings and as they have a garden at their house he is able to enjoy the fresh air. Of course Madame Bigeon takes care of him most of the time—his mother is too busy driving out and attending parties of pleasure—but I am sure that fresh air and sea bathing will do him more good than any amount of medicine.

It is now plain to me why the military are made so much of in Suffolk, as they are here in Kent and even in Hampshire. Everyone is taken up with the fear of invasion. I am becoming fearful of reading the newspapers, which now contain almost nothing but details of pending invasion by the French. It seems that Bonaparte is at Boulogne and awaits only fair weather before crossing the channel. When the sun shines people speak of 'raft weather,' since this is how the French mean to cross the water—by means of giant rafts with paddles powered by windmills—the *Morning Post* carried a print of such a contraption this morning. They could carry many hundreds of armed soldiers and we could all be overpowered in no time. They would come by night and the long dark nights of this month when there is no moon is when we are most at risk. Great beacons have been built on every hilltop to pass on the alarm of any landing and we are told to listen for the church bells ringing backwards, as that will be the sign that the invasion has begun. Mama has told our servants to lay in stocks of food, but so many people are doing the same that flour is now in short supply. My cousins Frank and Charles are both at sea and have told Jane that there is no risk at all and that the newspapers are spreading panic. They believe that Bonaparte has other fish to fry and that he intends to invade in the Mediterranean, not in England.

I am sure that Jane has passed this news to Eliza, as they are regular correspondents, but even if it is true—for which I sincerely pray—it will not stop the new Mrs Austen from parading herself in her new frogged riding habit, for all the world as though she herself were to be the defender of our realm.

I have to ask her a favour, which I am reluctant to do, but I need her to intercede with Warren Hastings on behalf of my friend—perhaps I might even call him 'my admirer'—Mr George Whitaker. Now that I am left alone with my mother, who is not in good health, and that he has been cut off by his father, we shall never be in a position to marry if Mr Whitaker does not receive preferment from somewhere, and as he knows of my connection with the great Warren Hastings he has asked me to intercede with Eliza to seek commissions from him so that we might have enough to marry on. He has not actually made me an offer, but we both know that this is dependent on him securing a position. We would be quite prepared for him to undertake some business abroad. I cannot at present leave Mama and it may be some years before . . . I shall write back immediately and seek her support.

May 1798

Well, that did not take her long! When I think how she has often teased me about Mr Whitaker and wished me joy with him but when it comes to giving practical support . . . she can say only that it is utterly out of her power to comply with my request. She actually tells me she has the most insuperable aversion to asking favours and that she could never approach Warren Hastings as he is so teased with requests and supplications. She does give me his address for Mr Whitaker to write himself but actually forbids us to use her name in the matter—so what good would that do? She is as shamelessly selfish as ever—having had two husbands herself she does not scruple to deny the opportunity of marriage to one whom she professes to love. She merely says that she has observed there is a tide in the affairs of this life and she hopes mine will take a turn for the better soon.

Henry's regiment is to be posted to Ireland soon I gather. She will not accompany him—it would serve her right if Henry found some consolation there.

# NINETEEN

## *Letter from Henry Austen to Eliza Austen*
### Ireland, September 1799

My dearest wife,

My longing to see you and the boy again grows ever stronger with each month we are apart. It is now almost a year since I saw your dear face, though your charming letters are a great joy and consolation. I was so glad that in your last you were able to tell me of some improvement in your health. I had hoped that the air at Dorking would do you good, being drier and more bracing than that of East Anglia. I know that you, too, had thought that the quiet country life and early hours would suit your constitution. We had hoped the same for dear Hastings, too, and I know that he was the principle reason that you moved to Surrey when I was posted to Ireland. Alas, his seizures, or epileptic fits as you say the doctors now call them, seem to have grown worse and are a source of great grief to you and I assure you to his devoted stepfather. My love, I cannot help believing that your own poor health can be attributed in large measure to the worry of his condition. And I hope when the current emergency is over we shall be able to devise for ourselves a more stable life that will have the effect of soothing your spirits as well as his. More of this anon.

    Now that we are stationed in Dublin, my life with the militia is considerably more agreeable. This is largely due to the kind attentions I have received from the Lord Lieutenant since our dear friend Charles Spencer did me the honour of making the introduction. He keeps a fine table and cellar and we dine with him twice weekly at least.

I know you say that you are content at home with your harp and your books, but I do feel that if you partake of some agreeable company it would lift the spirits of one who has always been so sociable. I know that Lady Burrell and Lady Talbot have sought you out and I do recommend that you take up their invitations when they next call. In truth, I would find our separation intolerable were it not for the friendships of the fine gentlemen I have mentioned.

It is of a conversation with them that I now wish to speak. The Lord Lieutenant, in company with most of the officers, thinks that the militia will be stood down next year if the war continues to go our way. Lord Nelson's great victory in Egypt has raised morale and the navy now feels the French are almost vanquished. Now my dear, do not allow your hopes to rise too much on the subject of your French property—it will be a considerable time before we can address that issue—but when I am stood down, how should you like to be the wife of a banker and live in a fine house in London? This is a prospect I am now seriously considering. I can arrange a partnership with Henry Maunde who has much experience in this field and once trade begins again all the fellows think more banks will be needed so why should not I take the opportunity? We could also be agents for army transactions and many of my acquaintance would give us commissions, I am convinced.

Do let me know, dear girl, what is your view of this scheme. Apart from my friends I have mentioned it to no one but you, though I am in frequent correspondence with my sisters and my father. My brothers Frank and Charles are not the best of correspondents, as you know, but they have the excuse of being at sea and indeed in action from time to time. Brother Edward writes little but I have received a long letter from Jane, which I enclose, and from that you will see what a fine life he now enjoys. As to brother James, you will have heard that Mary ([Jane calls her Mrs JA to distinguish her from you—Mrs HA) is safely delivered. It is to be hoped that now she has a boy of her own, she will be more kindly towards little Anna. If I were as bad a stepparent to your dear boy as Mary is to Anna, I should be ashamed.

Jane is scribbling again, as you will see from her letter. It was good for her to have space to spread her papers at Godmersham and I hope that with this book she might eventually find a larger audience than her family. She deserves that, does she not? I wonder if I could interest a publisher in her work once we are settled in London.

I now bid you adieu and send my fondest love. I have hopes of returning to England in December but that still seems too long to be apart.

Your most devoted cousin and husband

*Henry Austen*

My dear,

On rereading Jane's letter before sealing this I wonder if I should add a warning about heeding Jane's misgivings about cousin Philly. I know you are inordinately fond of her but the rest of my family thinks her a mischief maker, often given to saying cruel things. I wonder if they have heard her say such things about you? Might it be wise to be a little guarded in your intercourse with her?

Letter enclosed with This,
From Jane Austen to Her Brother Henry

My dear Brother,

I expect you have heard from Papa that Mary is brought to bed of a boy—named James Edward for his father. Things did not go too well with her and Mama made the journey to Deane in the dark to be at the lying-in. Thank God they both came through and we are all thankful. In presenting James with a son and heir it is to be hoped that Mrs JA will have overcome her resentment of poor little Anna, who quite dotes upon her new brother, though as you know she can rarely please her stepmother. Mary does not manage things as well as Elizabeth, who always looks so neat and tidy at her lyings-in. Henry I entreat you , do not tease—I expect you are saying that E has so much more practice—after all she has had seven already and shows no sign of stopping!

I certainly must not tease about Elizabeth as the real purport of this letter is to tell you all about our family visit to their new—and very splendid—abode. Rowlings, where they have lived since their marriage, is a fine enough house, but as for Godmersham! As Cassandra and I walked around we agreed it was like a fairy tale or the Palace Beautiful in *Pilgrim's Progress*.

It would have been nice to be conveyed to Kent in our own carriage, but as you know, we were unable to continue its upkeep and were obliged to give it up. So we went post as far as Canterbury but our discomfort was forgotten when we arrived at Godmersham. It is a fine brick house, with two wings and a most imposing façade with a set of steps to the front entrance where Elizabeth, Edward, and five of the children were waiting to great us, their coachman having collected us in the finest of their carriages (they have four!) from the Inn in Wye for the last stage of the journey.

Edward says he was reluctant to move in when Mrs Knight became a widow, but as she said, when they adopted him and he agreed to change his name from Austen to Knight, with that came all the privileges of an eldest son, which certainly include inheriting the family property and taking his own family to live in it. It is the rule, of course, and I am certain that Edward and Elizabeth are more gracious about it than my John and Fanny Dashwood—I am sure you remember them from my readings to you from Elinor and Marianne. Edward was very proud to show his family around, as well he might be.

It is a lovely house, long and low, built of warm red brick with decoration in white stone. It is most favourably situated in a green valley, surrounded by parkland and woods, which abound with game for the shooting parties. The trees were a fine sight, with their leaves just turning gold. We went in by the north front up a flight of steps and Edward proudly led our mother in. He is becoming quite portly, which I suppose is fitting for a landed gentleman. Elizabeth is as pretty as ever despite her many confinements.

All the rooms are magnificent but especially the main drawing room, which is very ornate and decorated with plaster depictions of fruit, flowers, and leaves. The chimney piece is vastly superior to any I have ever seen and I dearly wish I had had it as a model for the fixtures at Rosings or even Pemberley! The furniture is very fine, with silken chairs and gilt mouldings and embroidered chair backs. My favourite room, you will not be surprised to hear, was the library. Edward is not much of a reader as the estate takes up so much of his time—or at least that is what he says, though his steward seems very able and my father enjoyed walking the farms with him. But what a delight the library was to me and to Cassandra!

And we sat there often just the two of us, with two fires, five tables, and twenty-eight chairs; we did not mind a wet day in the least! The other joy for us was that we had not only our own room but our own sitting room and dressing room, too, with a fire lit all day and all night—such a comfort to be able to rise in the early morning if I had an idea to set down and not sit shivering by a cold grate. Yes, I have been scribbling again and have started a whole new story that I believe will amuse you all. I have called my heroine Susan and she is young and impressionable and a great reader of novels such as *Udolpho*. What I hope will amuse in the story is that she has a little difficulty distinguishing fiction from reality. The story is set in Bath and I found our recent visit there useful for description, though to tell the truth staying with Aunt and Uncle Leigh-Perrot was not the most pleasant experience. Anyway, during the stay at Godmersham I found that I could increase my rate of writing because of not having to tidy away my papers so frequently. I could leave my work spread out, secure in the knowledge that no one needed to lay a table for dining and that the servants were too much in awe of 'The Master' to spy on his sister's writing.

I made a new friend there, too—Miss Sharpe, the governess. Now Henry, do not scold me for calling a servant a friend. She is part of the family, a gentlewoman, and only obliged to shift for herself as her family fell upon hard times. I am only too aware that your sisters might find themselves in the same plight if our brothers are not generous to us after the death of our father, which I hope and pray may be long delayed. Miss Sharpe and I both enjoy walking and Edward's estate gives us plenty of opportunity, with a large shrubbery, a park near ten miles round, a river, and even a Doric temple. Elizabeth took us visiting to the neighbours round about, principally the Knatchbulls and the Wildmans, and we went several times into Canterbury, where old Mrs Knight now lives. She is a kind lady and is prodigiously fond of Edward. What a lucky thing it was for him, and I suppose for all of us, that she and the late Mr Knight took such a fancy to our Edward on their honeymoon journey that they wished immediately to adopt him, for they never had any other children and their estate might have passed to a very distant family or been broken up. I remember at the time that you and I thought it heartless of Mama and Papa to agree to the arrangement, but I am sure they now feel their decision was vindicated as we can all enjoy Godmersham—as I told Cass 'Everyone is rich in Kent.'

I confess I found it difficult to adjust to the different standards here at Steventon. I became used to dining at six on partridge and French wine, whereas here we dine on mutton at three thirty. I miss my sister greatly—you know that she has stayed on with Elizabeth and Edward as Elizabeth is to be confined again soon and would like Cass to help. I know full well that my sister will be a greater favourite than I at Godmersham as her sweet and docile temperament is more acceptable to them. Much though I enjoy the luxury I fear that their neighbours somewhat look down on us as Edward's 'old maid' sisters and poor relations and I do not find that comfortable. But my mother's poor health at present means I have much to concern me with household matters and when I have no time for my writing I become cross and ill tempered.

Speaking of cross and ill tempered, I beg you when you write to dear Eliza to suggest to her that she is less open in her correspondence with Philly. Your dear wife is so frank and open that sometimes she is easily taken in and I am sure she does not realise that Philly is always critical of her and does not hesitate to tell my mother or other members of the family of what she calls ' her latest extravagance' or ' her ridiculous aspirations.' She even criticises her mothering, which is especially wicked since we all

know that there could be no more devoted a mother than your
wife. I pray you remember me most kindly to her and send a kiss
to dear Hastings.

I hope that this emergency situation is soon over and that you
may be free to return to your family, of whom no one thinks of you
with more affection than

Your devoted sister

*Jane*

# TWENTY

## *Eliza at Her Residence in Dorking*
### September 1799

I confess that the letter received from dear cousin Cassandra this morning gives me some alarm. The most extraordinary event seems to have overtaken Aunt Leigh-Perrot in Bath. She has been arrested and imprisoned on account of a stolen piece of lace! Of course it is a most malicious falsehood and there has clearly been some terrible mistake. I have enough confidence in the legal systems of dear England to believe it may all turn out well, though do not deny there is a period of distress ahead for all my dear family. If found guilty she could be sentenced to transportation to the colonies! I cannot believe that this will happen to the old lady. My family here in England have not experienced a truly unreliable system of law as I have had the misfortune to do, or they would not be so alarmed. I can well believe such a transgression in France at present, but in England, in Bath, impossible!

I do feel that Aunt Cassandra has gone somewhat too far in offering the services of her daughters to support their aunt, to send unmarried young women to be with her in prison—a dreadful thought. Their innocence would soon be corrupted, and were I on more cordial terms with my mother-in-law I would strongly counsel against it. I know enough of my aunt, my mother-in-law, to understand this would not persuade her and my dear husband cannot be expected to take up the situation at present, concerned as he is with our own future.

But leaving aside the plight of Aunt Leigh-Perrot, there is, I believe, more to concern us about dear Jane. I hear from Cassandra that Tom Lefroy is recently married—he did not let the grass grow under his feet when it came to securing his future; I understand the lady in question is well provided for. And Jane feigns indifference, but she gave her heart to him, of that there is no doubt, and though I believe Cassandra can well survive her own loss, I do not feel so confident of Jane. She needs love and romance to fuel her writing. She has been diverted by having Charles home and truly delighted that he is made. How fine he must look in his new lieutenant's uniform! During the summer she sent me long letters from Bath while on a visit there with Edward, Elizabeth, and her mother. They were full of her usual wit. She told me that Edward had decided to take the cure in Bath as he had now reached the age and station where it was proper for him to suffer from gout! He had taken two whole floors in Queen Square, so they were tolerably comfortable, but I always felt a touch of melancholy in her correspondence. Edward went into the baths every other evening and Aunt Cassandra took the waters each day, but they had very little other diversion aside from shopping. Jane bought artificial bunches of fruit to trim a hat given her by Elizabeth and bought some small gifts for Cassandra, sounding sprightly enough, but when I heard that Edward had bought a matched pair of carriage horses for sixty guineas I was forced to wonder if Jane felt her own poverty and obligation to be constantly watching her pennies rather trying. I did feel, too, that Edward and Elizabeth might have made an effort to see that Jane went about a little more. They scarcely dined out at all and strolling about Barton Fields is unlikely to result in suitable introductions. When I heard they were to attend an entertainment in Sydney Gardens with music and a fine display of fireworks, the first thing I thought of was that Edward and Elizabeth would have made up a party that included at least one single man. They must know some and surely Jane, modest though she is, would have expected such a favour. Surely every parent, especially those in straightened circumstances like my aunt and uncle, have a responsibility to try to get their daughters married off. A brother may not feel the same obligation, yet Edward must know that Jane and Cassandra will be entirely dependent on him and the other brothers once Uncle George is dead. Not that I would begrudge that support to my dear sisters-in-law but if other arrangements can be made is it not wise to try to bring them about? They may now despair of Cassandra and marriage but Jane still has a great deal to offer and deserves more opportunity. Surely Charles has a dashing officer or two among his acquaintance? Was there not a young clergyman in the Pump Room with whom my uncle could have made contact? When I consider that even cousin Philly, who with the best will in the world one cannot call attractive either in looks or personality, has a suitor, it seems monstrous unfair that dear Jane is denied. Which thought reminds me that I had perhaps better heed my husband's warning about Philly, since I have displeased her by my reaction to her request for intercession with my godfather.

When my dear husband returns from Ireland at last and we take up residence in London, to which I greatly look forward, I shall make it my business to invite Jane and take her about with me. So many of my French acquaintance are now in London that I am sure we shall have a fine time. There is no prospect of their returning to France in the immediate future, since Bonaparte now makes himself First Consul and is to rule France in the antique manner of three consuls. I doubt that the other two will have a great deal of influence!

## TWENTY-ONE

### *Mary Austen [Mrs JA] at Deane Parsonage*

#### March 1800

I t is always my luck to miss out whenever anything pleasant is occurring. How I should like to have seen Aunt Leigh-Perrot return in triumph to Bath. She managed it all with great aplomb, I believe. It is reported that she said: 'Alls well that ends well. The man who accused me is fled, the shop is ruined, and my character is cleared. Lace, I am glad to say, is not necessary to my happiness.' A brave speech, indeed, but without her husband being willing and able to spend nigh on two thousand pounds to collect witnesses and pay for her keep and food and laundry while incarcerated she would have been in a fine pickle. Lucky they are to have it to spend and have no children to consider.

Then shortly afterwards I was kept from seeing brother Frank on his return from the Mediterranean with his decoration for bravery. What a fine evening they all had, and I deprived as usual because little James fell from a tree and broke his collarbone. I do not see why James was excused duty and could leave his son while I was expected to stay with the boy.

Now I hear that cousin Eliza is to have a fine new house in London. Henry wishes always to give her the best—even if he does it with *her* money. I do not suppose she will have to scrimp and save to furnish that fine place like I have to do here. Not that this small house is worthy of much attention anyway. We have been married now three years and James is thirty-five, after all. High time he had a stipend worthy of his fine mind and great preaching ability. He deserves more respect than he gets as a humble curate. Why, father Austen is looked up to almost like a squire in his parish at Steventon. The parsonage is spacious, too—far bigger than they need for two old people and two unmarried girls. We have James and Anna and could have more in the future. They really ought to be thinking of us and of retiring—he is not far off seventy.

## May 1800

That east wind is still bitter in spite of it being spring. I said to my mother-in-law as we sat together at the parsonage that I did not think it wise for the old gentleman to be out in it at his age and that he should consider a warmer location than Hampshire.

'Oh,' she replied, 'his parishioners like to see him and they are used to expecting him to call when they are sick or bereaved.'

'But do you not find the winters dull here, as well as cold? I wonder you do not consider a place like Bath, where there would always be something to amuse you both—the book shops, the library, the Pump Room. Here you are so shut off from the world, whereas in Bath you would have your relations to hand, as well as much more amusement.'

'Oh, I own it is dull in winter. I have lived here most of my life, you know, and would quite fancy a change. But we have the girls to consider. Cassy is so fond of the countryside, and Jane dislikes Bath intensely.'

'Well, as to that, the girls should not be allowed to rule your lives. They should permit their parents to know what is good for them.'

'I think it is good for them to be happy in the home they have always known.'

'But Mama, have you not considered how they are ever to get husbands here? Jane will be twenty-five in December and Cassy is almost thirty. If we do not take them in hand, they will both die old maids. A larger society would greatly improve their chances. Cassandra is handsome enough, but she wants liveliness. If she could but meet a widower with a family in need of care, what a wife she would make.'

Mama smiled. 'I do not think Jane would be suited to such a role, do you?'

I could not but agree. 'No, but she is becoming sharp and disagreeable, making fun of the few young men she does meet and saying they are not clever enough to tempt her. She would be greatly improved by a larger society. She says herself, I have heard her on many occasions, that she often wants for partners at the balls and assemblies hereabouts. I do not like to see her passed over and I am sure you do not either.'

'To be sure Bath is a good place to look for husbands, and perhaps Mr Austen would benefit from an easier life. I do not wish to see him work himself into the grave. You are a thoughtful girl, dear Mary, to consider us so kindly.'

I believe she may be warming to the idea. I am sure I can soon make her see that Mr Austen should be making way for a younger, fitter, cleverer man. A man like my husband.

November 1800

I have had an unaccustomed stroke of luck this autumn. It is very unusual for Jane and Cassandra to be absent from home together but that has happened these last six weeks. Cassandra is gone to

Godmersham, where Elizabeth is to be confined yet again, while Jane is staying with the Lloyds at Ibthorpe. It gave me the opportunity to sit with Mama and discuss what we have started to call 'our plan.' I can see she is becoming quite animated about the idea of removal to Bath, and best of all, has now contrived to make Mr Austen equally enthusiastic. At first James was astonished and tried to dissuade them.

'But dear Mama, is your health fit for such a change of scene? Would you not find it too taxing?'

I soon put him off that I can tell you, and made him see that this was entirely the right course for everyone concerned. Who could quarrel with an easier life for his father, more diversion for his mother, and a wider society, with all that implies, for his sisters?

'No James,' I said, 'do not let your own unwillingness to inherit your father's parish divert you from doing what is clearly the right thing.'

'I am not at all unwilling to take on the parish,' he responded. 'I am as willing as the next man to do my duty. I am only unwilling to put undue pressure on my father and mother for our benefit—we shall be moving into a much larger house and no doubt inheriting most of their property. I would not wish there to be any impropriety, real or perceived.'

'Impropriety?' I almost shouted. 'Many would think the only impropriety was in their keeping you waiting so long.'

December 26th, 1800

We have not passed a cheerful Christmas, though it has been pleasant to have my sister, Martha, staying at Steventon. I was astonished by Jane's reaction to the news of the removal to Bath. True, my mother-in-law was not very tactful in announcing it the minute

Martha and Jane walked through the door—tired and cold from their journey back to the parsonage.

'Well girls, it is all settled. Your father and I have decided to leave Steventon and go to Bath.' But yet for Jane to faint away entirely was a great shock—I have never seen her overpowered before, and she was as white as a sheet.

She has done her best since to put a brave face on it, but whenever the conversation veers towards the move or arrangements connected with it, a strange look comes over her and she is often sharp and even rude in her responses to me. She misses having Cassandra about to support her, I think, but Cassandra shows no sign of wanting to return and indeed has said she will stay away until after the move is accomplished. This is not kind of her and may not make my life easier, as Jane is far from compliant. If truth be told, she has never liked me, or at least not since I married her brother. She was tolerably kind before that, but I believe she thinks I have not been a good enough stepmother to Anna, of whom she is inordinately fond. She has not seen how difficult the child can be and how hard I have had to work to make her mind me. In my opinion, it is all due to the child's being vastly spoiled by Jane and Cassandra after the sad death of her mother. Then again, Jane has always been too greatly influenced by cousin Eliza, 'Madame la Comtesse,' as my father-in-law still calls her. She gives herself so many airs I do not think she needs more flattery from *him*. Of course James was misguided enough to ask Eliza to marry him, though only because he was still mourning Anne and had not quite come to his senses. La Comtesse as the wife of a parish priest—I do not think so! Surely Jane did not really wish for that match—Henry is more suitable a husband by far for such a woman. It might perhaps add to Jane's reasons for being hostile to me. None of them consider what a trial it is to have the woman your husband wanted to marry in the same family as yourself. I always wonder if they are thinking that James took me only because Eliza refused him. Few women have as much to endure as I and a larger house and grounds and more possessions would be scant reward.

April 1801
Letter from Mary [Mrs JA] to Eliza [Mrs HA]
Deane Parsonage

Dear Cousin Eliza,

I address you as cousin, though of course we are sisters. But as I understand that you still sign yourself by your French name as well as Mrs Henry Austen, it seems appropriate.

First, may I wish you joy of your new abode and assure you of the very best wishes of James and myself for your new life in London. I understand that dear Henry is finding life as a banker most agreeable and that your house is very fine. I shall look forward to receiving firsthand reports of it when Cassandra returns to us after her visit to you, which I believe is to take place soon.

I was disconcerted by the letter I have recently received from you. I quite fail to understand why you felt it necessary to intercede on Jane's and Cassandra's behalf about their move to Bath. Cassandra seems so little concerned about it all that she has scarcely been at home since the plan was fixed upon. Indeed she is to depart again shortly for her visit to you. Jane, meanwhile, after her initial distress seems quite reconciled and even looking forward to the relocation. We are overwhelmed with callers who come almost daily to pay their farewell visits. The Bigg Withers, the Chutes, and the Harwoods were here only yesterday, and Jane had them all in gales of laughter about the servants they are to keep, 'a steady cook and a giddy housemaid,' and as they left professed themselves envious of the life the family was to enjoy in Bath, with much warmer winters and the prospect of summers at the seaside in Wales or Devon.

I know Jane expected to receive more money for her father's library, but James did not want it, so you must see that selling it was the only option. It is hardly our responsibility that only £70 was received. They were perfectly at liberty to take any furniture they wanted and I only offered to take Jane's pianoforte as a favour, as I thought it would save the cost of transporting it, especially as they have not yet finally settled on where they are to live in Bath. I did not intend her to make a present of it to me, though she might indeed have done better to do so as she received only a derisory sum from the auctioneer. But as for Jane's accusation that 'the whole world is in conspiracy to enrich one half of the family at the expense of another' I really must beg you to seek confirmation of such behaviour before you take it upon yourself to criticise my husband and me. They have yet one month more here in the Parsonage as the Rector wishes to celebrate his last Easter Festival and to visit each of his parishioners. James has made no quarrel with this, even though many might say that it would have been an ideal time for *him* to become acquainted with his new flock.

In short, dear Eliza, I feel my husband and I need attract no criticism for the manner in which we have conducted this difficult situation. It is clearly time for the Rector to take life a little easier in order that his health may be preserved for as long as possible, thus ensuring that his wife and daughters are not thrown upon the mercy and generosity of the brothers, which we all know will be the case once his income ceases. In taking on the parish, my husband is fulfilling his filial obligations, and I am sure his sisters will benefit from his dutiful behaviour. Once they have grown used to their new abode and the wider society it affords them I am sure they will be grateful and that the discontent that has been expressed to you will be a thing of the past.

I believe you are planning a visit to Edward at Godmersham soon. I am sure you will receive a warm welcome and I trust you will pass an enjoyable stay.

Please remember me kindly to Henry.

Your affectionate cousin and sister-in-law,

*Mary Austen*

## TWENTY-TWO

## Eliza in Upper Brook Street, London
### May 1801

What a fine view of Portman Square is offered by this drawing room window. I can sit here and await the arrival of dear cousin Cassandra. How I wish both sisters were to be here, but Jane seems so preoccupied with the move to Bath, which is to take place this week. Henry was cross with me for writing to Mary and James, but I felt I had to try to take Jane's part. Without husbands or money of their own, those girls are so powerless. Jane is making the best of it, but I know she is unhappy and I long to receive up-to-date news of her spirits from Cassandra.

I have often reflected on my own good fortune in terms of money and preferment and never more than now, when I see Jane and Cassandra being forced, yes forced, there is no other way to put it, to adopt a life they have no wish for simply because they are totally dependent on their parents. To be fair, Cassandra has £1,000 left her by her dead fiancé, but that is not sufficient to support a household even if it were deemed proper for unmarried ladies to live alone. It is fortunate that Charles is home on leave so that he can escort Cassandra here, otherwise the duty may have fallen to James, and I would not have relished such a meeting after the recent falling out. Indeed, I doubt that Mary would have permitted it!

We shall have a fine celebration this evening. I have ordered a splendid dinner—how good it is to have a French chef again after the efforts of those cooks in Surrey—and our two drawing rooms are so suitable for entertaining now that the new hangings are arrived and the plate and silver are all unpacked. Henry's partners in the bank, Mr Maunde and Mr Tilson, are to join us, and I expect they will both invite Charles to visit their offices in Cleveland Court. While they do so I shall take Cassandra shopping. She is not as interested in her appearance as Jane, but I expect she could be prevailed upon to accept a present of something special to wear when we go to see Mrs Jordan at the Opera.

Oh, I think I see the post chaise on the other side of the square— yes, there is Charles waving from the window!

June 1801

Cassandra is to leave us tomorrow and I cannot tell whether she looks forward to going to Bath or not. At first the news received in Jane's letters was tolerably cheerful. Having her own room at her aunt and uncle's residence seemed welcome to her. But clearly seeking accommodation became a depressing task—how well I understand that, having done it so very frequently myself!— especially as they had constantly to confront their financial limi- tations. They looked at lodgings that were damp, that flooded, where the sun never reached or that were in entirely the wrong part of town.

'When you arrive,' she wrote to Cassandra, 'we shall have the pleasure of examining some of these putrefying houses all over again. But for the moment I have nothing more to say on the subject of housing.'

Cassandra is worried, I know, even though they have now settled on Number 4 Sydney Place, which seems to meet their requirements tolerably well. The rent is low, there is a lease for three years, and it is near both the Leigh-Perrots and the Pump Room for my aunt and uncle's daily walk. Jane has made a sketch and sent it to her sister and it certainly looks most acceptable.

'What is it, Cassy?' I asked her this morning. 'surely now that your have good lodgings and you and Jane can once again settle into your easy life together, you can look forward to Bath? Yet you seem unhappy and I beg to know the reason.'

Cassy, always reluctant to reveal her feelings, hesitated and then said: 'I am a little anxious about poor Hastings, I confess.'

'How kind you are—it is a source of great worry to his stepfather and to me. That seizure he had yesterday was one of the most violent and his doctor tells me we must expect more of them.'

'Dr Baillie seems a very competent physician—is there nothing more he can do for the boy?'

'He says not. As you know, it is my belief that the fits are due to epilepsy, but it defies all treatment. I can only hope that God will give me the strength to bear the worst if—'

'Oh surely you do not expect . . .'

'I am afraid we must be prepared, my dear, and sometimes when I see him in those painful paroxysms I can only wish him peace.'

Her eyes filled with tears.

'At least you have the devotion of my brother to help you through, although that cough of his . . .'

I needed no reminding of the worries Henry's hacking cough caused me, though Dr Baillie had assured me he was *not* consumptive, so I sought to divert Cassandra's attention.

'Is that all my dear? I fear you have more worries about Jane that you have not yet confided.'

Reluctantly she drew from her pocket Jane's last letter, received yesterday, and laid it upon the worktable that stood between us.

'The last line,' she said, pointing.

I read:

**Unless something particular occurs, I shall not write again.**

I read it and looked at her curiously.

'I would not expect her to write again, as you return home so very soon.'

'No, she does not mean letters, she means her real writing—her stories, her novels.'

'Oh,' I said, understanding at last. 'But perhaps she just means she will be too busy in your new life.'

Cassandra spoke more sharply than I had ever heard her. 'Allow me to know my sister better than anyone. Without her writing she will shrivel, she will die inside. You might as well tell her never to laugh again. On the last night we spent together at Steventon in our sweet blue room—the night before I came here—Jane looked all around, then clasped her little mahogany writing desk to her bosom, the one my father gave her for her nineteenth birthday and is her most treasured possession, and sobbed as if her heart would break. 'I shall not be able to do it, Cass,' she said. 'Without this place I cannot do it. I must have a settled place—we shall be nomads. I shall no longer be able to compose.'

'I tried to comfort her,' Cassandra went on, the tears shining in her eyes, 'but it was in vain.'

I was shocked by her vehemence and could think of no way to respond but to try to take her out of herself.

'Come, Cass, let us change for the Opera. We are to meet Lord and Lady Acton. Put on your sweet gold muslin, which so well sets off the topaz cross dear Charles brought you from his last voyage.'

She smiled wanly.

'Even those sweet crosses did not raise Jane's spirits. "How foolish our brother is to spend his prize money on his sisters," she said to me. "We shall be intolerably fine."'

'"Yet it is an incident you could use in a story, my dear, is it not? That is, er . . ."—I hesitated, as I am only too well aware of my own limits as to composition—"if you had a naval gentleman in your story."'

'"I shall never have another gentleman of any kind in a story" was her retort,' and as she related this, Cassandra turned to go to her room.

In the face of her distress I could think of nothing comforting to say to her.

October 1801

For a short time after her departure I waited eagerly upon correspondence from Bath to hear how my dear cousins progressed in their new abode. But within a few weeks all such thoughts were driven from my mind by the anxieties I myself suffered. First, my husband did not enjoy a day, indeed scarcely an hour, of good health. His complaints of a cough, a pain in the side, and the loss of weight and energy were so clearly an indication of galloping consumption that I could not entirely believe Dr Baillie's assurances, and I am sure all our acquaintance had the same fears. Knowing that Dr Baillie is one of the most respected physicians in London and even consulted by royalty prevented me from seeking another opinion—a wise decision as it turned out, because at length, one of the good doctor's prescriptions proved to be efficacious and removed most of the symptoms. I am glad to say he is well again, and how I have had need of him these last terrible weeks as we have endured the loss of my poor dear Hastings. His sufferings were dreadful, so dreadful, in fact, that the end came as something of a release, as I am writing at present in response to the letter of condolence from cousin Philly—how many touching letters I have received.

> So awful a dissolution of a near and tender tie must ever be a severe shock, and my mind was already weakened by witnessing the sad variety and long series of pain that the dear sufferer underwent—but deeply impressed as I am with the heartrending scenes I have beheld I am most thankful for their termination, and the exchange that I humbly hope my dear Child has made of a most painful existence for a blissful immortality.

We buried him with his grandmother, which is also a comfort to me when I think of them together. The inscription reads:

> *Also in Memory of her Grandson Hastings only Child of Jean Capot Comte de Feuillide and Elizabeth his wife. Born 25th June 1786. Died 9th October 1801.*

Henry wishes us to go to stay at Godmersham Park with his brother and sister-in-law. They live in great style, as I have heard from many sources, so perhaps I might accept their invitation at last. I am mindful that it is near four years since they first asked us. Elizabeth is in the increasing way yet again, having produced her last only at the beginning of this year. She is bent on setting records I vow—perhaps His Majesty may reward his subjects who add most to the population! Still, I shall go and hope that Jane and Cassandra may also be visiting that I may have up-to-date news of them.

# TWENTY-THREE

## *Philly Walter at Tunbridge Wells*
### May 1802

Something is going on and I am not being told about it. I am
only picking up hints from letters and it is most frustrating. I
should have thought my intimacy with Eliza was sufficient for her
to confide in me, and if she cannot confide the whole truth, why
mention it at all?

I had thought that Henry and Eliza might pay a visit here on
their way from Godmersham—after all, the distance to this part of
the county is not that great from there—but no, they decided to go
to Bath.

'That I might have the great consolation of my dear uncle George
in my bereavement,' she wrote to me.

Well, she won't get much consolation from Aunt Cassandra,
who to my certain knowledge has never liked her and was delighted
when she did not accept James—anyway, what a dreadful wife for
a clergyman she would have made. Driving out in Elizabeth's fine
carriages is more her style, and they did a prodigious amount of
that while at Godmersham, so I gather. Well, Eliza would not be
content to sit inside while the men were hunting, sewing Edward's
shirts, as the women are usually expected to do there. Henry would
go out with a gun, I daresay, while Elizabeth and Eliza drove about

calling on all those fine neighbours. Eliza wrote to me about how pleasantly they were received by this one and that one. At least it would have been a relief from being plagued by those endless children of whom she complains. She tells me that Lizzie is always undoing her ribbons and that Georgie pulls her hair whenever she comes near him.

She has written to me from Bath, where they have now been for a sennight at least. There are some intriguing passages in her letters about Jane and Cassandra—'the girls,' as uncle George calls them, which for my part I think a most unsuitable way of referring to two women who are almost middle-aged and who everyone now thinks are beyond hopes of marriage. At least that is what I thought, but Eliza hints that Jane has recently met someone of whom she is fond. I believe it was in Lyme, where she and Cassandra spent some weeks earlier this spring. I said at the time that it was not fitting for them to be there alone, even though Charles was able to escort them there. Sure enough, Jane, no doubt without the restraint of her mother, was able to run wild and flirt as she was wont to do in earlier years when everyone described her as 'madly husband hunting.' It is highly annoying to have no details, but Eliza hints that another meeting is planned because she and Henry have been asked to escort her back to Lyme later in the year. I wonder if he lives there? Eliza refers to him as 'the reverend gentleman,' so I wonder if his parish is nearby? If only I had a name I could look him up in *Crockford's Directory of Clergy* and find out more. He must be a widower or he would have no interest in a woman of Jane's age. But I am sure he must be childless, else he would have more sense than to pay court to Jane. Cassandra is much more suitable for such a position.

I cannot ask Eliza more and I am certain Cassandra would not answer any question—I am sure their mother and father are ignorant of these developments. They are so taken up with their life in Bath—I hear they are to move again, though what was wrong with Sydney Place I do not know. Perhaps Green Park Buildings is nearer the Pump Room, where I believe they walk each day, and there is no doubt that Uncle George is growing frailer.

Eliza has told me about Jane only because she is planning to go to France and must fit the escorting of Jane in with this. The packet boat has begun to sail between Dover and Calais again.

It is of course another mad scheme. This 'peace' which our government has negotiated with the French will surely be short-lived and I cannot imagine how they will be able to recover her property, although she keeps hoping. Of course Henry will have an eye to more wealth as the life they lead in London must cost a pretty penny. They still keep that French servant—Madame Bigeon—on. I thought she was there to be nurse and governess to Hastings, but even now that the poor unfortunate is in his grave she still resides there and no doubt is in receipt of a handsome salary. They, too, are to move again. This time to Brompton, just outside London—though 'near enough for Madame and myself to walk into the Town without the bother of a carriage,' as E told me. She says she needs to be separated from the memories of the child, but I suspect she just wants a grander house.

It makes me feel very out of spirits—everyone moving and travelling about and now even Jane, whom I thought forever an unloved spinster, with perhaps the prospect of marriage. And if that took place Cassandra, whom I thought would be forever with their parents, would have the prospect of relocation as I daresay Jane would want her to live with them, whatever the opinion of this mysterious clergyman on the matter.

It does seem so unfair. There is no prospect for me with Mr

Whitaker, what with his commitment to his mother and mine to Mama, who since father passed away daily grows more confused. What have I done to deserve this as my lot? Mary Austen has no love either for Eliza or Jane—I wonder if I could find out more from her?

## TWENTY-FOUR

## Mary Austen [Mrs JA] at Steventon
### December 1802

The carriage taking Jane, Cassandra, and James back to Bath has just now left and I am shaking with emotion as I sit down amid the scarcely touched breakfast things. We were still abed when to our astonishment we heard the sound of a large carriage approaching our front door. I looked out and recognised it immediately as that of the Bigg Withers family, as they had collected Jane and Cassandra not three days since to take them for a week's stay. The girls set off in such high spirits and to tell the truth I thought they were heartily pleased to be leaving Steventon. Their visit had not been a success, as they were constantly comparing the way things are here now with the way they were when they both lived here.

I told them and told them that our income was not as great as their father's had been and though they might think me penny-pinching I was only trying to be a prudent housekeeper for their brother, and is there anything wrong with trying to give the place the air of a gentleman's residence?

My mother- and father-in-law certainly lived well when they were here, better than we are able to do. They had good food, of course, which I never begrudge—I always make sure James has a little treat, such as a sweet bread or a piece of Stilton, even if the children and I have to be content with mutton stew. But really there was no need for them to be so generous to the parishioners—roast beef and plum pudding and ale at Christmas indeed! They have grown to expect it but, as I told James, they must understand things are different now and there can be no such largesse. The maids can just as well eat dripping as butter—they have been used to no better in their own homes in the village after all. And most mistresses lock up the stores and give them out weekly—you can never tell whether servants are honest and my mother-in-law was altogether too trusting in my view.

Jane may look askance, but it is the way of the world that when a son inherits, his wife changes the housekeeping arrangements. I daresay she may scribble something about it and amuse her family— as long as it is not at my expense I shall try to be amused.

Just after they arrived Jane said: 'I hardly recognised the garden, Mary, you have certainly been busy—a greenhouse indeed? Quite the look of a squire's dwelling it will have before long.'

Cassandra, as always, was kinder and tried to compliment me on the changes, but I felt Jane liked them ill and was always looking for something to criticise. I was heartily relieved by the invitation from the Bigg Withers that they should go to them for a week and attend the ball they were arranging at Manydown. Then we expected Jane to stay here until her birthday on December 16th and James would escort them back to Bath in time for Christmas.

Now here they were so early on a bitter cold morning returning without notice—was one of them taken ill?

James and I hurried down and were amazed to find that Catherine and Althea Bigg were of the party, and as they got out we saw that they and Cassandra were all in tears.

'Oh what on earth is the matter?' cried James. 'And where is Jane?'

Cassandra gestured at the coach and I looked inside. Jane sat against the far side, her face stiff and expressionless, looking out of the frosted over window, her breath coming out in clouds in the icy air.

'Jane,' I said, 'are you unwell? What is the matter?'

She did not respond and Cassandra, taking my arm, put her finger to her lips.

'Go into the house,' she said, 'and we shall join you there presently.'

The coachman was unloading their boxes and James was telling our manservant to take them to the girl's room.

'No,' said Cassandra, 'leave them in the hall, for we must leave again immediately.'

James and I returned to the house, and I asked him what he thought was happening.

'What does she mean, leave again immediately? They can go nowhere without you and you cannot go to Bath at present—what about your sermon the day after tomorrow?'

'I am as puzzled as you my dear,' he said, 'but let us wait for an explanation from my sisters.'

Looking out the parlour window, I saw Jane descend slowly from the carriage and bid an affectionate farewell to the two Bigg girls as they drove off.

I hurried out to the hall and saw that Jane, refusing to shed her cloak, was seated on the settle beside their boxes and saying in a low voice to Cassandra: 'Tell James that we must go to Bath immediately, and if he cannot take us we must travel post .'

'Two young women travel post alone?' I burst out. 'It is impossible and just as impossible for James to abandon his parish and escort you on a whim.'

'A whim?' she cried, and I swear I had never before seen such a look of despair on anyone's face. It quite frightened me and I was glad when James suggested that we leave Jane where she was and ask Cassandra to come into the parlour to explain.

It was then that we heard the whole sorry story. Harris Bigg Wither, the eldest son and heir of Manydown, last evening asked Jane to marry him and she accepted! There had been much celebration and everyone had gone to bed happy. Sometime in the night though, Jane had changed her mind, or, as Cassandra put it 'come to her senses'.

I could not believe my ears.

'Come to her senses?' I burst out. 'Is it sensible to refuse a man of twenty-one, and moreover a man of wealth and property, when you are seven and twenty? What was her reason?'

'She simply cannot love him enough to marry him,' said Cassandra.

'Love him enough? What is she about? Has she no thought for the well-being of her family? Think of the home she could have given you, Cass. Think of the worry about the future taken off the shoulders of your parents and your brothers. How are the two of you to be provided for in future? Did she not think of that?'

James stopped me with a look, but said that he himself found her refusal difficult to understand.

'I never thought young Harris an appealing young man—he has a strange way of speaking and is awkward in company—but to be mistress of Manydown would be something to be sure, can she easily give up such a prospect?'

'All this we discussed endlessly in the small hours, believe me,' said Cassandra in a weary voice. 'In the end she felt that the match, with all its advantages, was so horrible a prospect that she must see Harris as soon as the household stirred and tell him her decision. We were most anxious, you see, to ensure that the news did not spread further, for Harris had gone to bed saying he would ride down the valley in the morning to tell all their neighbours his good news.'

'Oh the mortification!' I said. 'How was it accomplished?'

'She saw him alone in the library and when he emerged I never saw a man more affected. The kindness of his sisters is beyond measure. They were so grief-stricken themselves—you know how they have always loved Jane—but insisted upon coming with us as you see.'

'A sorry story indeed,' said James, 'and one that is bound to lead to a degree of awkwardness between our families in future but now that you are both here, why the urgency to remove to Bath? Can you not stay here as arranged?'

'Yes,' I added, 'surely it will be soon enough for James to escort you as arranged on Monday.'

'I fear not,' returned Cassandra. 'Jane is afraid that Harris, knowing she remains in the vicinity, may call here to press his suit again. She is insistent that we leave, and brother, I fear so much for her spirits that if it is in your power, I beg you to agree. Things have gone so ill with her this year what with the move to Bath, which as you know distressed her greatly. . . . No Mary,' she continued as I was about to put our side of that event, 'she knows it was inevitable but that did not make it easy, and then of course—'

She stopped and would have gone no further but I suddenly remembered the hints I had received from cousin Philly Walter.

'Is it true, Cass, that Jane formed an attachment recently? When you were in Lyme last summer? Is that perhaps the reason she has refused Mr Bigg Wither?'

'I think it may be—though I am sworn to secrecy. She may have had hopes and indeed I believe she had hoped to meet the gentleman again—Eliza and Henry were to escort her there—but she has heard nothing from him and her disappointment is dreadful to behold. I beg you do not mention it. I have said this much only to excuse the demands we now make on you.'

James was ever the considerate brother and of course agreed that they should go to Bath immediately. He quickly arranged for his curate to take the Sunday services, and I have just seen them into the carriage.

I have not always admired Jane or even found her tolerably agreeable, but I have gained a new respect for her this morning. Many would have taken Bigg Wither without love, for the comfort and fortune and position. She could not and knows that place and fortune cannot alter the man.

I will not tell Philly of this new development. I think she wants the news only to gloat over the misfortunes of others and I shall not give her the satisfaction. When James returns from Bath I shall make Eliza's plans to visit France the subject of my letter. That will give Philly her share of gossip and Uncle George is sure to have been full of the scheme, as he quite dotes upon La Comtesse. I think without such diversion it will be a sorry Christmas in their household.

## TWENTY-FIVE

## Eliza at Brompton
### May 1803

O h that dreadful man Napoléon—how near he came to putting my dear Henry and me behind bars for goodness knows how long now that hostilities have been resumed. How guilty I should have felt as *'mon cher mari'* did not really wish to travel to France in the first place. When we heard the news of the Peace of Amiens, as they now call it, he and brother Edward declared that we should be mad to trust those Frenchies and that to travel there was foolhardy. But Henry has no will but mine and like most bankers knows only too well the value of property, so when I insisted that I was determined to recover what was rightfully mine—and of course now rightfully his—he agreed.

How lovely it was to set foot in my beloved France again after so many years! The countryside is much the same, but the towns and cities are so changed. In Paris the populace is rude, arrogant, and without respect. Where once my title would have gained admittance to officials, notaries, and lawyers, now we were kept waiting for hours by people we once would not even have employed as gardeners or under footmen.

Not one of them would use my title and insisted on calling me Citizeness Austen. I did not have the heart to visit the scene of the Comte's murder, though Henry walked about the square they now call Republique and told me the cobbles are still stained with the blood of the thousands who were executed.

I had been wild to see Paris again and I had heard that the First Consul was willing to be indulgent to members of the ancient regime. They said that General Bonaparte was a vulgar little fellow, but I thought he had a most distinguished profile and looked very fine on his horse as he reviewed his troops on the Champ de Mars. In particular I looked forward to going to one of the magnificent drawing rooms that I had heard his wife was now holding regularly at the Tuileries. True, she is only the daughter of a planter from—where was it? Martinique? They say she cannot smile very much as her teeth are so bad, but she is certainly elegant and it would be lovely to mix with French nobility again, even if they come from peasant stock. Josephine was a widow as I have been and you cannot blame any woman for trying to better herself.

But sadly we spent all our time in Paris fighting the officials and with little outcome.

When eventually we were admitted to the presence of the Notaire Publique—we had to call him Citizen, too, though I daresay Napoléon will soon do away with this nonsense—I expected him to be a reasonable man and to tell me how we might go about retrieving my rights to the property in Guines. Alas, he did nothing of the sort but merely confirmed that the man who, as he put it, 'called himself a count' had died a confessed murderer and a thief. All his property therefore was ceded to the state and he advised us to leave France immediately and to think no more of the matter. Scarcely bothering to be civil, he then had us shown out! I was all for engaging lawyers to advocate on our behalf, but Henry reminded me that few lawyers would now be sympathetic to my claims.

'In order to survive in this regime, my dear,' he said, 'they needs must be seen to support the current government, however disagreeable they may find it.'

He persuaded me that the prudent thing would be to return to England forthwith and to try to press the matter further from a distance. I agreed, which as it turned out was very fortunate. I did manage to buy a new bonnet in Paris, where some elegant shops have been reestablished, but what adventure we and the new hat had on the way home!

We had just settled ourselves in a tolerably pleasant inn near Verdun on our way to Calais when the patron told us that the Peace was at an end and that the First Consul had ordered that all the Channel ports be closed and all English travellers were to be imprisoned forthwith. We were in danger of capture as enemies of France!

Henry was highly alarmed, of course, but I said to him: 'Fear not my love, I have escaped from France before, you remember—some eight years ago—and we shall do so again.'

'But how?'

'We shall simply become French for the purposes of our journey—a loyal French couple who are called to visit a sick French relative who resides in—where shall we say? London? Brighton? Winchester?'

'Now my love, be serious—you know I could no more pass for a French man than fly to the moon.'

That I saw immediately was true—Henry's French accent leaves a great deal to be desired. Like most Englishmen, he is incapable of moving his mouth enough to make the proper sounds.

'I have it—you shall be an invalid and I will do all the talking!'

It went against his instinct not to be the man in charge, but he saw the sense of it and that indeed is how we got through. At each posting house he wrapped himself in his cloak and lay back in the carriage with his eyes closed while I conversed with the staff of each post. On one occasion, when I thought a groom showed too much interest in my fellow passenger, I made a great show of scolding the waiter who served our cold meat, to provide a distraction. I am pleased to say that though out of practice, my French is still so perfect that not a single person even suspected my nationality and we passed through to Calais without mishap. As we boarded the ship I ventured to say to Henry how distressing I found it to see that dreaded tricolour flying at the quayside in place of the fleur-de-lys, but luckily by this time no Frenchman could hear me.

It is a relief to be safely home, to be sure, though I own the excitement of our flight has stimulated me and quite helped me to find consolation. Indeed, for the first time in months I have not been thinking of the loss of my dear boy. All officers are being recalled, so Henry's decision to leave the militia was a wise one. Dear Uncle George and Aunt Cassandra are missing Captain Frank—now promoted again and enjoying the opportunity to introduce his intended bride to his family. I suppose there will soon be hopes of yet more little Austens. They certainly are a prolific family! Uncle George hints that they are also concerned about Jane. She is in such low spirits that a visit from us—Henry is after all her favourite brother—is requested to help distract her. He begs, too, that we would travel there to see their new lodgings as well as to tell them firsthand about what he calls 'your daring escape from the enemy.' We shall go as soon as Henry has settled some business matters.

Eliza at Green Park Buildings, Bath
June 1803

Dear Uncle George! How happy he appears to be in this new situation. I enjoy once more the acquaintance I had made when the

Comte and I were here at an earlier and happier time, but most of all I revel in spending time with my dear family. Aunt Cassandra has been tolerably kind and I know that as a mother she would be sympathetic to the trials I have undergone.

I cannot say that Green Park Buildings is the most congenial of dwellings—the reception rooms are somewhat small and the offices dark and forbidding. They keep only two servants, which is just as well since there would be no room for more. My aunt and uncle, however, seem vastly content with their life here.

Uncle George said to me and Henry: 'It was a good day's work when we decided on the move from Steventon.'

I can see that the routine of their days suits them both perfectly. He walks down Great Pulteney Street each morning, usually with Jane or Cassandra or sometimes both, to accompany him. He drinks his two glasses of that foul yellow water—how I have always hated the smell!—and discusses the day's news with his friends, many of them retired clergy like himself. He might then call at the butcher or the fishmonger on an errand from his wife or go as far as the library in Milson Street if 'the girls' have to change their books. On Sundays they now attend St Swithin's in Walcot, though to please me he agreed to the Abbey on the Sunday of our visit.

'The Abbey is too lofty for me nowadays, you know,' he said, 'and Mrs Austen and I were married at Walcot so we feel comfortable there.'

My aunt, too, appears content. Cassandra now seems to have most of the housekeeping to her share and my aunt is free to make a four at whist or bezique with her sister-in-law or other friends.

But anyone with half an eye about them could see that it is 'the girls' one should have concern for—especially Jane. She does not like cards, so she is often left out of evening parties, which are the thing in Bath. Many of the residents lack the resources for dinners so give such parties as an alternative. I have always loved her quick wit but have to own that it can be disconcerting when she allows one of her sharp remarks to escape her. There are few balls and I think she spends many an evening, even in company, sitting quiet in a corner, just observing. I cannot help noticing that her gaiety and sparkle are not in such abundance as they were and she has even taken to dressing in subdued tones, like the spinster she is fast becoming. I do not think it fitting either for Jane and Cassandra to dress alike as they do—nothing proclaims the fact that they believe themselves past marriage more than those dull matching bonnets.

They are a contrast to their parents, who are a fine sight arm in arm, both tall and well looking. I understand he is a great favourite in the Pump Room, where his company and that of my aunt is sought out by their large acquaintance. I tell him again and again about our French adventure and he never tires of hearing about it. But one day when we walked on the Royal Crescent he took my arm and Henry's and confided his worries about Jane.

'Cassandra somehow seems to have recovered from her terrible loss, but as for Jane . . . She was ever a dear child to me but somehow at present I cannot seem to reach her. Mrs Austen says it is because she resents our move to Bath. Perhaps that is so, but you know part of our reason for coming here was so that she and Cassy could go about a little more. We were beginning to fear that our somewhat confined life at Steventon was denying them opportunities for . . . well, for . . . well, to speak plain, we thought Bath might afford them more opportunities for meeting potential suitors.'

'And it has not done so?' asked my husband, though nothing after all could be more clear.

'No, and it seems that Jane has had a further disappointment this year—my knowledge of this is sketchy and gained only from overheard snatches of conversation. And then there was the business at Manydown . . .'

'What was this business at Manydown?' I asked. 'We hear references to it but no one speaks plain and I have not asked Jane herself as I feared to distress her.'

My uncle explained the whole sorry business to us as we turned back to Green Park Buildings.

'So you see, I do not know if she now regrets refusing Harris Bigg Wither and sees that possibly her last chance of matrimony is gone . . . or it is something else? Henry, you have always been close to her and she admires you prodigiously, Eliza, so I wondered if you could ask her, or perhaps find ways of cheering her?'

'She is welcome to return to London with us Papa,' said Henry, 'and we could distract her with concerts and dinners.'

I put my hand in his arm, for I, too, had been struck by the change in Jane's appearance and manner. Her eyes had lost their sparkle and she, who would once have delighted in our French adventure and thought how she could turn it into a story, had scarcely paid us any heed.

'No, my dear, she needs more than distraction and diversion. She needs occupation. Think, when was Jane happiest? Think of times she seemed fulfilled and content.'

They were both silent.

'Think—is it not when she is scribbling and reading her work to the family? Let us encourage her in that and I guarantee her spirits will lift.'

Uncle George smiled broadly and his eyes lit up. 'Yes, I am minded that she began a tale some while back about an impressionable young lady in Bath. When we return, take her on one side, Eliza, and encourage her to take it out again.'

# TWENTY-SIX

## Henry Austen at Bath

### Summer 1803

N ow, my dear,' said my wife, 'have you the conversation clear in your mind—you know how you are going to put it to her?'

Dear Eliza, she was longing to bring the matter of *Susan* up with Jane herself, but we had agreed that it was better coming from me and today, our last in Bath, was to be the time when I suggested to my sister that she should take out the work again and update it.

'Yes, my love, fear not, I shall suggest we take a turn upon the Crescent this afternoon and bring the matter up.'

'Be sure to let her know that we have connections with publishers who would be amenable to reading the work—that may encourage her.'

I was surprised. 'Have we such connections, my dear? I never heard of them.'

She laughed—I always love the sound of her laugh.

'Dearest husband, did you not hear Mr Seymour boast at our last dinner with him that he can find a connection with anyone in London? That surely includes publishers.'

I was not so sure but could see that the thought would be an encouragement to Jane. Cassandra had told me that although Jane made light of it, she had shed tears about the rejection of *First Impressions* in such a heartless manner—clearly no one at Cadell's had even bothered to read the work.

I made certain that no one else accompanied us on our walk and was at first somewhat heartened by the animation of Jane's manner.

'Do you know who we saw on our morning walk to the Pump Room with Papa today?'

'No. Someone important?'

'Why yes, no one other than the wife of Admiral Nelson himself and she looked as disagreeable as everyone says she is.'

'So it is no wonder then that he has taken up with Lady Hamilton?'

She looked for a minute as mischievous as she was wont to do in happy times at Steventon.

'Brother, do not let Mama hear you talk so; she will not countenance an unfaithful spouse as you know, but'—putting her hand in front of her mouth and speaking low—'I do not find it at all surprising.'

We shared the joke and strolled harmoniously for a few more yards. We passed some volunteers from the militia drilling furiously as all leave had been cancelled since the peace was at an end.

'Are you content, Henry, that you are now a banker not a soldier in these troubled times? I am sure your wife is, even if you are not.'

'But I am—I think I will make an adequate if not a fine banker and I am certainly pleased to be living with my dear Eliza again.' She had given me my opportunity: 'And you Jane—are you content?'

She looked at me warily.

'Why do you ask?'

'Oh, it strikes me that you want animation at present and I wonder how this life in Bath suits you.'

She stopped and looked at me, her hazel eyes suddenly shining with tears.

'I like it not at all, but as you know I am powerless to change it. It suits Mama and Papa vastly well and that has to be enough.'

'You know we are always glad to welcome you in London for a change of scene, but I do wonder if more could not be done to make your time here more enjoyable.'

'Please do not mention going more into company—that is what people always suggest and Henry, you know me well enough to know that is not what I want.'

'No, my dear, nothing was farther from my mind—in fact the opposite was what I was thinking of, staying at home and taking up your writing again.'

She looked into the distance. 'Cassy tries, the dear girl, to persuade me but, but . . .'

'But what?'

'I fear I have lost the ability to do it. It used to be such a source of pleasure but somehow now . . .'

'Will you not try again? For your brother and sister who love you so? There is that story you began about the young girl who visits Bath—it sounded a fine plan and one that would be most entertaining.'

'Do you think so? I fear the fashion has rather passed for those sorts of tales—you know I meant it as a sort of joke on *Udolpho* and I am not sure that anyone would be interested.'

'Your family most certainly would and you used to find delight in entertaining us.'

'True. They were good evenings, were they not, when I read *First Impressions* to you all—or even Elinor and Marianne. Eliza loved that one I believe?'

'Indeed she did—she often wonders what became of those two young ladies.'

'Does she? Well, perhaps . . . but I do not know even where the manuscript is.'

'Cassy does.'

'Why you sly dog, Henry—have you been plotting?'

She looked merry and I decided to leave the matter there and not to mention the possibility of publication. It would surely be sufficient to get her started.

When we returned to Green Park Buildings she went immediately upstairs and when the dinner bell went, Cassandra whispered to me that she had been rummaging in her trunk.

After dinner this evening, she retired early and I hoped she was setting to work again.

We return to London tomorrow, but I am to be here again in a month or so. I hope progress will have been made.

September 1803

My business in Bath has proved satisfactory in more ways than one.

I have persuaded Uncle Leigh-Perrot to invest more money in my business—Mr Maunde and Mr Tilson will be delighted. I may not know much about banking but I am confident of my ability to persuade investors. I could, of course, put in more money of my own—or rather *our* own, since it is Eliza's really—but my uncle was pleased enough and I am sure my promise to him of a good return will be fulfilled.

But the real excitement was hearing Jane's progress with her story. It is delightful! There is a young man in it named Henry— how flattering that she has named him for me—and he is a fine handsome young man and an excellent dancer. There is a wonderful character, a fearsome General Tilney—I wonder if Jane took as a model the general who was James's first wife's father. Best not say if she did—Mrs JA does not like to be reminded of any rivals, alive or dead!

At Eliza's suggestion I contacted Messrs Crosby of Paternoster Row—a tolerably respected publisher—and they put me in touch with their Bath branch. I called in on them on my way home from my uncle. They have agreed to read the story when Jane and Cassandra have copied it out freshly. They did suggest that Susan was not now a very fashionable name for a heroine—I cannot think why Jane has persisted in using it again. Eliza thinks Georgiana would be a more suitable name or even Charlotte for Her Majesty the queen, but I do not think Jane will be persuaded.

November 1803, London

I am just now in receipt of an express telling me that Crosby's have accepted the manuscript for publication and will pay Jane £10! She is touching in her gratitude to Eliza and me both for the introduction to Crosby's but also for, as she puts it, 'persuading me that I had something tolerably interesting to say.'

The £10 is a fortune to my sister—how proud everyone will be that her talent is recognised outside the family at last. We shall invite her to stay and take her about with us. I wonder how long before *Catherine*—that is the name she settled upon—is published and how it will be received?

## TWENTY-SEVEN

### *Jane Austen at Brompton, London*
### Spring 1804

How I wish Eliza would not do that! As we go about, she will insist on telling all her acquaintance that my 'charming novel' has been accepted for publication. That inevitably leads to them asking when it is to appear and of course there is nothing to say.

'Soon,' she says, with her charming laugh and a little shrug of her shoulders, 'and we shall give a large evening party to celebrate.'

But clearly it is not to be soon. I have heard nothing at all. Henry set Mr Seymour to make enquiries, as he had made the original introduction, and he brought back the news that my work *Catherine* had been advertised in a journal or a sort of brochure called *Flowers of Literature*.

'The advertisement says that it is "in the press,"' announced Henry when he returned from dining with Mr Seymour, 'so it will surely be completed very soon.'

That was almost three weeks ago, when I first arrived here, and still there is nothing definite to be heard. I begin to fear that it is all an illusion. I did receive the £10, which raised my hopes at the beginning, but now I feel this to be an even worse situation than the rejection of *First Impressions*. At least that happened by return of post so I did not suffer this agonising wait.

Eliza and Henry try to distract me and pay me no end of attention, always arranging new amusements, and I have to own I enjoy many of the activities that are always so plentiful. I cannot believe that Eliza's fortune, large though it may have been, will last forever when they seem to spend at such a rate. A French cook—Eliza calls him a *chef de cuisine*—fine wines, boxes at the opera, and lavish parties are a great change for me, but it seems this is how they live every day.

They seem to have no end of servants, too, and it is extraordinarily nice to have the fire made up and hot water brought before one gets out of bed in the morning. I like Madame Bigeon very much, although I find her difficult to understand sometimes because of her charming French accent and yesterday walked into London with her and her daughter Madame Perigord, who seems now to have joined Eliza's household, too. I cannot quite make out if these two ladies are servants or friends. They call Eliza 'Madame la Comtesse' and address Henry as 'Milord,' which he loves of course. They do not sit at table with us if Henry is present but do dine with us if he is dining out, and Eliza seems to treat them more as equals than as servants. It is very puzzling. At Godmersham the distinction is always clear whereas here . . .

I am glad though to have their company when Eliza is out on her endless calls. I often ask to be excused and sit or walk with the two Frenchwomen instead. I like to hear how they have managed to shift for themselves and earn their living. I know only too well that the time may come when I shall have to do the same. Henry, of course, protests that he will always look after his sisters, come what may, but I wake at night worried about what will become of Cassandra and me when our father dies. Henry is profligate, James mean, Charles and Frank are at sea and anyway have growing families of their own. Edward, of course, does not lack resources but I have never been a favourite with Elizabeth. It is clear that Cassandra would ever be welcome at her lyings-in but I am only tolerated. My brothers will help our mother, of course, as she, too, will need support but I had best think of becoming a governess if I cannot earn my living with my pen.

If only my meeting with my dear friend in Lyme had led to . . . I had hopes, of course, though I confided them only to Cassandra. But like all my other hopes, they have been dashed. He was a fine man, not rich like Harris Bigg Wither, but noble in his thoughts and inspirational in his ideals. I could have made a life with him—a clergyman's wife is a suitable occupation for me. But perhaps I should not have told him about my wish to be a writer. Many men find it a less than respectable aspiration for a lady, especially if done for publication rather than for the amusement of the family. I believed him though, when he said that he wanted to meet again. I even asked Henry and Eliza to accompany me to Lyme so that I could see him. They have been extremely tactful and never asked me about it, but it is as much an embarrassment as the book. How cruel it is to have so many hopes raised, only to be dashed again.

One week later

How different I feel after this morning's outing! How much more enjoyable I found it than the calls and card parties to which Eliza subjects me! I was not inclined to accompany her to church this morning and to think what I might have missed! She rose from the breakfast table and said: 'Now Jane, today we shall not attend church locally as we have done on each Sunday you have been here.'

'What, shall we walk to Kensington? 'Tis a fine morning and I would enjoy a walk.'

'No, today we shall take the carriage and be conveyed to Blooms-
bury to attend church in Coram Fields. It has become quite the
fashion and afterwards we shall—'

I interrupted her with a laugh but I must own, quite sharply:
'Fie, Eliza must even going to church be to follow fashion now?'

Eliza was not one to take offence easily and simply replied, 'It is
not the church that is fashionable so much as the visits that are paid
afterwards to the Foundling Hospital. One goes to see how the poor
street children fare and some ladies and gentlemen even decide to
adopt one if they like the look of them.'

'What, you choose a child as you might choose a puppy? For
shame, I shall not go.' I was horrified and did not mind if she knew.
But she only said gently: 'It is kindly meant and the children thrive,
I believe. The hospital has a Royal Charter and attracts the attention of the finest in the land—the children are not only trained as
servants but also are taught music and drawing and altogether have a
fine education. Adoption can be a great advantage for a child, as we
in our family have reason to know. I shall make ready and hope you
will decide to accompany Henry and me.'

She turned away and repaired upstairs, the silk of her skirt
swishing on the marble of the curving staircase.

I accepted her rebuke. My family after all rejoiced in the good
fortune Edward had received by being adopted by the Knights. But
it was Henry, coming into the room in his new grey morning coat,
who tempted me to go with them.

'What, do you not wish to hear Mr Handel himself play the
organ in church—you who are so fond of music? He is a great sup-
porter of Thomas Coram's enterprises, you know, and I believe that
today there is an exhibition of Mr Hogarth's work in the Great Hall
of the hospital—you need not see the children if it upsets you, but
do come!'

How right he was to persuade me! There was nothing at all unpleasant about the visit. Though a large number of ladies and gentlemen—all very fashionably dressed, no wonder Eliza is intent on joining such a throng—strolled about talking to the children and viewing the exhibition, they were all so beautifully dressed and with such excellent manners that it was clear they were happy in their surroundings and that by being taken in there, they were being enabled to enjoy a life that would have been denied them, even if they had survived being abandoned as babies. We were told that more than one thousand babes are abandoned in London each and every year. A shocking figure! I did not dare to approach Mr Handel and kept the other side the room when I saw Eliza and Henry being introduced, but of course his playing was sublime. Eliza told me that she had asked him to attend one of her musical parties but was disappointed that he did not immediately say yes. I suspect he is sought after by every hostess in London, but Eliza is not noted for her modesty about the importance of her drawing room!

The sun shone upon us as we drove home, the coachman brought us along the river and the new Battersea Bridge looked very fine. My spirits are so lifted by the morning's engagement and I am so grateful for my loving and considerate family compared with the fate of those poor abandoned children that I think I may find the heart for a new composition. Families, for all their faults, well perhaps *because* of all their faults, are the source of many stories.

# TWENTY-EIGHT

## Mrs Austen at Lyme
### Summer 1804

Perhaps I have misjudged Eliza. While I was always aware that she had been a dutiful daughter and a most devoted mother to poor little Hastings, I must own that as a wife for my son she was not my first choice. But I begin to see that perhaps she *is* right for him. They contrive to be apart more than is suitable for most married couples. He visits James and Mary and always seems to be at Godmersham. Eliza stay at home with the excuse that she neither hunts nor shoots, which are the pastimes he enjoys—shooting indeed; I expect that is where Jane got the strange idea that she would like to go out with a gun!

Still, it seems to be good arrangement for them both. He looks content and satisfied, but I am pleased to say is not growing stout as so many married men do. He takes morning exercise very diligently and I am sure Eliza monitors his food lest he become too fond of puddings and fat meat. I expect her French cook makes ragouts and fricassees, which are healthier than the mutton broth and hashes that Mary serves to James—no wonder he is growing fat.

I never thought I would say it, but I have found Eliza's company on our summer journey more congenial than that of Mary, who seems to grow more ill-tempered with each passing year. She complains constantly of little Anna, who is very much a favourite with her aunts and myself. Eliza by contrast is sweet-tempered and charming—always so respectful of her uncle George and even towards me her manners are impeccable. She has done wonders for Jane, too. Ever since she returned from her last visit to London, Jane has been more her old self—certainly not the carefree high-spirited girl she was but tolerably good humoured at least.

So though I was not at first delighted with the suggestion that Henry and Eliza should accompany Mr Austen and the girls and me to Lyme and Weymouth, it has proved to be a memorable and enjoyable holiday. I shall be sorry when Henry and Eliza leave us tomorrow for Weymouth. We had hoped to travel with them, but Mr Austen is not at all well. He grows stooped and seems short of breath. Even to walk the length of the Cobb tires him now, so it is best that we stay here and await their return. At first I had thought that Cassy would stay with us—she is ever more willing to be the dutiful daughter than Jane—and Jane does so delight in the company of Henry and Eliza. But Jane seems to be writing again and does not want to leave her manuscript, so she is to stay. Jane and I are not the easiest of companions—I think our characters are too alike—but she is much less difficult and more content in spirit when she is writing.

She has just come back to the lodgings with Cassandra and told us of the merry time they have had sea bathing.

'It is most delightful to splash about Mama,' she said, 'and the bathing machine ladies are so amusing—great fat arms they have and they can bodily lift you back into the machine if you are too tired to climb the ladder.'

I was glad to see her cheeks flushed and pink—she had been looking so pale lately.

'What do you think, dear aunt?' joined in Eliza. 'Jane is to read to us tonight—not from Mr Cowper but from her own work!'

I clapped my hands. 'Oh I knew it—I knew you were composing again Jane. What is it, what is the piece called? When may we hear it?'

'I shall finish putting it in order directly and read it in the parlour when dinner is over. Fortunately the other guests here are dining out, so we shall have the place to ourselves.'

'And so to hear more of the Watsons and the fate of all the sisters, please ask the author to tell you when the next instalment will be ready.'

Jane looked around expectantly. There was silence. We had always greeted a reading of her work with applause, but this time even Mr Austen clapped only very faintly. Eliza roused herself and said: 'Bravo Jane—you try a new style I see.'

Cassandra looked at the floor.

Henry rang the bell and when the waiter entered ordered more wine.

Jane looked angry. 'So none of you like it—is that what I must presume?'

'My dear, it is just that it has a much different tone. When I heard it was about four sisters I expected the Bennets or a family such as that—'

'The Bennets?' she interrupted, her face growing red. 'How untrue to life are the Bennets—no wonder they were declined by return of post. How could anyone imagine that girls without fortunes would make such fine matches? The reality is more like the Watsons, I assure you, and if you do not like it, I pity you.' And turning, she fled from the room.

'Go after her Cassy, I beg you,' I said. 'She is distressed and in need of comfort'.

Cassy left the room to follow Jane upstairs and as she did so

Henry said, 'I think we are all distressed, Mama. I did not realise she was so bitter.'

How shall I describe the Watsons? It is a mournful bitter description of the fate of the daughters of a clergyman who see that when he dies, they will be thrown upon the mercy of their brother. Their misery is compounded because they have been forced to leave their childhood home and make a home in Bath. She had read us six chapters and there appeared not a ray of hope or amusement anywhere. On the contrary, the sisters appeared to dislike one another, hate their parents, and see that their only hope was in pursuing a man, any man it seemed, in order to be rescued by marriage. It was too close for comfort.

'Well Eliza,' said my husband, 'when you encouraged Jane to take up her pen again, I warrant you did not expect this.'

'Indeed not Uncle. I am as shocked as you at the content. But'—Eliza was ever one to look on the bright side—'there are one or two scenes that show her old flair, are there not? What about the charming little boy Charles—so like her own dear brother when he was learning to dance, did you not think?'

But there was little comfort to be had and I dreaded the morrow when Papa and I should be left alone with Jane.

Cassandra came back into the room. I could see from her eyes she had been crying.

'We were saying, Cass,' said Henry, 'that we did not realise that Jane was so bitter.'

'Bitter? Bitter?' Cassandra raised her voice in a way she never normally did.' She is not bitter, she is just suffering from disappointment such as would make a weaker person than my sister unable to function, unable to speak, let alone write.'

'You mean about the publication?' put in Eliza. 'I must say, Cass, that no one could have tried harder than Henry.'

'She knows that—but that is not all. It comes on top of the rejection of what we all thought her finest work and then the Manydown incident but before that here in Lyme the business with the reverend gentleman who she thought admired her and wished to continue—'

'What *was* his name?' interrupted Eliza. 'Though we were to convey her here to meet him again, she never disclosed his name.'

I was astonished. 'Mr Austen,' I said, 'what know you of this clergyman? How is it that half our family know and I do not?'

Cassandra blushed deeply. 'Forgive me, Mama, I forget myself in my worry about Jane. He was to be our secret.'

'It is highly improper for young girls to have secrets from their parents.'

'My dear,' my husband tried as ever to calm me, 'we should perhaps realise that neither of our daughters are young girls anymore and may be entitled to some privacy. . . . But I wonder if I might be permitted to ask what is the situation between Jane and this clergyman now?'

Cassandra was silent looking steadfastly at the floor.

After what seemed like several minutes but was probably barely one, Eliza said: 'Dear aunt, we should not press Cassandra, who is sworn to secrecy. So far as I know they agreed to correspond until they were able to meet again and did so for a while.'

'Nonsense,' I said. 'No letters ever came for her at Bath, Mr Austen or I should have seen them if they did.'

'As I understand it,' Eliza went on calmly, 'she would walk to the post office to collect them and take them straight up to her room.'

I had to concede that this was a possibility.

'Are they still corresponding?'

'No, I understand that the letters ceased abruptly after some small disagreement.' I looked to Cassy for confirmation and she nodded imperceptibly.

As her mother, I was of course unhappy that Jane had been having a secret relationship—it is certainly not proper and she had not been brought up to throw decorum to the winds. I blamed myself for allowing her and Cassy the freedom to go on holiday last year with only Martha as chaperone. How my sister-in-law will upbraid me should she find out and as for what that minx Philly will make of it and what gossip she will spread abroad, why, it hardly bears thinking about. And yet my heart goes out to Jane. Disappointment piled on disappointment; I could see now the emotions that had made their way into the Watsons. I must be especially kind to her when we are left alone with her.

Bath, December 17th, 1804

In fact, the rest of that stay in Lyme was remarkably pleasant. Jane's spirits seemed to improve greatly and she seemed vastly more content. By the time Cassandra and Eliza and Henry returned to collect us, I had rarely seen her looking so well. Eliza whispered to me that Jane has somehow found out that the clergyman died suddenly and this is the reason for the improvement in her disposition. I should have thought this would make her more melancholy yet, but Eliza explained that she was relieved to know that she had not been mistaken, he had loved her and not rejected her and it was only his death that had parted them. This both Cassandra and I could easily understand—look how content *she* is after all to know that she was loved by Tom even though their happiness was so short-lived.

But I have just had news that I fear will send Jane into the depths of grief again—her dear friend Mrs Lefroy was thrown from her horse yesterday as she rode out and was taken up dead. That this should happen on Jane's birthday—she was twenty-nine yesterday—is a particularly cruel blow. I have always been puzzled by how friendly Jane has been towards Mrs Lefroy, who after all sent that young Tom of whom Jane was so fond, back home to Ireland with scarce time to bid anyone good-bye. She was also obliged to give Jane news of his marriage and of how well he is doing in the law in Ireland. Yet Jane has a nature sweet enough to disregard all such difficulties if she likes someone—just as if she dislikes, well, her tongue can be horribly sharp. She and Cassandra will be home from their walk soon. I shall try to get Mr Austen to break the news to Jane, but do not know if he is strong enough. He is failing before my eyes after that bad cold and feverish attacks, but I do not know if the girls see it. They were able to divert him very much this morning by reading a letter from Eliza with a long account of the awful Bonaparte being crowned emperor in Paris. We had read some report in the *Morning Post* but did not know that the pope himself was there. Much good it did him, apparently, as when the moment for the crowning came, Boney took the crown from the pope's hands and put it on his own head! The impudence of it! And all of them done up in satins and laces and purple velvet—including Josephine, now an empress if you please. Eliza tells us that the court of the new emperor promised to be even more splendid than that of the old king, whose head they cut off. I said that you could expect no better of the French, but Mr Austen reminded me that the English had done the same to a king and then restored one not a dozen years later. We all laughed at the thought of Eliza, torn between her dislike of the new emperor and her taste for fashion and court life! Since this morning though, my poor husband has scarcely been able to lift his head from the pillow. I shall have to break the news about this death myself. I fear it may not be long before there is news of another much closer to home.

## TWENTY-NINE

### *Philly Walter at Tunbridge Wells*
#### February 1805

S o the old man is dead! I had heard he was failing, but the Christmas letters from Bath were tolerably cheerful. He did not last long, though. I have had no fewer that three letters telling me of his last hours—from Cassandra, Jane, and Eliza. Not that Eliza was present, but as soon as the news reached London she and Henry rushed there 'with only a short stop for a glass of porter at the inn at Reading and the post house at Chippenham,' as Eliza put it. I cannot see why Henry was needed—after all James is the eldest son and much closer at hand—let alone why Madame thought her presence was necessary. On the contrary, I should have thought her being there would cause extra work for my aunt and cousins, which they could well do without at such a time. But of course where there is drama Madame wishes to be at the centre of it. Her letter about Uncle George's death is far more emotional than that of either of his daughters.

> He was so very dear to me and had ever been my guide and mentor. His dear face looks so tranquil and we are all thankful that he did not suffer but only gradually became insensible. Doctor Bowen and Doctor Gibbs both attended him and bled him but to no avail and he slipped away as if in sleep.

Jane and Cassandra are not so overcome but busy themselves with all the necessary letters—both Frank and Charles are at sea and it will be weeks before they have the news, but James is at Green Park Buildings and he and Henry represented the family at the funeral. Eliza is remaining there 'so as to be of comfort to my aunt and cousins in their dreadful loss.'

Well, she has nothing else to do and a great deal of comfort is going to be needed, especially where money is concerned. I wonder if any of them have thought how they are going to live? My uncle's small income will die with him and the church does nothing for widows and children, as I have reason to know. Aunt Cassandra has nothing of her own. Cassy has that £1,000 from her dead fiancé but that won't take them far. Jane, of course, has nothing either and this idea that she would be able to support herself through her writing, which I have heard talked about, clearly has no future. I know for a fact that the lease on Green Park Buildings runs out soon and they could not afford it now anyway. I wonder what will become of them?

May 1805

I expected to hear from Aunt Cassandra before this. I wrote immediately on hearing the news of Uncle George's death and received no reply. I wondered if she was offended because my mother did not pen the letter of condolence herself, but I explained fully enough I hope that she is no longer able to write for herself. I think none of my family have any idea of how difficult Mama is and now how incapable. Anyway, I have finally received a reply and I must own it is a long and detailed one. It seems the reason for her silence was the difficulty of making what she calls 'the new arrangements.' They have had to move house as I expected and now reside in Trim

Street. I have never heard of such a street in Bath and am confident it is not in a very smart part of the town. However, this seems to be of no consequence to my aunt, as she intends to spend only winters in Bath in 'comfortable lodgings' and to spend her summers travelling about the country staying with relatives. I do not know if this was meant as a hint for an invitation but if it was it will not be taken up. I have enough on my hands with my mother and it is not as though the only visitor would be my aunt. Not only will Jane and Cassandra be of the party in these summer ramblings but also Martha Lloyd, who, now that she has lost her mother, is to leave Ibthorpe and take up residence with the Austens! My aunt does not seem to find anything wrong with this plan—I should be ashamed if it were me to put myself on the comfort of others.

She writes at great length of the generosity of her wonderful sons:

> No mother could be more fortunate than I. No sooner did the news of his father's death reach him than dear Frank offered me £100 a year. James and Henry offered £50 each. James has his family to consider and Henry's current income is precarious, though he promises more if his firm prospers. We believe Edward may offer us as much as £100 a year and though we have not heard from Charles as yet since his ship is so far away we believe he may manage £50 once he is promoted. Cassandra and I each have £200 from our capital, so we shall be delightfully easy in our circumstances. In fact, I shall not accept Frank's offer but will take only £50 from him. The dear boy will need all he has when he sets up house.

How I should love to know what Jane makes of this—there is no mention of her and I doubt any of the brothers have given her a thought. In my opinion they are not as generous as their mother seems to think. Edward has wealth beyond the understanding of most of us—look how they all boast about his property constantly—only £100 a year from him is derisory. He could not even shift himself to attend his father's funeral—the excuse of his wife being confined is no excuse, it is hardly the first time! Mrs JA will have been involved in limiting James' contribution—she is a wise housekeeper by all accounts—but considering he has inherited not only his father's home but his stipend he could certainly give more. Frank's offer seems generous to be sure but I have heard that he has just taken command of a splendid new ship—the *Canopus*. Well, not new as she was a French-built ship captured at the Battle of the Nile but has been refitted and will bring him in at least £500 a year. But as for Henry—why is his situation precarious? What pray, has happened to his wife's fortune? There is certainly enough of it to keep a French cook, two housekeepers, endless underservants and enough carriages and coachmen to keep him and Eliza in comfort as they cavort about the country. They are to be at Godmersham soon.

July 1805

So my aunt's summer progress is begun. Does she think herself Queen Elizabeth? She is certainly travelling with a big enough entourage. Jane and Cassandra are with her, of course, and now Martha accompanies them everywhere. As they left Bath they stopped at Steventon to collect little Anna. Mary is just brought to bed of another daughter—called Caroline—so I suppose they thought it would be good to remove Anna from her stepmother, who is bad-tempered with her at the best of times and no doubt will be even more impatient with her now. She is much preoccu-

pied, as she does not put her children out to nurse as many mothers
do. They all arrived at Godmersham at the same time as Eliza and
Henry, so it was a large party. I have received a letter from Eliza
describing it all to me:

> It would be especially agreeable, dear cousin, if you were present
> at this time and I wish you might be prevailed upon to accept the
> invitation I know Elizabeth has bestowed.

No one realises that I am simply unable to accept even an invitation
to dine with Mr Whitaker as Mama cannot be left even for a few
hours. She goes on:

> Though the household is large I want congenial female company.
> Elizabeth is much preoccupied with her new baby, while Aunt
> Cassandra and Cassy amuse the little ones. Anna and Fanny, the
> eldest girl, have a fine time together reading romances and taking
> picnics into the fine woods hereabouts. I do not begrudge them
> that—indeed it is heartwarming to see Anna so content, as we
> all know life at home with Mrs JA is not always easy. Fanny, too,
> deserves the leisure. In my view she is called upon too often to
> be 'little mother' to her brothers and sisters. I would be content
> to walk and ride with Jane, who is such a good companion to me
> and revels in my company usually. But here at present she seems
> to spend every spare moment with Miss Sharpe, the children's
> governess. She has been intimate with her before when staying
> here I think, but this time they are inseparable. I have warned
> Jane before, and Henry has too, about the indelicacy of making
> too intimate a friend of a servant, but she hotly denies that Miss
> Sharpe is anything of the kind. I cannot quite see why Jane
> admires her so much and feels she has more in common with her

than with me, who has been her close friend for so many years and who is now truly her sister.

This aside, we have much merriment here and are to have some theatricals, which as you know will please me greatly. We are to put on *The Spoiled Child* when we return next month for the shooting. Before that though, Henry and I are to take Edward and Fanny to stay with us in London. It is high time a girl of her age was introduced to London society. We shall take them to the theatre and Lord Charles Spencer will come to dine—I know Fanny will enjoy the company of so charming a man.

Do not fear, dear cousin, if you hear further rumours of an invasion. In this part of Kent the only worry the gentlemen have is that the Emperor's army might disturb their game birds by trying to land. I think Bonaparte is turning his attention to Spain and may leave us in peace.

Eliza cannot see it—she never sees anything which does not affect her directly—but it is clear to me why Jane spends time with Miss Sharpe. She is thinking that she may have to become a governess and wishes to find out all she can about such a life. 'Tis likened often enough to slavery but if one were placed within a good family it might be tolerable. Better for a woman like Jane perhaps than being endlessly at the beck and call of her mother and forced to rely on the generosity or otherwise of her brothers. I know what the former is like but at least I do not have to ask for money to pay my laundress or to have to make a case for a new muslin. I have never liked Jane, but I do not envy her that.

# THIRTY

## Jane Austen at Bath
### November 1805

I am glad that Eliza is to come to Bath again. Now that we are moved into Trim Street and Martha lives with us permanently there is no room for her in our lodgings but she has friends enough in the city and Henry does not stay—he only escorted her before journeying back to Steventon to visit James and Mary on his way to Godmersham. I have never known my brother to be such a devoted gun. I think the attraction is not so much the covers and the pheasants as the luxury and the ability to live grandly at someone else's expense. Dear Henry, I love him so, but we have to own he is not sensible with money. Nor do his duties as a banker seem particularly onerous. He talks airily of 'seeking new business,' but I cannot see how he does that with a gun in his hand at Godmersham. I do not think Eliza likes Godmersham as Henry does—she often describes it 'delightfully rural,' which is not entirely a compliment. Of course, she would not accompany him to Steventon either. Between Mrs HA and Mrs JA the atmosphere remains decidedly frosty. I suspect this can be laid almost entirely at Mary's door. She is the one who bears grudges—Eliza would simply shrug off the past. It is hardly as though she covets James, or ever did come to that—that is all in Mary's mind. Eliza will not mind the chance to stay with her French friends here—I have no doubt they enjoy planning for a return to France that will never come. Some of them are so poor now they make even my family seem comfortable, but Eliza will as ever be generous to them and ensure that for a while at least their tables are plentifully supplied.

She enlivens us too, as we are not a merry party most evenings. Yesterday was an exception though. Eliza was walking through the yard of the White Horse Inn on her way to dine with us at our usual hour of 4 p.m.

'I could not believe it my dear,' she said as she arrived breathless on our doorstep. 'I was actually in the yard when the London coach came in. It was so thrilling to see—the whole coach was dressed in laurels, greenery hanging from every part and the passengers leaning out and waving their hats. "What is it?" I asked an ostler?

'"Why Madame, have ye not heard? Lord Nelson has won a great victory at sea—sent the Frenchies packing he has and them Spaniards, too." Oh Jane, it was so thrilling—everyone in the street running and cheering. Do put on your bonnet and come out.'

I could not wait to do so and shouting to Mama that I would return soon, I joined Eliza in the street. Everyone was running towards the Abbey and as we reached the square the bells in the tower began to ring high above the rooftops. Such a sight it was and such a crowd to be part of. But suddenly even as we laughed and shook hands with strangers, the bells stopped and a single deep passing bell began to toll. The crowd fell silent. 'What is amiss?' they began to ask. A messenger galloped up, an express in his hand.

'We have lost the admiral. Lord Nelson is dead—a great victory but sad news.'

Eliza clutched my hand, tears in her eyes. 'Oh Jane, it cannot be—to lose the admiral, it is too cruel.'

But suddenly I had no thought for his lordship—only for my brother.

'Frank serves under Lord Nelson—pray God he is safe, for I warrant we shall have lost many ships and many men.'

'*Mon Dieu!*' she exclaimed. 'What shall we tell my aunt of this?'

'As little as possible—do not alarm her unnecessarily until we know more.'

She did as I bid her and was charming all the evening in her distraction of Mama—playing bezique for hours on end and though we have no instrument, of course, she sang in her sweet voice and the evening passed very pleasantly. I realised that neither Mama, Cassy, nor Martha had thought about the possible danger to Frank, and when I mentioned it to Cassy as we retired to our room she agreed with me that we should keep silent on the matter until firm news was to hand.

December 1805

It did not take long. We looked again and again for the name of the *Canopus* to be mentioned in the newspaper accounts of the battle but saw nothing. But a letter is now arrived telling us of Frank's huge distress that he entirely missed the battle! They had actually been on their way to join the fleet but a huge gale kept them so long beating past the Rock that they did not sight Cape Trafalgar until the day after the engagement. Oh he is so frustrated! He writes:

> It is heartbreaking after so many months in a state of constant and unremitting fag to be cut out by a parcel of folks just come from their homes where some of them were staying at their ease the greater part of the last war and the whole of this.

He has hopes of coming home soon to his new bride and warns us not the mention the Trafalgar action!

I shall write to him to send Christmas wishes and to tell him Eliza and I had the great pleasure of seeing Mr Pitt, the prime minister, in Bath this week. He has a gouty foot and hopes the waters will cure it. In the Pump Room the crowd fell back and made way for him, but he looked very pale and was clearly in pain. He lodges in Laura Place, which, Eliza reminds me, is a much more fashionable address than Trim Street!

She is to return to London to spend Christmas there with Henry. To my great surprise she tells me that they find the house at Brompton 'somewhat on the small side' and are seeking a dwelling both larger and nearer the city. They do not seem to mind the constant moving about, while for my part I find it both distressing and debilitating.

I noticed that Eliza did not once ask me during this visit how my writing was progressing. She, like the rest of my family, does not like *The Watsons* and cares not if it is ever finished. I am beginning to feel the same. My mind is quite dry, nothing grows in it. How I wish I could leave Bath forever.

# THIRTY-ONE

## Henry Austen at Brompton, London
### Spring 1806

Frank's comments disturbed me, I must own—nay, caused me much distress. We were sitting in our drawing room after Eliza had retired. It had been, I thought, a splendid evening. Eliza and Frank had scarcely met since he went away to sea at the age of twelve and it had been a joy to me to see how they revelled in each other's company. My dear wife is, of course, a clever and subtle flirt, and Frank was vastly flattered by her interest in life at sea and in his exploits on the *Canopus*. She had been warned not to mention the Trafalgar action but he brought it up himself when she admired his captain's uniform with his new decoration for bravery in battle.

'I am proud to wear it, but shall not leave off the black arm band for the dear Lord Nelson. The victory was ashes for many of his sailors when we heard of his death.'

'What think you of his successor?' I asked.

'Collingwood?' He is a fair sailor but not fit to wipe the boots of the admiral we lost and most of the navy think so.'

My brother was, of course, eager to speak to us of Mary Gibson, his betrothed. He had a miniature of her in his wallet and Eliza, in one of her typical sweet gestures, said she would take it on the morrow to our jewellers to have it properly set.

'Such an extremely pretty face merits a fine frame. Fear not dear brother, I shall choose the best,' and kissing him and me on the cheek she left us to our port.

'I am glad to see you happy with our cousin,' he began when she had departed. 'You keep a fine establishment here—the banking business must be profitable.' He looked around him. 'In fact, Henry, there is something I wish to raise with you, a little sensitive perhaps. . . .'

I rose and refilled his glass. I found myself rather anxious about what he was going to say and for a moment wondered if he was going to ask me to lend him money to set up his marital home. I was preparing my excuses but realised it could not be that as he received splendid prize money after the Battle of Santo Domingo—no less than three French ships had been taken and he had been telling us of this earlier at dinner. I was astonished when he suddenly burst out: 'To speak plain, Henry, I am astonished that you and my other brothers, living in luxury as you all do, tolerate the dreadful conditions in which our mother and sisters are living.'

'Dreadful conditions? What on earth do you mean? Their lodgings are not luxurious, to be sure, but perfectly tolerable surely and they are to leave there anyway shortly to spend the summer travelling and staying with relatives, as I am sure you know.'

'You admit then that Trim Street is not suitable for permanent occupation?'

I was angry and did not care if he knew it.

'I admit nothing of the sort—it is perfectly suitable and they seem quite content.'

'Content? What else can they be but content? It seems it is the best they can afford.'

'You must remember, Frank, that the arrangements had to be made in a hurry after our father died. The lease on Green Park Buildings was about to expire and their income diminished dramatically upon his death. We did the best we could, you know—you must remember that you and Charles were a long way off and those of us present had to turn to as we could.'

'I know, I know,' he said. ' I do not seek to cast blame, but Henry, I confess I was shocked to see our loved ones sunk so low.'

'Oh Frank, pray do not exaggerate. Eliza was with them only before Christmas and says they seem content—with the exception of Jane perhaps. . . .'

'Yes, Jane is the one who worries me most. She looks thin and pale and has settled into the maiden aunt role too soon. You know how she ever had a sense of fun and her quick wit was a delight. What has happened to her?'

Again I felt resentful and hurt. 'We have done our best. We invite her here as often as she wants to come and we have encouraged her to take up her writing again—but she—'

'I know. She confessed to me she finds no pleasure in it anymore. I tell you, Henry, I fear for her. I have never seen her spirits so low.'

'I am as fond of Jane, and indeed as dutiful to my mother as anyone,' I replied, rather sharply, 'but tell me, have you any suggestions as to how we may help further?'

'I do think they would be better in different lodgings—I was shocked to find them in such poor and dark quarters and not even in a respectable part of Bath. They had described it to me in letters, but I suppose I had thought of them as living in, well, a smaller version of the parsonage.'

'Frank, be reasonable! Smaller versions of Steventon are beyond their means and ours now. We went through all this when Papa died.'

'Was Edward present at that discussion?'

'No, he was unable to attend the funeral. Why?'

'Well, Edward owns a grand estate does he not? I am to visit there next week, as you know. Is there not a cottage or a dower house somewhere that the dear three could take on and that would be more suitable a dwelling?'

'We have to think of 'dear four' now, you know, I said as an aside. 'Martha Lloyd is to make her home with them permanently.'

'I have no objection to her—she brings a small income with her, I believe, and does her share of housekeeping. She may also keep the peace between Jane and Mama. But what think you of my plan?'

'I only wonder no one has thought of it before—'tis a good idea certainly, but surely if Edward had such accommodation he would have offered it? Let us ask Eliza her view in the morning.'

Eliza was not hopeful.

'You may suggest it to Edward, but I think you will find it is Elizabeth who makes the decisions in that household.'

'But, my dear, I have thought further on this since last evening,' I said, 'and I remember that Edward has another estate in Hampshire as well as Godmersham—it is scarcely possible that somewhere there is not a suitable dwelling for the four ladies.'

Eliza, with that tolerant, affectionate look she often gives me, said: 'My dear for Elizabeth, as mistress of Godmersham—'

'And of Chawton,' I added.

'Yes indeed, as mistress of two grand estates and as the mother of a very large family—I hear she may be expecting a tenth!—she sees her husband's mother and sisters as something of an embarrassment, the poor relations who must be tolerated.'

'Surely not. She is always generous in her hospitality and glad to welcome Jane and Cassandra there at any time.'

'No my dear , not at any time—only at times they can be useful, such as her endless confinements. I myself have heard her being somewhat patronising to them—in fact, last time I was there she asked the hairdresser to dress Jane's hair for half the price he charges the other ladies. She was mortally offended I can tell you, though of course cannot say anything as she is in receipt of Elizabeth's hospitality.'

Frank and I exchanged mystified glances—such things were not part of our life. What happened between ladies when they were alone was a closed book to us.

'So you do not think Elizabeth would welcome having them there as close neighbours?' said Frank.

'I am certain she would not and to ask Edward would cause awkwardness, I am sure. I advise you to avoid the subject,' said Eliza firmly.

'I am sure you know more about the delicacies of family life than I,' said Frank. 'I am but a simple sailor and see things more straightforward. If I cannot bring that about though, I am determined to see to it that my mother and sisters are better housed before I return to sea. They say I might have a year on shore and I will grow impatient at being idle. I will think of something.'

'Frank my dear,' said my wife, laughing, 'you are to be married— surely that will give you occupation enough for the time being!'

# THIRTY-TWO

## *Philly Walter at Tunbridge Wells*
### January 1807

I said to Mr Whitaker, 'I have rarely heard of a more foolish plan. Five women in one household and one a new bride—has Frank taken leave of his senses?'

Mr Whitaker agreed with me and said that one family of his acquaintance had tried such an arrangement and been obliged to give it up before the first quarter was out.

When I first heard in a letter from Eliza that Frank planned to set up an establishment in Southampton for himself and his new bride and that his mother and sisters were to accompany them, I thought it was for a visit only. That would be perfectly proper, as they do not know Mary Gibson and it is right for her to become more intimate with her husband's family. But then I heard that it is to be a permanent arrangement. Not only that, but Martha is to be included, too! I wonder what Mary Gibson makes of it? I cannot say that if I should be so fortunate as to achieve an establishment of my own—and I sometimes despair of that ever happening—I should want my mother-in-law, his two old-maid sisters, and another unrelated spinster to be constantly present. What sort of life is that for a bride? I know he is to be off to sea again shortly and will not like to leave her alone, especially as I understand she is to be confined soon, but oh dear—five women under one roof—it will not do!

I am amazed at how cheerfully they all write of it. Aunt Cassandra says:

> The house in Castle Square that Frank has taken for us all is large and commodious—quite airy and light compared with our last place in Bath. Frank is a practical fellow, as you know, and has erected shelves and hanging closets. Like all sailors he is good with his hands and never happier than when he has a hammer in his hands or is mending a rusted window frame. Mary is a dear girl, though somewhat unwell at present, but as sensible as Frank and sits sewing baby clothes while Jane reads aloud to her.
>
> My great delight is the garden. You will recall how I loved the garden and dairy at Steventon and have missed it since we have been in Bath. Jane bids me plant a syringa, though my taste is more to currant bushes.

When I read that I thought they would do better to plant potatoes if they were so proud of being practical. I know that Cassandra went to Godmersham at Christmas and Martha to her family so that will have left Jane with the housekeeping, which will not have pleased her. Cassandra was rewarded for her endless service at Godmersham by having the new baby named after her. Ten children is surely enough, even for Elizabeth. It seems they are to visit at Southampton as soon as she is well enough to travel. Eliza plans to go, too—perhaps everyone is curious to see how this foolish arrangement is working out.

## THIRTY-THREE

### *Eliza at Brompton*
#### Summer 1808

It would not have been my choice but I cannot say it has done Jane any harm. Life in Southampton seems to suit her so much better than life in Bath, and she has confided to me that she hopes never to return to that city.

'I hate the white glare of the buildings and the falseness of its society,' she said as we sat sewing yesterday. 'I may set another story there one day but I have enough in mind of the place not to need any more visits.'

I looked up, startled and pleased by this easy reference to 'another story'—was she thinking of composing again? I did not dare ask. By mutual agreement Henry and I never mention the manuscript still languishing at Crosby's but we know it must be on her mind still and I wondered if I should suggest that enquiries be made again. I know Jane too well to press her too much on this topic though, and thought she would confide in me if and when she had anything to say. Her spirits certainly seem considerably higher than when we last met and she was almost flirtatious at the dinner I gave last night.

'Your sweet émigrés are so amusing,' she said as we sat with Henry after they had gone. 'They were so downcast about the defeat of Austria but seem to have high hopes of Wellington in Spain. Do they really believe that Napoléon can be vanquished?' Her eyes had something of their old sparkle. 'Surely Boney carries all before him now and conquers the whole of Europe?'

I knew she was joking and joined in. 'For shame, Jane, you know there can be no talk of defeat in this house. The Allies will triumph in the end and our friends will be restored to glory! At least'—lowering my voice—'that is what we all pretend.'

'You are kindness itself to them, cousin,' she said, 'you and my brother, but I swear many of them are so thin and pale yours is the only house in which they have a good meal.'

''Tis too true, sadly, as you will see for yourself. They will be sure to ask you with us when they return our hospitality.'

Henry laughed. 'Yes, Eliza and I always eat before we attend one of their soirees, as you are likely to be served an omelette and tea as any meat or wine.'

'And is the conversation always the same? Of past glories, when they were at Versailles, and of the wickedness of Napoléon?'

'Indeed, yes, it never palls for them. We tolerate it but I know it can be trying for others.'

Jane was good enough to accompany us to one evening party given by the Comte Julien, but the next time one of the refugees asked us she begged to be permitted to stay at home.

'Of course, my dear, you stay here. Madame Bigeon can see to your dinner and tomorrow we are to attend the opera so there will be amusement enough then.'

When we returned at about eleven o'clock, I went to her room to bid her good night and was amazed to find her still sitting, fully dressed at the writing table, with piles of paper spread out around her. So intent was she that she did not hear my knock or my entry.

'Why Jane,' I said, 'what are you about?' I glanced at the sheets, covered with her neat handwriting. 'You surely cannot have done all this since we left you?'

She laughed. 'No cousin—even at my most industrious I could not accomplish that. Perhaps you did not know that I carry my manuscripts everywhere with me.'

'Oh, that mahogany box? I wondered what was in there.'

'I had an idea for a revision of the story you liked—you know *Elinor and Marianne*—and have been trying it out.'

I was pleased and excited and I clapped my hands. 'Oh do tell—how is it to be revised? Dare I hope Elinor and Edward will still find happiness?'

'How good you are to remember them. Yes, it is just that I was discussing it with Cassandra and she pointed out that writing it in the form of letters between the sisters means that the plot can move on only when they are apart, so I wonder if I could use another form. . . .'

'Just a telling of the story perhaps?' I interrupted.

'Yes. I have revised a few chapters and think it might be possible.'

I kissed her, quite overcome at the cheerful and productive mood that seemed to be upon her.

'Do not think of coming to call on Mrs Tilson tomorrow,' I said. 'You have more important work to do.'

Though Henry and I both pressed her, she would not be prevailed upon to read us any more of the work, but I noticed that when she and Henry entered the carriage a few days later as he was to convey her to Godmersham for another visit, she would not let her mahogany box be strapped behind with her trunk, but cradled it carefully on her lap, much as a mother might hold a baby.

I have just received a letter from her:

Godmersham is in its summer glory and the walks are beautiful. James and Mary have arrived, bringing all the children. I am glad to

see that Anna and Fanny are as intimate as hitherto, although there
is the usual ill feeling apparent between Anna and her stepmother.
... Elizabeth looks pale as any woman expecting her eleventh
confinement might do. I know you will be glad to hear that my
revisions are proceeding well and of course it is a joy to be able to
leave my papers undisturbed instead of having to clear everything
away each day before mealtimes as I have to do at home.

I have told Henry that I mean to write to Crosby's to ask that
they either publish my manuscript or return it to me. Henry offers
to do it for me but I mean to do it myself. I will use a false name
as they never knew my true identity and of course I would wish to
preserve that anonymity if they do decide to publish.

How confident she sounds! I wish her luck with it.

## THIRTY-FOUR

## Letter from Cassandra Austen to Eliza and Henry Austen

Godmersham, October 10th, 1808

My dear brother and sister,

I know you will be stricken by the sad news I have to impart. Elizabeth is dead! I cannot describe the shock and grief that overtakes us all. I am much needed downstairs but must find a few moments to give this news to all the family immediately. Edward is too overcome but his man is to send expresses shortly and I must have them ready. I have written already to Jane and Mama at Southampton but anticipate that you may be the first to receive the news as the coach to London departs from Wye every two hours.

As you know, I am only just arrived in Kent as the confinement was not expected for another two weeks. I was amazed to find that little Brooke John had been safely delivered even as I alighted from the coach conveying me here. Fanny ran to greet me, saying that all was well, and when I saw Elizabeth, the babe in her arms, she looked as well and as pretty as she has always looked at such times. The following morning, however, she awoke with a small fever and the apothecary who always attends her suggested finding a wet nurse, which was done without difficulty as there are a multitude of fine young women hereabouts who are able to fulfil that function. Still, we thought that perhaps E had only a little milk fever, which would soon pass. Indeed, she ate a hearty dinner of chicken followed by custard tart that same evening. As she was alternately hot and cold, I sat with her all that night, sponging her, and began to grow concerned when she did not seem to know me or Edward, who was ever beside her. At dawn she looked at us with a faint smile and before we could respond she was gone! Edward gathered the children, save for little Cassandra, who slept on, and the scene around the deathbed was enough to break your heart—how they wept and sobbed, yet tried to comfort their father. Fanny, though barely sixteen, takes a mothering role and is a great comfort to poor Edward, who cannot keep away from the deathbed where she lies, pale but beautiful still and surrounded by flowers the children have laid.

The two older boys are away at school, of course, and my first letter was to their headmaster that he might break the sad news as gently as possible. I have asked Jane to receive them at Southampton to try to occupy them until after the funeral, which Edward's steward is arranging. I have also asked Jane to send my mourning clothes, which I hope will arrive in time. The family are sending to Canterbury for theirs—how sad it will be to see the little ones in deepest black.

In haste and with the heaviest of hearts,<br>
*Cassandra*

Letter from Eliza to Edward Austen
October 13th, 1808

My dear brother,

On receipt of the terrible news, your faithful brother determined on coming immediately to Godmersham to bring you the comfort that only close family can bring, and I write hastily to enable him to convey my letter by his own hand. I know he will exert himself to be of use and comfort to you all.

Only those who have lost a spouse can begin to understand what you are undergoing at present. The joy that you and Elizabeth found in your union is an example to many married people but vouchsafed to very few. May she rest in peace and may God grant comfort to you and all the children.

In truth, any man who fathers eleven children may expect to be a widower at some time in his life and I know that dear Elizabeth would be the first to urge you, after a decent period of mourning, to seek another mother for your large family. You may be sure that your family will certainly support you in this endeavour, for your sake but most of all for the sake of your motherless flock. In particular, I entreat you to have a care that dear Fanny does not take on too easily the role of substitute mother. I have seen this happen only too frequently and though it may seem natural enough to a father in your position it undoubtedly is a great disadvantage to a young woman to have too much responsibility for her brothers and sisters. It would surely result in her losing her bloom and might mean that her chances of making a suitable match are much diminished. I am sure that as a loving father, you will have regard to that.

You know me as a practical soul, so I hope you are not disconcerted by my advice. It does not, believe me, reflect any lack of sympathy for you all. My tears wet the paper as I write and my thoughts and prayers are with you all.

Your devoted and grieving sister-in-law and cousin,

*Eliza Austen*

## Letter from Eliza to Jane Austen
## Brompton, November 1808

My dear Jane,

Henry is returned from Godmersham with mournful tales of
the devastation wrought by the death of Elizabeth. How dreadful
an affliction giving birth, especially so many times, can be to us
women. I have calculated that Elizabeth must have been in the
increasing way for most of her married life and I hear that Frank's
little Mary seems set to follow her example. According to your
news, however, she does not bear it as well as the dear departed one
and is often upon the sofa and very ill. I often give thanks that you,
my dear Jane, and Cassandra have been spared the dangers of this
state and that my dear mother and I myself had but one experience
each.

 I am concerned to hear that Cassandra is to stay on at
Godmersham for some while as I know you must miss her. She
takes charge of the housekeeping, I understand, while Fanny looks
to the children. I have warned Edward of the dangers of this but
suppose he is too grief-stricken to notice. I am glad to hear that you
cared so well for the two older boys when they stayed with you—an
aunt is a rare blessing in such circumstances. Henry and I were both
angry that Crosby's gave you such a rebuff when you wrote to them
about your manuscript. Whatever they now say, they *did* promise
publication, and to ask you for £10 to buy back what is your own
is too terrible. But be assured, dear Jane, that your brother and I
realise that such a sum is impossible for you to find in your current
circumstances. He bids me tell you that we shall gladly advance
you the sum needed—do not hesitate to write by return to confirm
whether you wish us to pay the sum to you or directly to Crosby's.

But I have a further reason for writing now and that is to urge
you to approach your brother Edward about a settled home for you,
Cassy, my aunt, and Martha. Henry has confirmed with him that he
has two properties that would suit—one is near Godmersham, but
the other in Hampshire, near to your old home, within easy reach of
James and Mary. Henry is setting up a branch of his bank in Alton
so is to travel in that direction shortly. He will take the liberty,
I believe, of viewing the property. Do consider it—I know you
would find a settled home more helpful to your composition. Frank,
I know, is gone to China but when he returns and if he and Mary
continue to increase their family, is he not likely to want his house
in Southampton for their sole occupation? I beg you, if the offer is
made to consider it at least.

Your loving cousin and sister,
*Eliza*

Letter from Henry Austen to His Wife
From the French Horn Inn, Alton, Hampshire
January 1809

It is settled! Your plan has taken a long time to come to its fruition
but how right you were! I am just come from Chawton Cottage and
can report on its being the ideal place for my mother and sisters.
It is not commodious but quite adequate for the four ladies with
room even for visitors, as I am sure that Jane and Cassandra will
continue to share a room. It will be easily run and there is a large
kitchen garden and a dairy, which will vastly please my mother as it
will remind her of Steventon. They will be within easy distance of
James, too, and of many of their old acquaintance. My business will

frequently take me to Alton, which is not much more than a mile away, so they will not want for visitors. I believe that my mother at first favoured the other cottage that Edward offered at Wye, since it was nearer to Godmersham, but could not hold out against the wishes of the three others and was easily persuaded. Only a very little refurbishment is necessary—a new privy is badly required!—which Edward undertakes to have completed by the summer, allowing them to move in by July at the latest.

You will understand what a weight this is off my mind, as Frank is not the only one who has been uneasy about the dear group since the death of my father. How ironic it is that it is another death—that of Elizabeth—that now makes this new arrangement possible.

I return with a light heart to my dearest wife as soon as my business here is completed.

Your devoted husband,

*Henry*

## THIRTY-FIVE

## Mary Austen [Mrs JA] at Steventon
### June 1810

Well, it has been an exceedingly pleasant visit to Chawton. The cottage is charmingly appointed now and Alton is a pretty little town. I enjoyed walking there each morning, usually with Cassandra, though sometimes Jane accompanied us. More frequently though she remained at home and Anna stayed with her, which was a relief to me. We were received very warmly by the staff at the bank—Henry's bank they call it, though of course he is only a partner with two other gentlemen—which occupies a prime position in the town, next door to the splendid new town hall, the sign above it proclaiming Austen, Gray, and Vincent.

I said to Cassandra as we passed it one morning: 'It is to be hoped that Henry's bank prospers as I believe the HAs are to move to an even more grand house in Sloane Street.'

'I believe so,' she answered. 'I think Eliza wishes to entertain on a grander scale than she could in Brompton, though I confess I always thought the house they had in Berkeley Street grand enough.'

I could not help but say rather sharply: 'But then for Eliza, nothing is ever quite grand enough until she can compete with Godmersham.'

'Oh no,' came the reply, 'she does not aspire to be a lady of the manor, rather she sees herself as a hostess—you know, keeping salons like the French ladies of whom we read.'

'You and Jane may read of such ladies—I am too busy helping my husband run his parish to read such things.'

Cassandra linked her arm through mine.

'Come, dear Mary, let us change the subject—you know that talk of Eliza always makes you disagreeable.'

I could not help but smile and reflected that the move to Chawton had even benefited Cassandra—she had always been even-tempered, and now she teased and laughed as I had not seen her do since her terrible disappointment of so many years ago.

'Now that you and James have spent a week with us, what think you of our new situation?'

I told her candidly that I had not seen any one of them as content before.

'Jane especially seems to be so happy—she radiates contentment but I cannot believe it can be laid at the door of the Reverend Mr Papillon. He is agreeable enough, but I cannot see her accepting if he makes an offer can you?'

The reverend gentleman had called once or twice during our visit as he was a great friend of their near neighbour, Miss Benn.

'It is not a man who makes Jane seem content, it is her writing— have you not seen how engaged she is with that?'

'To be sure, I thought that no one could spend so long on letter writing as does dear Jane, but when we go into the room she covers her work up, so that I have begun to wonder if letters of the heart were involved.'

'She is working on something she wrote a while ago and it is so amusing, so well observed, that I sometimes dare to hope that this time, at last, she may achieve publication.'

'You have heard it then?'

'She reads me extracts but I long to read it all when it is complete.'

'She once used to enjoy reading to the family—might she be prevailed upon when Edward and his family join us next week?'

'I am not sure; she may find that too large a group.'

There was, of course, insufficient room at Chawton Cottage for Edward, Fanny, and the two other children who were to join our party soon, but they would occupy the Great House just next to the church, also owned by Edward. Cassandra continued: 'She has always valued Henry's opinion though, so perhaps when he arrives on Tuesday she—'

Startled, I interrupted: 'What are the HAs to be with us? I did not know that and fear I . . .'

'No Mary, do not be alarmed. Eliza is not to be of the party, we are all aware that you would not wish to be in company with her. Henry is coming alone on bank business, and I was thinking that if Jane has her work in order we might ask for a reading then.'

Somewhat to my surprise, Jane agreed to this scheme and on the afternoon Henry arrived, after we had dined, we settled in the parlour. My mother-in-law busied herself with the patchwork quilt she is working while Anna sat at her feet, cutting her pieces out for her. Cassandra sat in the window seat, Henry, James, and I upon the sofa. Jane took an upright chair, a small table in front of her holding the piles of small sheets of paper that were, she told us, an almost completed novel that she now called *Sense and Sensibility*.

She read for almost an hour and not one of us wanted her to stop. Her mother stopped sewing, Anna looked at her aunt openmouthed with astonishment, and James and Henry exchanged admiring glances. I own that I was quite overcome—it was so good! The sad situation of the three young ladies, their widowed mother having to move out of a house that was her own, the monstrous behaviour of the daughter-in-law—oh it was all so fascinating, like being at a play reading—no, better than the theatre, for this was all our own dear Jane's work. I had heard only her rather silly stories before and always thought the family's opinion of her writing rather flattering. I had been wont to think that James was a finer writer and only needed to have more opportunity and time to do something very fine. But this, this was quite astonishing, and when she drew to a conclusion after Willoughby had asked permission to call on Marianne next day, having rescued her after a fall in a most exciting scene, we all clapped and begged, 'More, More.'

'Oh do tell us,' cried Anna, her eyes shining, 'do Elinor and Edward meet again? Will Marianne find happiness with Willoughby? Oh, when may we hear more?'

'Have a care for your aunt's voice now,' said Henry, but he went on, 'Seriously Jane, this work is by far the best we have heard. Will you not let me—'

'No Henry, not again,' Cassandra, who scarcely ever raised her voice, almost shouted at her brother. 'She has been disappointed often enough—do not tempt her again.'

But Jane quite calmly responded, 'I am ready to try my talents upon the world, Henry, if you will do me the honour. This time I am hopeful that we will have more luck. Next time you visit us, Henry, I shall have a fresh copied manuscript for you to take to London with you.'

She was as good as her word. She and Cassandra spent most days busily bent over the writing table. We enjoyed some pleasant outings in Edward's barouche-landau though, and came back in the evening to a fine dinner prepared by Martha and the cook. The evening entertainment was always a reading from the newly copied pages, so that by the end of our three-week stay at Chawton we knew the Dashwood family very well. Anna and Fanny renewed their acquaintance and gossiped as young girls do about affairs of the heart. Anna is turning into something of a flirt and will have to be watched. I thought Edward looked alarmed at times and may fear that she will lead his little Fanny astray—poor thing, she deserves a little fun to be sure. She is turning into quite a drudge. The girls, of course, hoped that Marianne and Willoughby would make a match: 'I cannot abide that old Brandon,' Fanny would say, but delighted in Elinor and Edward's coming together after so many misunderstandings.

It has been an altogether delightful summer. It will give me something pleasant with which to respond to cousin Philly. Her letter awaits an answer these five weeks. She will certainly scold!

## THIRTY-SIX

## *Jane Austen, Sloane Street, London*

### April 1811

'Cassandra is so droll,' I said to Eliza as I read the latest letter from her this morning.

Eliza looked up from her perusal of the Court Circular in the *Morning Post*—she always reads this first each day.

'How so? I should not have thought Godmersham a merry place to be staying, even near three years after Elizabeth's death,'

'No, it is sadly changed—they read prayers now instead of plays in the evenings. But what made me laugh is that Cassandra asks if I forget *S&S* in the round of entertainment you and Henry are arranging for me,'

Eliza laughed. 'Oh, I see. And what shall you tell her about your 'darling child'?

'Why, that I could no more forget it than a mother could forget her sucking child of course!'

We were laughing merrily when Henry came in to bid us good-bye as he went off to his office. He looked exceedingly handsome in his blue coat with gilt buttons and quite a dandy as he mounted his chestnut mare and rode off. I have never quite fathomed just what he does at what he calls 'his' bank but it seems to provide income enough for them to live in even better style than when I visited them at Brompton.

I knew Cassy would be wild to know about their new abode,

and I fear she is feeling somewhat neglected since my book has been taken up. I try very hard to let her see she is as important to me as ever, but of course this London life is very entertaining and I confess to a certain sense of pride in saying that I am to collect my proofs from Egerton's next week and shall spend a week correcting them. The publication date was set for July but they now say it may be September or even later.

When Henry first told me that Egerton's would publish I was so excited that I did not think to ask what 'on commission' meant. It was Eliza who gently explained: 'It means my dear, that the publisher thinks your work is good but not good enough to ensure sales to cover his costs. Thus the author must be prepared to cover the costs if the book does not sell. But never fear, Jane, Henry, and I are more than prepared to stand surety for that eventuality, which we sincerely believe will not occur. The book will sell and Egerton's will not only recoup the costs but be delighted to publish more— you wait and see.'

I was touched by their generosity and their faith in me. After all, with two major disappointments behind me success is far from assured. But Cassandra told me, as did Mama, that they could afford such a risk and that Eliza would be willing to risk much more to be associated with an author who would soon be the talk of London. Even if the book does sell I will hardly be the talk of London, since I have stipulated that my name must not be revealed. The title page will say only that the author is 'A Lady.'

I wanted to make Cassy feel included in the excitement, so I sent her a full description of the new house:

The new house is very fine and is situated next door to that of Captain Tilson, Henry's partner. It is part of a terrace, long and narrow like most London houses but most advantageously situated

with views over Five Fields towards Piccadilly. The reception
rooms are ideal for the sort of entertaining Eliza loves—there is
a wide parlour at the front, and an octagon room overlooking the
garden. The passage between the two affords access to the staircase
and there our fair cousin stands when she receives guests as they
mount the stairs. She is as beautiful as ever, though rather thin and
a little pale. There is to be a very grand musical party next week at
which as many as eighty guests are expected! Do not ask me where
they will all be accommodated but they will surely be well fed.
Madame Bigeon and Madame Perigord are already preparing the
white soup! I shall send you a full account.

Preparation for the party takes up much of Eliza's attention but she
has other things on her mind, too. When we were walking out in
Hyde Park with Henry last Sunday she suddenly said: 'Jane, I have
been thinking again about the situation of poor dear Fanny at Godmersham and am resolved to ask her on a visit to us in London that
she may be relieved of those onerous duties she has to undertake at
home—what think you of the idea?'

'She has been to stay with you since you moved to Sloane Street
has she not?'

'Why yes, she came with Edward, young Edward, and her sister
Marianne not long after we moved. We had a fine time—we took
them to see Mrs Jordan in her new play and gave two dinners in
their honour.'

'I remember—she wrote to Mama saying how much she had enjoyed it.'

'I think I should not have difficulty persuading her to come again
but my scheme is to invite her on her own, that she might enjoy relief
from her family for a while. But I also have another plan and you
must tell me if it is a good one or if it would cause a family upset.'

I was curious. 'Eliza you are looking mischievous—what do you have in mind?'

'Yes, my love, do tell us—are we likely to approve your scheme?' asked Henry, drawing her arm through his and looking down at her fondly.

'I think you will approve, but its execution depends on the approval of others. What I have in mind is to invite Anna to join Fanny here. You know how much they enjoy each other's company and I do think a few weeks in London in the autumn would do them both good.'

Henry looked at me while answering Eliza: "Tis a good plan certainly but the difficulty might be—'

'Henry there is no "might" about it,' I said, immediately understanding him. 'Mary would never agree.'

'I thought you would say so,' said Eliza, 'and we may speak frankly among ourselves. I know that Mrs JA has never cared for me and we all know the reason.'

'You cannot deny, my love,' said Henry with an indulgent smile at her, 'that it is a hard thing for a woman to know that her husband made an offer to another woman and only married her when refused!'

'I know, Henry, but this family feud has gone on long enough. That Mary and I have never been in the same room since we each married two brothers is ridiculous, you must allow.'

'So you wish to repair the breach by issuing the invitation to Anna?' I enquired.

She nodded vigorously. 'Yes. I thought it would show that I was willing to extend a hand of friendship and that in turn might make her forget the past.'

Henry looked doubtful. 'What think you Jane? Would Mary see it as a gesture of friendship?'

I was not sure. 'She might perhaps, and I think James would support Anna coming to London, if only because there is always friction between his wife and daughter—yet she is not a woman of warm feelings, as we all know, and she might interpret it differently. She might even think it a provocation—you know flaunting the amusements of London against the dullness of the parsonage.'

But Eliza was determined. 'I shall do it and take my chances. If she rejects my offer we shall all be no worse off than at present and if she accepts—why, think how much easier family parties will be. We might even ask Mary and James to fetch Anna at the end of the stay and we could give a fine dinner for them.'

Henry laughed. 'You are always too quick with such plans, my love. One step at a time will be enough, I beg you!'

She was prevented from replying by a disturbance in the park. We heard cheering and clapping and the sound of a carriage and horses.

'Oh do look, Jane,' cried Eliza, running back to the path we had just turned off, 'it is Princess Charlotte—I recognise her equipage. She must be going to visit her mother.'

We had a very good view as she passed by and I tried to take it all in to tell the family in Chawton. She is rather stout, somewhat like her father, the regent, I believe, and wore a pretty bonnet trimmed with blue and silver feathers. The horses and the livery were very fine, of course, and two footmen sat behind on the rear box as the princess and her lady in waiting waved amicably to the crowd. Eliza says that she often drives this way from St James's as she goes to visit her mother at Kensington Palace. Of course her parents are estranged, and I believe there is even talk of divorce. That is just such another aspect of London society that I know would not find favour with Mary.

Eliza will certainly extend the invitation, but I doubt that Mary

will allow it, even though she is usually glad for Anna to be anywhere but at home. For the moment though, Eliza will concentrate
on the musical party. Even I begin to grow excited at the prospect.

Letter from Jane Austen to Cassandra, Sloane Street
April 25th, 1811

> Our party went off extremely well. There were many solicitudes,
> alarms, and vexations beforehand, of course, but at last everything
> was quite right. The rooms were dressed up with flowers and
> looked very pretty. The musicians arrived at half past seven in two
> hackney coaches and by eight the lordly company began to appear.
> The drawing room soon became hotter than we liked, so we placed
> ourselves in the adjoining passage, which was comparatively cool
> and gave us the advantage of the music at a pleasant distance as well
> as the first view of every newcomer. Including everybody we were
> sixty-six—which was considerably more than Eliza had expected.
> She looked truly beautiful in a gown of pale yellow silk with a gold
> scarf wound about her arms and her hair dressed in little curls. I
> wore the mew muslin I bought for the occasion. It has a raised red
> spot and I wore red ribbons in my hair to match. The music was
> extremely good. Between the songs were lessons on the harp or harp
> and pianoforte together—the players were famous names, though
> unknown to me. All the performers gave great satisfaction by doing
> what they were paid for and gave themselves no airs. The house was
> not clear till after twelve.

I did not detail the food to my sister, fearing she would be envious
of our excesses now she is back at Chawton and eating mutton pies!
But Madame Bigeon excelled herself. There was hot lobster, oyster
patties, and chicken in aspic jelly. There were ices of every flavour

and little cakes soaked in rum. There was even French champagne, as Henry had found someone who could supply it and of course all the émigrés quite raved about it.

I did tell Cassandra that I was flattered to be surrounded by gentlemen all evening but worry that they all seem to know about S&S—how are we to keep it a secret when the publication date arrives?

Just as I sealed my letter, Eliza came into room, the *Morning Post* in her hand.

'Only see Jane,' she cried, 'our party is in the newspaper, but how stupid they are—they have not spelled my name right.'

I looked and saw the notice: 'On Tuesday Mrs H Austin had a musical party at her home in Sloane Street.'

'How well it looks.' Eliza was delighted. 'I must get the butler to go out and buy more copies. I am sure your dear mama would like to see it when you return home.'

I wondered what Mary would think but did not mention it.

## May 12th, 1811

I am to return home tomorrow and will be escorted not only by Henry but Mr Tilson also, as they both have business in Alton. If Eliza did not have her good companions with her I should have suggested putting off the journey because she is not at all well. She caught cold a week or so ago and it seems to have gone to her chest. Her cough is quite troubling. She is also not sleeping well and has left off having tea in the evening, as her friend Madame D'Entraigues says it impedes proper rest. In fact, it was on the way to visit these friends that Eliza caught cold.

As we approached Hyde Park Gate the horses seemed very restive and the coachman could not settle them. A fresh load of gravel had been put down and this made the going hard for the poor beasts and one of them, it seems, had a sore shoulder. He reared up and made a great noise, which was alarming I confess. Nothing would placate Eliza but to get down until the horses had gained the hill and so we must walk up. The evening was chill and damp and Eliza had only a thin shawl about her, though Henry solicitously wrapped her in his evening coat when he saw her shivering. She is not robust and has such a delicate frame—she looked quite done in when we reached our destination. The D'Entraigues were kindness itself when we arrived, setting Eliza close by the fire and proffering gruel as well as warm wine. But Eliza, as ever, responded to being in company and was soon her usual gay self. We had a most pleasant party, as they were all in high spirits about Lord Wellington becoming colonel in chief of the army in the Peninsula.

'At last Boney has met his match—his lordship is not afraid of him and will wear him down, you mark my words,' said Monsieur. The gentlemen all seemed to agree while the ladies were more interested in the new empress.

'The emperor did well to choose a Hapsburg,' said Madame. 'Through Marie Louise the little Corsican upstart can claim kinship to every royal house in Europe.'

'Oh surely the nobility will not recognise him, however astutely he marries,' said Eliza, horrified.

'Perhaps not, but their son, the king of Rome, as they have created him, will make him more secure on his throne.'

I was curious about what had become of Josephine since the divorce and was told that Napoléon still visited her at Malmaison and that they were on the best of terms!

'It was only her lack of ability to conceive, you know, that led to him to putting her aside for a young princess who looked fertile,' said Madame.

I felt myself blushing and reflected, not for the first time, on the differences between this society and the one I was used to in the country. I was greatly diverted by the evening in spite of the some-times shocking nature of the conversation and was as reluctant to leave as Eliza. Henry had noticed that she was feverish and finally insisted upon calling the carriage.

'We must ask Madame Bigeon to take good care of you while we are away, my love,' he said. 'You are too precious to us all for us to take any risks with your health.'

I would have expected her to laugh off such thoughts as she usu-ally did, but she only smiled rather weakly and leaned back against the cushions.

## THIRTY-SEVEN

## *Philly Walter Whitaker at Pembury, Kent*
### August 1811

S o Cassandra at least has finally stirred herself to write to congratulate me on my marriage. She says they heard of it only from the notice in the paper.

> I hope you do not need to be assured of our good wishes. I think I cannot give you a better wish than that you may be as happy as you deserve and that as a wife you may meet the reward you so well earned as a daughter. Mr Whitaker will, of course, feel himself included in every good wish we desire for you; pray assure him that it will give us great pleasure to have an opportunity of being introduced to our new relative. I shall hope soon to receive from you a very particular account of your new home.
>
> Mrs Henry has been spending a fortnight with us lately and I think I never saw her in such good health before—she is quite recovered from a nasty inflammation of the chest. We frequently talked over your plans and prospects but we did not get the newspaper that contained the announcement of your marriage until an hour after she left us or I am sure she would have united with my mother, Jane, and me in our good wishes on the occasion.
>
> We have been delighted to see dear brother Charles again— after seven long years. His wife, Fanny, is very pleasing and their two

little girls are a joy to us all. They, too, join in sending good wishes on your marriage.

So they talked about me did they? Well I suppose it made a change from boasting about Eliza's smart parties and this nonsense about Jane being a lady novelist. She wrote to me from London and mentioned nothing, but Eliza wrote that she had been seeing 'her publisher' or some such tale. She did not elaborate further and the rest of her letter was taken up with describing the piece of porcelain she was painting for her godfather. She is to take it when she visits him in Oxfordshire in the autumn. He is not much in the public eye these days, I suppose because so many believe he was guilty as charged even though they acquitted him. Eliza will be sure to stay in touch so as to be remembered in the will—Henry, too, will never forget those prospects and by the rate at which the HAs continue to spend money, it won't come a moment too soon. Although, unfortunately for them, I hear that Mr Hastings continues in tolerable good health. She did extend a pretty enough invitation for me and my husband to stay at Sloane Street, but we shall not take it up. I fear my cousin would be too outrageous for Mr Whitaker's taste and his health is not good at present.

March 1812

Well, of all the deceits this part of my family have practised on me all these years, I call this the worst. I have just heard from the apothecary who attends Mr Whitaker that my cousin is the talk of London! She is the author of *Sense and Sensibility*—a book that our circulating library has told me is the most borrowed book in their stock! At first I could not believe it to be true and am still struggling to take it in.

I have heard from Cassandra and Eliza regularly and not a word has been mentioned. It seems that the book came out last October. It costs 15 shillings and is in three volumes. I have just been amusing my husband—who is confined to his room again—by trying to work out how much money will accrue to Jane, but he says that will all depend on the volume of sales. But according to the apothecary it sells in quantity, so perhaps Jane will finally get some money of her own. I shall never forgive them for keeping it from me. Cassandra wrote to me at Christmas as she had heard that Mr Whitaker was unwell and hoped that he would soon shake off his complaints. The book was already in circulation by then but not a word!

Even Eliza said nothing in her Christmas letter, though she is never one to keep a secret. All I can say is that they must be so ashamed about having a lady novelist in the family that they wanted to ensure that no one knew. In that they have failed because the secret is out—to everyone it seems but their own family. There is a conspiracy among them all to keep me out of things. The secret was even known to Mary, and she is all of a flutter about it. I enquired of her whether she knew—feeling sure that it would be a surprise to her, too. After all, she has never approved of Jane and as the wife of a clergyman I should not have thought she would be happy about having a lady novelist as a close relative. But no—in her reply she seems to be as excited and silly as the rest:

It is all most exciting is it not? I know that dear Jane did not want her name known and Cassandra was quite set against it. But the book is so taken up that the cat is out of the bag. Jane spent some days with us last November and told us the news then, though we kept it from Anna, who is such a gossip that she could not be trusted. In fact have you heard of the amusing incident in the library at Alton? Anna was there with her aunt Jane and actually picked up a copy of *S&S*, looked at it, and threw it aside, saying to her aunt, 'Oh that must be rubbish I am sure from the title!' How Jane kept her countenance I do not know and we often laugh at the incident now. Of course Anna is in on the secret now, as cousin Eliza seemed to believe we all knew and mentioned it when she wrote to Anna. You will perhaps be surprised to know that she wrote to ask Anna to spend a few weeks in London in company with Fanny. It is a kind thought, but unfortunately Anna is unable to accept.

Jane's success seems to have set off a wave of writing in the family. James, who has not put pen to paper for years except to write his sermons, has written a poem of congratulations to Jane while Anna and Fanny have each started a novel! I expect they will have a fine time exchanging plots when Anna goes to Godmersham soon. For the present as Anna is so impressionable, her father and I both feel that staying in the country is preferable to a season in London.

I am not surprised they will not let Anna go to London. Eliza is hardly suitable to have charge of a young girl—not a good example at the best of times and certainly not when she is busy arranging social activities for the new lady novelist!

# THIRTY-EIGHT

## *Eliza, Sloane Street, London*
### May 1812

Henry and Jane were in the highest of spirits when they returned from their morning spent with Egerton. He came running upstairs to my sitting room.

'What, my love, not yet dressed? Do finish your toilette and come down. Jane and I have such news to impart.'

'I gather Mr Egerton was pleased then?'

'Pleased? A man could not be more so. He believes she will clear £140 on the book and when we told him there was another almost ready, you should have seen his face! Come down, my love. Madame Bigeon has fruit and cake and wine laid out but I told her to open some more of that French champagne! Shall I call your maid to help you dress?'

'No, I can manage alone, but ask Madame Perigord to come up if you will. I shall be down presently.'

I waited for him to quit the room before I rose from the seat in front of my mirror. I could not resist another look and drew my chemise away from my bosom. Yes, it can quite clearly be seen now, the change in shape, the unevenness. I have seen it before and know its meaning too well to be mistaken. Had I had any doubt, the look on Madame Perigord's face as she came in and saw my reflection in the mirror was confirmation enough.

'Oh Madame!' she exclaimed, her hand covering her mouth.

'*Non, non pas possible, quel horreur!*' Then recovering herself: 'Only a cyst or an abscess perhaps. Shall we summon the doctor?'

'We shall not ask him to come here but I shall call on him in Wimpole Street tomorrow, and I am sure he will be able to treat me. Medicine has moved on a great deal since my mother . . .'

'Oh Madame, do not speak of it, I pray you. We shall not think of it, but take the greatest care and we shall—'

'Yes, yes, you are right and for the moment—not a word of this to the master or Miss Austen.'

She came over and kissed me on both cheeks and that was proof enough of her alarm. Unlike her mother, she is not a demonstrative woman.

It was easy to forget my anxieties with Jane and Henry as their excitement about the future was so infectious.

'Only think, Henry, of Mr Egerton's reaction when he asked how long before my next work was ready and I said but a week or two!'

'And can you do it so quick, Jane?' I asked. 'Do you intend to give him *Catherine* if you buy it back from Crosby's?'

'Well, she certainly can buy it back now—there is ample available for that from her earnings.' Henry laughed.

'I know, but I am to give him *First Impressions*. I have been—'

'The one with Elizabeth and Darcy? Oh, how we all loved that one—the one rejected by Cadell's? How they must be gnashing their teeth now.' I loved the thought of those dreadful men who I am sure sent that manuscript back without reading it hearing about the lady's success.

'Yes, I had the manuscript still in the packaging they used to return it and have been working on it for some weeks—lopping and cropping as I think it needed. May I read you some of the rewritten scenes tonight?' asked Jane.

I had always liked this the best of any of Jane's work and found I was not mistaken when she read to us that evening. How we laughed at Mr Collins.

'Jane, you are wicked—is he not like so many clergymen of our acquaintance?' said Henry.

I thought that every young lady would be a little in love with Darcy and said how glad I was that the sweet character of the sister Jane had been given her own name.

'That was Cassy's suggestion,' Jane admitted. 'I had named her differently in the original. Now do tell me what you think of Lady Catherine?' She had just finished reading a scene where that lady scolds Elizabeth unmercifully and sweeps out.

'She is very fine and rather puts me in mind of Aunt Leigh-Perrot,' said Henry. 'Did you have her as a model?'

'Now you must stop seeking people we know in all my characters.' said Jane. 'I do not write from life, as I have told you all these many times.'

'The great joy of your writing, Jane,' I said, 'and with each piece I read or hear I understand it more, is that each reader will think they know a character such as the ones you draw. Why, we should not forget that even Princess Charlotte has said that Marianne is very like her!'

I was not in truth surprised that Mr Egerton was eager to publish another book and this time would advertise it as being 'by the author of *Sense and Sensibility*,' for the reviews have been most pleasing and every salon one attends in London is talking about it. I long to take Jane about with me more and to give dinners for her. But she is as ever modest and reluctant to be the centre of attention except within her close family. The only difference I can notice in her is that she is enjoying spending some of her money and is even a little impatient with Cassandra that she is not wanting to accept gifts.

'Only think, Eliza,' she said to me later that evening, 'I have bought Cassy a new mauve silk and a velvet pelisse like the one Lady Bessborough was wearing. I warrant she will say she does not go anywhere fine enough to wear them but I shall insist. Now that I am very rich, well tolerably so anyway, I shall ensure that my presents are always in the finest taste and gratefully received by everyone.'

It really lifted my spirits to see her so gay and carefree after all the years when she had seemed so low in spirits.

'As to having nowhere to go to wear it, shall you not be dining frequently at the Great House at Chawton when Edward and his family are installed there?'

'Of course, you are right. They are to be there for four or five months I believe, so there will be many occasions for finery.'

'Are they to be there so long?'

'Yes, Godmersham is to be completely refurbished and redecorated, so they thought it best to move out. I hope you will spend time with us while they are there—you know how Edward and especially Fanny enjoy your company.'

'So long as we do not come at the same time as Mrs JA,' I said and we both laughed, understanding the joke.

Two weeks later

This morning I received confirmation from Dr Baillie, who also attended my mother, that my affliction is the same as hers. He has tried to be reassuring, telling me that he has developed a range of preparations and unctions that are often efficacious. I shall not give up hope—that is not my way—and if the worst comes, shall try to be as brave as my dear mother was. I have not yet told Henry and have contrived to hide the inflamed breast from him even in our most intimate moments. He remarks that I am growing thinner and asks Madame Bigeon to cook dishes to tempt me. I am finding it harder to hide my condition from Jane—I have found her looking at me curiously several times and she often enquires for my state of health. Luckily she has been much occupied in getting *First Impressions* ready for the publisher. She is relieved that it will be delivered to him before she leaves us tomorrow. She had to find another title, as *First Impressions* had been used already it seems. Henry and I sat hours with her to try to find the right one. We were almost settled on *Jane and Elizabeth*, having discarded *Mistaken Impressions*, *Learning to Love*, and *Maids of Meriton* when I found the expression *Pride and Prejudice* in the volume of Miss Burney's *Cecilia*, which I happened to be reading. Jane clapped her hands. 'Oh that is so right,' she cried. '*His* pride and *her* prejudice—how exactly it fits my story.'

Henry immediately saw another advantage: 'It fits so well with *Sense and Sensibility* that old Egerton can expect runaway sales and my sister runaway income!'

Henry is particularly good humoured at present, as he has been appointed Receiver General of Taxes for Oxfordshire. It is a credit to his reputation and will provide extra income for us, which is always welcome. We may have need of it for medical matters soon.

Henry is to dine out tonight and as the two Madames are visiting the theatre, Jane and I will be alone. I know I shall be tempted to confide to her my worries about my condition, so I must think of a way to divert her.

Well, I could hardly have hoped that the diversion would be so successful! In fact we were still deep in our intimate conversation when Henry returned, and knowing that Jane would not want him to see her tear-stained face, I called out to him to go straight upstairs and that I would join him later.

Jane looked at me gratefully.

'You were ever an understanding friend to me, dear cousin,' she said, 'I wish now I had told you my sad story earlier that I might have had comfort from you.'

'I am glad you have told me now,' I said, 'and I know that the story you are planning will be the better for the sorrow and sadness you have suffered.'

'And the joy, too,' she protested, 'the joy of knowing what it was like to love someone and have that love returned. You have known that more than once Eliza, but for me, I know there could be only a single time.'

Had I? In truth, I am not sure. I was not in love with the Comte, and though Henry is a dear man and I am inordinately fond of him, I do not know that I felt the depth of emotion that Jane has shared with me this evening.

Our conversation began quietly enough. Anxious to ensure I did not talk about myself, I began by asking her if my favourite lady novelist had another book planned.

'Oh indeed, yes,' she said. 'I have not yet begun to write but I know what its subject will be.'

'Oh, pray tell me, do!'

To my astonishment she replied, 'It is to be about good and evil.'

'Good and evil?' I repeated incredulously. But, Jane, is that not a subject for a book of sermons, not a novel?'

'It will be a novel, of course, about the nobility and set in a grand house but its characters will represent good and evil.'

'This is very different from what you have favoured us with before, and, dare I say, from what we and your publishers are expecting?'

'Perhaps, but be that as it may, I must write it.' She hesitated and looked out the window where the evening shadows were beginning to fall across the garden. I could see she was considering whether to say more, so I just kept silent. She took a deep breath and went on, 'You know a little, I think, about the gentleman I met at Lyme some years ago?'

'A little only. You had asked Henry and me to accompany you there the following year when you were to meet again, but it was never mentioned further so we assumed . . .'

'I, too, made assumptions, assumptions that he had rejected me, perhaps because I told him I wished to be a writer, but—'

I could not help interrupting: 'But why would anyone feel that was wrong?'

'He was a clergyman with a strong moral code and you know as well as I do that men of the cloth do not always approve of novels. Anyway, it was a foolish assumption on my part when I consider it now, because this was a man who had read the *Rights of Women* book you so kindly gave me and actually approved of it! No, as you know, I discovered much later when we were again at Lyme that in fact he had died suddenly and that was the reason he ceased to write to me, not because of any disapproval.'

'What a relief to your poor spirits that must have been!'

'Oh, indeed it was! And I realized that I must write the story I had discussed with him, about ordination, about how good people will win through, and how we all have a moral guide within us if we will only listen to it. He used to tell me such tales of the profligacy of the London society in which he had been curate and how he had sometimes thought God was ignoring him as he tried to remind his parishioners of their duties and responsibilities. He was particularly dismayed by the men he saw enter the church because it provided a good living, not because they felt a call from God.'

I felt my heart sink at the thought of Jane trying to make an entertaining novel of such a subject. I may lack some morality myself in thinking it, but I cannot see such a story selling well!

She smiled at me. 'I can see your dismay, Eliza, but I vow the characters will be amusing and infuriating and admirable and that there will be scenes of drama.'

'I am relieved to hear it!' I laughed.

'There is to be a displaced little girl in it and she really will be the 'good' while another young lady will represent the 'evil.'

'Oh, I cried, 'I warrant she is the more interesting one! But tell me, will the good one find her true love?'

'Yes, she will. I do like a happy ending, as you know.'

'How I wish your story could have had a happy ending, Jane.' I touched her hand as I spoke.

The tears that had been near all the while she was speaking of her gentleman friend began to fall.

'In a way it has. I am more content than I have ever been and thankful that I knew him and that he loved me. It is more than many women ever know.'

I could only agree.

# THIRTY-NINE

## Henry Austen at Sloane Street
### November 1812

I knew I must meet Jane at the door as she arrived so as to warn her about the change she might see in Eliza. Though I suspected that Cassandra might have made her aware that Eliza was often tired when we were together at Godmersham for the shooting, I think my dear wife has hidden her condition so well that it might not have been apparent that there was anything seriously wrong. Eliza has always made a point of being at the door herself to welcome visitors—it has been part of her talent as a hostess and she has always prided herself on making everyone who visits us feel cherished and special. So I have told her that Jane is not expected until the dinner hour, when in fact she will be here by three, I think. Mr Tilson is escorting her, as he had business in Alton. Even now she is a famous authoress, it is not considered proper for her to travel post alone but the bank connection in Alton has proved most useful this last year. It has been most agreeable to have Jane with us so frequently, and to see her 'correcting my proofs,' 'seeing my publisher,' 'negotiating my contracts' has been such a joy to Eliza and me, especially when we thought back to that time, not so long ago, when her spirits were so low that we feared she would never write again.

What amazed me most is how few corrections and changes she had to make to *Pride and Prejudice*, when one considers that she completed it some fifteen years ago. She said she had to cut it quite savagely, but you would never know. Eliza says that just shows the quality of the writing.

Tilson gave her his arm to help her down from the carriage and presented her to me with a bow.

'Henry, here is the lady of whom all London is talking!'

Jane's natural modesty makes her blush at such compliments but, as I said, ''Tis true and Egerton says yours will be his best-selling book this year!'

She thanked Tilson for his company and then looked around.

'Where is dear Eliza? I always expect to see her as soon as I arrive. Is she out calling on someone of great consequence?'

I put my finger to my lips. 'I wanted to see you alone before you saw her so as to warn you—'

'Henry, please, what is it? Pray tell me immediately.'

Worried that Eliza, upstairs in her chamber, might hear us, I took her arm and led her to the morning room.

As she sat down, she said in a dull voice, 'Cassandra told me that she was unwell at Godmersham and that she feared . . .'

'Feared what?'

She kept her eyes on my face. 'That she saw similarities, well, was reminded of, of, Aunt Philla.'

I took her hand. 'Cassandra was ever a good predictor; she is well named as we have often remarked.'

The tears sprang to Jane's eyes. 'I was praying it was not so, but when she was not here to greet me . . . Does she know?'

I sighed. 'We do not discuss it.'

Jane looked astonished. 'How can you not when you must both know . . . ?'

'It suits us both to pretend that she will recover. We speak of an inflammation of the chest, of an abscess such as she has had before. This is why I wanted to see you before you meet her. I knew you would see a change in her appearance but mostly I wanted to warn you not to discuss her possible fate. . . . It will do her no good and only upset her.'

'I am sure you have consulted the best doctors—what is their view?'

'As I told you, there is no hope of survival but she may have a year or two.'

'A year or two, our lovely Eliza? Oh, I cannot bear it!'

'You must, my dear, and I must ask you to contain your emotions in front of her. She needs to be encouraged to hope.'

I saw her draw back her shoulders and arrange her expression as she prepared to go upstairs; like my wife, she is a courageous woman.

That evening
Jane Austen with Eliza in Her Dressing Room

I am trying to keep a conversation going and to keep my eyes away from Eliza's face, not only because I hate to see the accustomed liveliness so depleted but also because I fear she will read my thoughts.

'Do tell me, my dear,' I said, 'about the visit to Godmersham. You have not been there as often as Henry and I long to know what you think of it.'

'Well, of course, it is a more sober place than it was those years ago and Edward shows not a sign of remarrying, which I think is rather selfish of him!'

I was delighted to see signs of her old spirit.

'I hear that Fanny is still housekeeper in chief, which has always concerned Cassy and me.'

'I have done my best to give her opportunities for other society, as you know, but Jane, you are the one who may influence her most.'

'Me?' I said. 'How so?'

'Why because she tries her hand at writing, of course—she longs to be a lady novelist like her famous aunt!'

'She did tell me something of the sort and asked for advice and you will be amused to know that Anna is writing, too. Perhaps all my nieces will be published, but I hope they will not have to wait as long as I.'

We both laughed, remembering the disappointments.

Eliza said: 'It is not unexpected they should hope talent runs in families. As you know, we were all at Godmersham when *P&P* came out. Cassy was there, too, so she will have told you of the excitement. The first copies came to the village by post chaise as Edward had ordered them, but in no time all the neighbours knew of it and were calling to congratulate us on having such a clever relation. In truth, I think they hoped you would be there and that they might be allowed to shake the hand that had created Elizabeth Bennet!'

'Oh Eliza, do not exaggerate so.'

'I do entreat you to stop this modesty—you are the lady of whom London is talking and you cannot get away from it. I am convinced that we shall have such excitement every time a book by Miss Jane Austen is announced and I shall be the one who gives handsome parties to celebrate each publication. Never again will I bear to hear of you being alone with your mama at Chawton when the whole of England celebrates.'

Her face grew suddenly serious.

'Jane, I must talk to you. While it gives me great joy to think of your continuing success, I must face the fact that I shall not see it. To speak plain, I am dying. Henry knows it, my doctors know it, and soon everyone must.'

'But my dear, surely it is only a small inflammation of the—'

'Did Henry tell you that? It suits us both to pretend. Dear man as he is, he is not strong and has not had to face the sort of difficulties that have plagued me all my life. He finds the truth hard, so I protect him from it. But we were ever dear friends, Jane, and I will be truthful with you.'

It did not surprise me, of course—how strong she has always been and how I shall miss her. I said so.

'Yes, I know you will, Jane, and that is why I am so desirous of telling you that you must not miss me too much.'

'But how could I avoid it?'

'What I mean is, miss me by all means but do not let the fact that I am no longer here deter you from your work. You must write and you must be published. Why, you are but five and thirty and could write perhaps twenty more books!'

'Oh, dearest Eliza, your ambition for me knows no bounds!'

'Nor should it, for your talent is boundless! Though I may not be here to congratulate you on every one of the twenty, I shall be with you in spirit and cheering you on.'

I could not hold back the tears then and we shed a few together, sitting on the small silk chaise longue with our arms about each other.

Presently, she recovered and dried her eyes.

'Now Jane, there is something else I must talk to you about, something else I require of you.'

'Anything, dear cousin, anything, you know that.'

'It is Henry. You must ensure he marries again.'

I could not help smiling. 'I am not sure anyone has the power to do that.'

'Nonsense, he is not yet forty and a fine, well-looking man; there will be ladies aplenty who see him as a fine catch!'

'I am sure that is true,' I replied, 'but you know he has been devoted to you since the age of fifteen. He may not easily—'

'Henry needs a wife,' Eliza interrupted. 'He is not practical, you know, and between ourselves has little talent for banking. Do try to ensure he does not overreach himself financially and that he finds another wife with a little money to her name.'

I could not help expressing surprise. 'But I always thought that there was ample money here?'

'Well, we have lived very well, perhaps too well, and Henry is no better a manager than I, in fact somewhat worse.' She smiled affectionately. 'Dear man, I shall rest easy knowing his sister takes him in hand, only Jane . . .'

'Yes?'

'Do not allow him too much access to your income, which I know will be prodigious if sales of *P&P* are anything to go by.'

We both laughed, joined in our affection for Henry and understanding that a woman must keep an eye on her own money.

'One day,' she said, 'I daresay all ladies will be able to control their own resources but until that time, let us allow our men folk to *think* they are in control, while being very cautious about how much we tell them!'

We laughed together and I wondered how many more times we should be able to do that.

'You are to be with us at Christmas at Chawton, I think?' I said. 'We are all looking forward to that.'

'I pray that I may be well enough to enjoy it. Dr Baillie is to treat me with leeches again in the week before—'

'Leeches?' I cried, horrified.

'Yes, they provide relief from the pain, you know, and I do not wish to take too much of the laudanum he prescribes.'

'But why not, if it helps with the pain?'

'It also has a tendency to make one insensible and I am too concerned to know what is going on about me to be content with that.' She laughed.

I wondered if I could be so brave were I in her position.

# FORTY

## *Jane Austen at Chawton*
### February 1813

O h, it is too too cruel!' My mother cried this out so loudly
we all feared that Henry and Eliza would hear her as they
climbed the stairs. But we all knew what she meant. To see Eliza,
who has always carried herself so well and taken such a pride in her
appearance, so enfeebled as to be unable to mount the stairs without
her husband's support was terrible. Her deterioration seems to be
happening so quickly now. It is but six weeks since they joined us
here at Christmas and only one week since they were here on their
way to Oxford, but the failing is rapid and only too apparent. Her
spirit is strong though—'Just like her mother's,' said Mama with admiration. Eliza had been the first to applaud when I finished reading
the scene about the theatricals at Mansfield Park and before Henry
took her upstairs had said: 'Now that Sir Thomas is returned, Jane,
I cannot wait to hear what is going to happen to those naughty play-
ers. Please, I beg you, read no more tonight so that we can continue
tomorrow where we have left off.'

I made the promise, of course. Henry had taken her hand as I
read and we all knew that they were thinking of the theatricals they
themselves used to engage in at Steventon—when Henry first fell in
love with her.

Up until the turn of the year most of the family were scarcely
aware of her illness. She was so excited with all the attention given

to *Pride and Prejudice* and so proud of its success. Eliza told everyone that I was 'the lady of whom all London was talking,' but it did me no good at home! All the family were kindness itself about the book, though—I should have found it hard to bear if people had *not* liked my Lizzie since I think her as delightful a creature as ever appeared in print.

With her usual candour, Cassandra had told me then that she saw in Eliza all the same symptoms that had carried Aunt Philadelphia off in such agony. Even when I returned from London I retained a hope that there might be a miracle, that she might recover, but it is very clear from seeing her now that she has not much longer to live.

We women face death more frequently than men; childbirth takes its toll, of course, and I am now thankful that I have not had to face that. Cassandra and I often speak of our good fortune in escaping its dangers. But just lately I have begun to think that I, too, might die without making old bones. I mentioned this once to Cassy, who said, 'What nonsense is this, Jane? Just look at Mama— eight children and looking as strong as a woman half her age. You and I will live until we are eighty at least, happily together in our cottage at Chawton, with you turning out novels by the dozen and me ensuring you do not have to be bothered with the housekeeping. Save for making tea and toast in the morning!'

We have all believed in my sister's ability to predict the future. I hope she is right in this, yet feel I must produce as much as I can, in case . . .

Henry quite dotes upon his wife and it is touching to see his concern for her. He knows that she will not survive long but they both still talk of it being 'a small inflammation of the chest that will be better when the warmer weather comes.'

She must be in great pain, but Eliza still contrives to laugh and joke. Her interest in my work is gratifying—she knows I have always valued her opinions, even if they do not always accord with mine, especially when it comes to *Mansfield Park*. I did not want to repeat the experience I had had with the first two published books of having to change their titles at a late stage, so I settled on *Mansfield Park* early on as the title for my next.

'Oh Jane,' Eliza had said when she heard this, 'is this the one you told me you would write? It sounds as though it is about nobility—is it a fine house with titled occupants?'

'One or two,' I said 'but the book is actually about ordination and the complications surrounding it.' It was clear to me that she had quite forgotten our conversation last year. I realised that the pain and suffering she was having to face was now affecting her mind and her memory as well as her body.

Her face, now even thinner than before, fell. 'Ordination—that is not an exciting topic, is it? I pray you, will there be no wicked characters in it? We do not find pictures of perfection so interesting you know.'

I laughed. 'Believe me there will be villains enough in this story.'

'Will there be villains like Willoughby?'

'One at least, but also some wicked women!'

'Wicked women—what say you, Henry? Shall you like to read of those?' said Eliza, turning to her husband.

Henry smiled at me. 'Once when you wrote of a woman with no redeeming features I scolded you—will these villains be like her?'

'One may be,' I replied, 'but one is so crotchety as to put us all in mind of cousin Philly.'

'Now Jane.' My mother looked up from her quilt and eyed me crossly. 'You know you always say that you do not write from life, so we wish to see no family portraits in this next.' But she could not help smiling to herself I could see.

Mama had been very pleased that I wrote to Frank to ask if he would tell me how a ship might be berthed at Spithead, because I am writing scenes of Portsmouth and do so want to capture it right. She is delighted with William Price as she sees he is like my own sailor brothers, though I think she does not admire Fanny Price as she did Elizabeth Bennet. But then, I fear no one will.

When Henry came down from upstairs he drew me to one side. He smiled. 'I know you always protest that you do not write from life but that scene where Mary Crawford tries to turn Edmund away from the church . . .'

'Yes, Henry?' I said, looking up at him.

'Did you not hear something of such a scene with dear Eliza and me?'

I made to interrupt but he held up his hand. 'And I think I do see something of dear Eliza in Mary—tell me, is Edmund to win her? Eliza was asking me my opinion as she retired.'

'I think he will,' I replied, 'and Cassy tries to persuade me to allow Henry Crawford to succeed at last—you know we always favour Henrys!'

'Jane,' he began again—I could see he was close to tears—'you see how things are with my dear wife. I beg you to grant me a favour.'

'Of course, anything, you know that brother.'

'Thank you, my dear. It is this: When the end comes . . .'

'Oh Henry do not talk so.'

'We must, my dear, it cannot be long delayed her doctors say. When the end comes, will you be with us? She has always loved you so well and would want you there I know.'

I gladly gave the promise, hoping with all my heart that she might live long enough to see *Mansfield Park* completed and published.

April 1813

It is not to be. An express is just come from Henry. He will be
here tomorrow and requests that I return immediately with him to
London, as she is failing fast. He writes:

> She is brave beyond imagining but her suffering is terrible to see
> and I can only wish her peace. To have you here, my dearest sister,
> will be the greatest comfort.

## FORTY-ONE

### *Jane and Henry Austen in Hampstead Cemetery*

#### November 1813

'T is a fine inscription Henry, and fitting that she should lie beside her mother and dear little Hastings.'

*Also in Memory of Elizabeth, wife of H. T. Austen Esq. formerly widow of Comte Feuillide, a woman of brilliant, cultivated and generous mind. Just, disinterested and charitable she died after long and severe suffering on 25th April 1813 aged 50. Much regretted by the wise and good and deeply lamented by the poor.*

'Thank you for coming with me. I have not been here since the funeral.'

'Well, you have been busy disposing of poor Eliza's things and of course moving to Henrietta Street.'

'Yes, I know you and Cassandra thought I did that too quickly, but I found it impossible to be in Sloane Street without her. The house was like a tomb—her presence there had been so all embracing—like the beautiful enchantress that she was.'

'We all understood, and that house was too big for a widower— anyway living over the bank is much more convenient for you, is it not?'

'I am as happy as I can be there and glad it is not too small for visitors, especially you, Jane. You will often be with me I hope—in fact, I am sure Mr Egerton will insist upon it when *Mansfield Park* is out. You will be so much in demand.'

'I do not think we can be sure of that. He accepts it only on commission again, remember. He is clearly not as confident of *MP* as he was of *P&P*.'

'My dear, you have no need to worry—your reputation is now assured and you tell me you are already planning another.'

'Yes, since no one finds my Fanny Price very attractive, I shall next time create a heroine whom no one will much like but me!'

'Oh Jane, how you lift my spirits! What is she to be called?'

'I have almost decided upon Emma. Come Henry, the wind grows chill. Give me your arm and let us leave dear Eliza here with her loved ones and return home.'

## FORTY-TWO

## *Henry Austen at Chawton Parsonage*
### August 1815

S o, I am to be a clergyman after all—I wonder what dear Eliza would say? I am advanced in years to be a curate to be sure, but it is comforting to be near my mother and sisters and a pleasant cottage and fifty guineas a year are welcome when you have endured bankruptcy. I think Eliza would approve, though she would understand, too, that such an income does not provide adequately for a wife. She was always of a practical disposition and knew that a widower has a duty to remarry—she assured me of that on her deathbed.

There is to be an evening party at the Great House tomorrow. Edward and some of his family are in residence and everyone wishes to celebrate the great victory at Waterloo and the war finally being over after so many years. I hope that Jane may be persuaded to read from *Emma*—such a delightful story and such an honour that the prince regent himself asked for it to be dedicated to him.

The rector's niece Miss Jackson is to be invited. She has an income of ten thousand pounds a year I believe, perhaps I may . . .

## EPILOGUE

H enry did marry Miss Jackson, who made him a loyal wife, but did not do so until 1820 when he took over the Steventon parish on the death of his brother James and moved back into the parsonage where he had been brought up.

Jane herself died, at the age of only forty-one, in July 1817, and it was Henry who oversaw the publication of her last novel, *Persuasion,* and of *Catherine*, which had eventually been bought back from Crosby's and called *Northanger Abbey*. Though Jane left Cassandra all rights to her work, Henry described himself as joint owner and negotiated a good deal with a new publisher, John Murray. Ever with an eye to making money, though never very good at it, he tried to supply more biographical material about the authoress, but could find little to say.

'My dear sister's life was not one of events. Indeed the farthest thing from her expectations or wishes was to be exhibited as a public character under any circumstances.'

## ACKNOWLEDGEMENTS

I warmly acknowledge all the encouragement and assistance I have received from Ruth Rendell, and I am indebted to all the wonderful biographers of Jane Austen.

# THE HISTORY

# BEHIND

# THE STORY

# AFTERWORD

A s Henry Austen said when he wrote a biographical note to the first edition of *Northanger Abbey* and *Persuasion*, published together after Jane's untimely death, 'my sister's life was not one of events.'

That is very clear to anyone who knows her story. She lived the modest life of the daughter of a clergyman, in a small village in the English countryside, never married, travelled very little, and she herself defined her work as being done with a fine brush on a two-inch square of ivory. Yet from that limited experience she wrote six almost perfect novels that are world famous, constantly analysed, always at the top of any favourite novel list, and that provide endless material not only for academic study but for popular film and television adaptation.

Her first cousin Eliza, by contrast, led a most eventful life. Born in India, quite possibly the illegitimate daughter of the great Warren Hastings, who stood trial for treason, she frequented the French court of King Louis XVI and Queen Marie Antoinette before the Revolution, married a French Comte who was executed in the Reign of Terror, escaped capture herself by the mob on two occasions, mixed with the cream of London society, was a brilliant hostess, and eventually married Jane's favourite brother before dying of breast cancer before she was fifty.

I have always been fascinated by the close and loving bond between Jane and this scandalous cousin and the more I know of this relationship, the more convinced I have become that Eliza exerted great influence on Jane's writing. That she encouraged her to write, at a time when literary composition was far from a respectable activity for a young woman, is clear but I am certain, too, that she provided a model—though Jane herself would always deny this—for some of Jane's more assertive characters—especially where flirting was concerned! Where else would Jane have met a woman like Mary Crawford or Lady Susan?

There is no definitive biography of Eliza, though she is mentioned extensively in every one of the wonderful biographies of Jane, but we do have many of her letters, especially those carefully preserved by her and Jane's waspish cousin Philly Walter. Her character leapt out at me from these letters. It was easy to imagine how fascinating she would seem to a young girl fourteen years her junior as she arrived at the parsonage in fine carriages, with servants, in fine silks and linens and laden down with presents for the whole family. She always brought books for Jane and encouraged her writing from a very early age.

From my previous book, *Cassandra and Jane,* I had grown used to imagining conversations between Jane and her sister. I was able to extend this to Eliza and also able to imagine letters passing between members of the family to add to the real ones. Eliza was sure to cause a stir wherever she went!

One criticism that is often levelled at Jane Austen is that she did not mention the wars that were raging in Europe all the time she was writing. She may not have made much direct mention of what was occurring, but there are many clues in her novels and she had two sailor brothers who were actively involved. Through this story of Eliza, I have tried to give a flavour of history beyond the immediate family. All dates are accurate and I have tried to be as faithful to reality as possible.

I find Eliza enchanting, and I hope others will, too.

# *The lighter side of* HISTORY

\* Look for this seal on select historical fiction titles from Harper. Books bearing it contain special bonus materials, including timelines, interviews with the author, and insights into the real-life events that inspired the book, as well as recommendations for further reading.

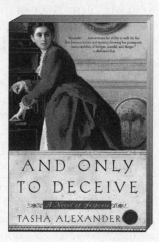

## AND ONLY TO DECEIVE:
### A Novel of Suspense
by Tasha Alexander
978-0-06-114844-6 (paperback)
Discover the dangerous secrets kept by the strait-laced English of the Victorian era.

## ANNETTE VALLON:
### A Novel of the French Revolution
by James Tipton
978-0-06-082222-4 (paperback)
For fans of Tracy Chevalier and Sarah Dunant comes this vibrant, alluring debut novel of a compelling, independent woman who would inspire one of the world's greatest poets and survive a nation's bloody transformation.

## BOUND: A Novel
by Sally Gunning
978-0-06-124026-3 (paperback)
An indentured servant finds herself bound by law, society, and her own heart in colonial Cape Cod.

## CASSANDRA & JANE: A Jane Austen Novel
by Jill Pitkeathley
978-0-06-144639-9 (paperback)
The relationship between Jane Austen and her sister—explored through the letters that might have been.

## CROSSED: A Tale of the Fourth Crusade
by Nicole Galland
978-0-06-084180-5 (paperback)
Under the banner of the Crusades, a pious knight and a British vagabond attempt a daring rescue.

## A CROWNING MERCY: A Novel

by Bernard Cornwell and Susannah Kells
978-0-06-172438-1 (paperback)
A rebellious young Puritan woman embarks on a daring journey to win
love and a secret fortune.

## DARCY'S STORY

by Janet Aylmer
978-0-06-114870-5 (paperback)
Read Mr. Darcy's side of the story—*Pride
and Prejudice* from a new perspective.

## DEAREST COUSIN JANE:
### A Jane Austen Novel

by Jill Pitkeathley
978-0-06-187598-4 (paperback)
An inventive reimagining of the intriguing
and scandalous life of Jane Austen's cousin.

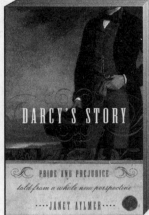

## THE FALLEN ANGELS: A Novel

by Bernard Cornwell and Susannah Kells
978-0-06-172545-6 (paperback)
In the sequel to *A Crowning Mercy*, Lady Campion Lazender's courage,
faith, and family loyalty are tested when she must complete a perilous
journey between two worlds.

## A FATAL WALTZ: A Novel of Suspense

by Tasha Alexander
978-0-06-117423-0 (paperback)
Caught in a murder mystery, Emily must do the unthinkable to save her
fiancé: bargain with her ultimate nemesis, the Countess von Lange.

## FIGURES IN SILK: A Novel

by Vanora Bennett
978-0-06-168985-7 (paperback)
The art of silk making, political intrigue, and a sweeping love story all
interwoven in the fate of two sisters.

## THE FIREMASTER'S MISTRESS: A Novel

by Christie Dickason
978-0-06-156826-8 (paperback)
Estranged lovers Francis and Kate rekindle their
romance in the midst of Guy Fawkes's plot to blow up
Parliament.

## JULIA AND THE MASTER OF MORANCOURT: A Novel
by Janet Aylmer
978-0-06-167295-8 (paperback)
Amidst family tragedy, Julia travels all over England, desperate to marry
the man she loves instead of the arranged suitor preferred by her mother.

## KEPT: A Novel
by D. J. Tayler
978-0-06-114609-1 (paperback)
A gorgeously intricate, dazzling reinvention of Victorian life and
passions that is also a riveting investigation into some of the darkest,
most secret chambers of the human heart.

## THE MIRACLES OF PRATO: A Novel
by Laurie Albanese and Laura Morowitz
978-0-06-155835-1 (paperback)
The unforgettable story of a nearly impossible romance between a
painter-monk (the renowned artist Fra Filippo Lippi) and the young
nun who becomes his muse, his lover, and the mother of his children.

## PILATE'S WIFE: A Novel of the Roman Empire
by Antoinette May
978-0-06-112866-0 (paperback)
Claudia foresaw the Romans' persecution of
Christians, but even she could not stop the
crucifixion.

## A POISONED SEASON:
### A Novel of Suspense
by Tasha Alexander
978-0-06-117421-6 (paperback)
As a cat-burglar torments Victorian London,
a mysterious gentleman fascinates high
society.

## PORTRAIT OF AN UNKNOWN
## WOMAN: A Novel
by Vanora Bennett
978-0-06-125256-3 (paperback)
Meg, adopted daughter of Sir Thomas More, narrates
the tale of a famous Holbein painting and the secrets
it holds.

### THE QUEEN'S SORROW: A Novel of Mary Tudor
by Suzannah Dunn
978-0-06-170427-7 (paperback)
Queen of England Mary Tudor's reign is brought low by abused power and a forbidden love.

### REBECCA: The Classic Tale of Romantic Suspense
by Daphne Du Maurier
978-0-380-73040-7 (paperback)
Follow the second Mrs. Maxim de Winter down the lonely drive to Manderley, where Rebecca once ruled.

### REBECCA'S TALE: A Novel
by Sally Beauman
978-0-06-117467-4 (paperback)
Unlock the dark secrets and old worlds of Rebecca de Winter's life with investigator Colonel Julyan.

### THE SIXTH WIFE: A Novel of Katherine Parr
by Suzannah Dunn
978-0-06-143156-2 (paperback)
Kate Parr survived four years of marriage to King Henry VIII, but a new love may undo a lifetime of caution.

### VIVALDI'S VIRGINS: A Novel
by Barbara Quick
978-0-06-089053-7 (paperback)
Abandoned as an infant, fourteen-year-old Anna Maria dal Violin is one of the elite musicians living in the foundling home where the "Red Priest," Antonio Vivaldi, is maestro and composer.

### WATERMARK: A Novel of the Middle Ages
by Vanitha Sankaran
978-0-06-184927-5 (paperback)
A compelling debut about the search for identiy, the power of self-expression, and value of the written word.

### THE WIDOW'S WAR: A Novel
by Sally Gunning
978-0-06-079158-2 (paperback)
Tread the shores of colonial Cape Cod with a lonely whaler's widow as she tries to build a new life.